IN THE
Dog House

AN APPLETREE COVE ROMANCE

IN THE
Dog House

AN APPLETREE
COVE ROMANCE

TRACI HALL

Entangled Publishing, LLC
2614 South Timberline Road
Suite 105, PMB 159
Fort Collins, CO 80525
rights@entangledpublishing.com

Bliss is an imprint of Entangled Publishing, LLC.

Edited by Alethea Spiridon
Cover design by Bree Archer
Cover photography by Vadymvdrobot and mythja/DepositPhotos

Manufactured in the United States of America

First Edition February 2019

Bliss

To Christopher Hawke, with love

Chapter One

"Stay," Emma Mercer commanded, following the word with a hand signal—her palm up as she faced her emotional support dogs, four varied breeds she'd rescued from the shelter and trained for another lease on life.

Ready to wrap up her presentation, she stood on the auditorium stage at Kingston Middle School in front of seventy restless sixth graders who just wanted to pet the pups.

The dogs on the far end of the wooden stage sat on their haunches, noses and ears up. Lulu, a beagle mix with long ears; a Maltese named Princess; and a mutt of indiscernible breed she'd dubbed Sheldon—but not her latest trainee. The three-year-old golden Lab, all sixty-five pounds of rambunctious love, was mesmerized by the kids in the audience.

Emma gave a warning snap of her clicker to keep the dog in place, but Zelda eyed a little girl in the front row and wagged her tail, adding a hopeful *woof.*

The girl waved.

Zelda barked and scooted on her butt toward the edge of the stage, inch by inch, as if Emma might not notice.

Ditching the clicker, Emma brought out the whistle and gave two trill bursts. The Lab stopped as if playing freeze tag and sent Emma a guilty and apologetic whine. She slowly crawled toward Emma despite the whistled command to stay.

The kids laughed, and Emma's cheeks heated.

Part of the ESD canine certification was that the dog had to follow the rules no matter what else was going on. *My mistake—the pup wasn't ready.* Emma tugged the dog's leash closer to her leg. "Sit, Zelda."

With a groan and a tongue loll, Zelda did, collapsing against Emma's calf. The kids laughed harder. "Good girl," she said softly.

Twenty-eight and never married, Emma had a master's degree in psychology, with her emphasis on therapy animals, as she worked toward her doctorate. Emma had been called to the school three years ago because Mrs. Mosher, the health teacher, had a student with special needs that required a therapy dog. Educating people about support dogs was the project of Emma's heart, and starting with kids she considered a fun bonus.

"Is Zelda in trouble?" a young boy with braces shouted from the second row.

"No." Emma smiled at the students, holding Zelda's leash with one hand and keeping her palm up toward the three dogs still waiting to be released from her "stay" command. "I use positive reinforcement when training these animals." She dug a treat from her khakis' pocket, looked down at Zelda and said, "Sit."

Zelda stopped wiggling and sat straight so Emma gave the Lab the kibble. "Good pup." She turned back to the kids. "Zelda here will need more training before I can match her with the right person."

"What if you can't?" a girl from the fourth row asked.

"Raise your hand, please," Mrs. Mosher instructed. "Go

ahead, Hannah."

"What happens to the dogs if they never learn? Do you send them to the pound to *die?*"

Emma sighed. It was just one of those days when nothing went smoothly, starting with the dead battery in her SUV, to spilling coffee on her shirt, to Zelda's exuberance. "No. We don't do that."

Which was why she needed that government grant approved, in order to build her training shelter. "Even if for some reason the dog can't be certified for use in therapy, at Heart to Heart Kennel we place the animal in a loving home."

Mrs. Mosher called on another child. "Matthew?"

"Can a support dog help with bad dreams?" a boy asked.

As Emma considered how best to answer, Zelda strained against her leash to join the pack at the far end of the stage—Princess's brown ears twitched, but Lulu didn't budge. Emma gave a quick two-trill whistle to remind the pups to stay.

"Nightmares can be scary," Emma said, and agreement rose in a murmur from the other children. "A family pet can snuggle with you and take away the bad feelings. What I do with my emotional support dogs is train them to counter distress in people with certain...anxieties that keep them from living a full life."

She liked to keep things light at the middle school and didn't go into accidents, war, or abduction. "If you'd like more information, I have brochures for you to share with your parents at home. Mrs. Mosher? If your students would like to pet the dogs now, have them get in single file and I will keep the pups here on the stage."

It was a routine they'd done a half dozen times before. She held up her palm and walked toward the dogs, not including Zelda, giving each pup a treat and a pat of assurance. The trio waited calmly as Mrs. Mosher had the kids form a line.

A man slipped inside the auditorium as if trying not

to disturb the class. His silhouette against the closed door showed melded-on jeans, a fitted T-shirt, the biceps of a male in his prime. Her mouth dried, and she cleared her throat, self-conscious in her baggy polo shirt and sneakers.

"Hi. Go ahead and scratch behind Sheldon's ears," she told the boy with braces. "He loves it." She handed each student a brochure that advertised her kennel and services, while suggesting a donation for the local Kingston animal shelter.

A boy about eleven, all big teeth and ears, in a gray T-shirt and jeans, patted Sheldon's fur. "How much does this dog cost?"

"Doesn't matter if they were free, Matty. Let's go."

The man with the muscles had navigated the auditorium in quiet strides and crossed his arms at the bottom of the stairs, his smooth jaw tight. Short hair, light brown, and a profile that dredged up memories of high school with a sickening twist to her stomach. He studied the boy and not Emma, which was good because her hands shook. Zelda, picking up on her emotions, whined at her feet. If she'd been able to think, she would have clicked to reward the intuitive behavior.

She snuck a glance as she bent down to pet Zelda. *Jackson Hardy.* He'd broken her heart, ending their relationship after graduation to run off and join the military.

His solid chest was much broader than it had been when he'd played football as a teen. She never thought she'd see him again, other than in her most secret dreams.

The boy looked longingly at the brochures, but after glancing at the man, he stuffed his hands in his pockets as he went down the stairs where Mrs. Mosher waited.

"I was just asking, Uncle Jackson," the boy said.

"Don't talk back," Jackson admonished in a low tone. "You've got some reading homework to do." He turned to

Mrs. Mosher. "He should have been catching up in study hall rather than wasting time here playing with animals."

Mrs. Mosher's wrinkled cheeks flushed at the rebuke. "Matthew has done well in my class and earned this reward."

Jackson put his hand on his nephew's narrow shoulder as he spoke to the teacher. Emma was close enough to hear but hoped the other kids wouldn't notice. "I was just talking with the principal. Seems he's behind the rest of his class in reading."

Mrs. Mosher removed her glasses to peer at Jackson over her long nose. "And you are?"

"Jackson Hardy, Matty's uncle. My sister was in a car accident." His jaw clenched tight. "I'll be filling in for this last week of school." He ruffled the boy's hair. "Guess what you'll be doing this summer?"

Zelda rumbled a protest from the stage.

"Hush," Emma said to Zelda as her heart went out to the boy. His mom had been hurt? She remembered Livvie, with long brown hair and a camera around her neck. She'd been two years ahead of them and had watched over Jackson after the death of their parents.

At Jackson's urging, the boy mumbled something that sounded like a goodbye to Mrs. Mosher. The military had molded the man. Straight posture, polite. A soldier. So different than her memory of him joking with his friends after football games. How she'd loved running her fingers along his sensitive nape—it always made him laugh.

He'd been her first love, the one to show her the stars over the beach, just the two of them wrapped in a blanket on a bed of smooth, oval river rock, protected by the sand dunes and driftwood. Like all first loves, she'd believed they'd have forever, but he'd left her without a backward glance.

Now, ten years later, she wasn't even a blip on Jackson's radar as he thanked the teacher and urged his nephew up the aisle toward the exit of the auditorium. Emma sank her fingers into Zelda's coat in an exchange of solace.

With effort, she peeled her gaze from Jackson's incredible backside and handed out brochures. His slight shouldn't hurt and yet…it was a solid reminder of why, most of the time, she preferred animals to people.

• • •

Jackson Hardy hesitated at the auditorium door, the tingling at the back of his neck hard to ignore. The last ten years in the Marines had trained him to trust his instincts, and he clasped his nephew's shoulder. "Hey, wait a sec."

Matty shrugged free and glared up at him.

Jackson peered into the bright lights at the auditorium stage, but there was no danger—only dogs and giggling children. The sensation at the back of his neck was probably Mrs. Mosher glaring daggers into his back. He might have been a little abrupt with the older teacher and with Matty.

He'd just come from Swedish Hospital where his older sis was laid out on a hospital bed, hooked up to all kinds of tubes, her head shaved—he'd agreed when the doctor suggested a medically induced coma as a way to keep her alive until the swelling went down and they could find the tiny bleed before it killed her. So, yeah, he might have been short, but he was barely holding on. He'd do anything for Livvie. Which included trying to figure out how to be in charge of his nephew and run a home rather than training his men overseas.

"What?" Matty shuffled into the quiet hall. Once the bell rang it would be an eruption of kids, and Jackson had no intention of being caught in the tide.

"Nothin'." He gave one last look into the dark. "I've got Mitch's truck." Jackson let the auditorium door close and led the way to the front entrance of the middle school and the parking lot. He'd been in Kingston a week to the day, and the transition hadn't been easy for either of them.

The doc, as well as Bonnie, Livvie's best friend, had suggested limited visitation for Matty because of the scare factor, and Jackson remembered damn good and well how it felt to be suddenly orphaned.

Jackson forced himself to relax. "Tell you what. Let's go get an ice cream before you hit the books."

Chapter Two

One week later

Emma rolled her windows down to enjoy the pine-scented summer breeze as she drove home from Kingston Animal Shelter. On the way, she passed the property she dreamed of owning to expand Heart to Heart Kennel. The gold and blue FOR SALE sign sat on the edge of the road as a daily reminder. Someday, she thought.

She parked in front of her seventies rancher after her morning shift where she'd accepted a Pomeranian that might be a good fit for the ESD program. Joy turned to apprehension as she realized that the barking from the kennel wasn't the usual "welcome home" greeting from her dogs.

Emma raced for the chain link gate that separated the house from the converted dog kennel. Bandit's deep growl, Princess's high yip—and there—Pedro's chest-rumbling woof. *Something is definitely wrong.* Emma hurried through the gate toward the closed door and pulled down on the silver padlock, her fingers slick with nervous perspiration. It was already undone.

She shouldered the door open and ducked inside the dark garage. Cool air shocked her summer-hot skin, and she flipped the light switch on with a shiver. Barks chorused in a painful cacophony as Emma blinked to bring the room into focus. She sensed she wasn't alone.

Her fingers dropped to her pants pockets. No cell phone, no keys. In her rush, she'd left them in the SUV.

Her eyes finally adjusted to the interior light, and she made out a rust-colored shadow kneeling at the far end of the garage. The space between the lines of kennels was wide open, so there was nowhere for the person in camouflage to hide. The stranger tugged on the door of her newest rescue, a golden retriever mix named Romeo.

Emma's legs refused to move. Was she interrupting a robbery? Someone trying to harm her dogs? In a commanding tone, she ordered, "Stop!"

The dogs quieted at her command. However, the slight, hunched-over figure with the knit ski mask ignored her and pulled at the handle of the crate. Romeo jumped up inside his crate, his tail wagging, his tongue to the side with excitement. Something glinted in the intruder's gloved hand, and Emma was torn between running back to the house for help or hustling to Romeo's aid.

The dog won.

The figure, rushing to get the crate open, dropped the object with a clank against the cement floor.

Emma sprinted by the dog kennels, and the pups barked once more, urging her forward. She neared the person dressed in army green and slowed. "Stop." It occurred to her that she had no weapon, nothing with which to protect Romeo or herself. "Please."

Emma reached the last kennel just as the thief yanked back on Romeo's crate door. Romeo barreled out, happy to see her, trampling his abductor to leap up with his front paws on Emma's chest. His wet tongue licked her cheek. Romeo was definitely a lover and not a fighter.

"Down," she ordered firmly. "*Sit.*"

Romeo, ears at attention, sat. So did the would-be kidnapper.

Emma instinctively reached out and peeled back the knit ski mask, revealing the frightened face and eyes of a boy.

"Who are you?" Her voice hitched. "What are you doing here?"

The boy's chin stuck out in silent mutiny. He looked familiar. Slight of build. Stubborn jaw. "Aren't you a little young to be a criminal?"

The words came without thought. To be fair, their small town in Washington State, across the Puget Sound from Seattle, had its share of seedy elements. Then she remembered exactly where she'd seen him before and who his uncle was: Jackson Hardy. His mom, Livvie, had been hurt in some sort of an accident.

"What's your name?" She kept her hand on Romeo's soft head.

"Matty."

Behind her, the dogs quieted. She bent down and picked up the metal piece she'd seen drop to the cement floor. It was the end of a wire hanger, sharpened to a point. Her stomach knotted. "Is this how you broke in?"

Why? Had he wanted to free the dogs? The army-green camouflage outfit was a costume, she saw now. A few years old, if the inches of visible ankle and wrist were anything to go by.

Matty averted his eyes, so she dropped to her knees, bringing them nose to nose. "Why did you do this?"

He didn't talk. His nostrils flared as his breaths came faster. Now that she was calming down from her adrenaline rush, Emma found room for anger. "You had no right to break into my kennel and frighten my dogs. They were *scared*."

"I didn't mean to scare them."

She held out one hand, palm up. "What *did* you want?"

Her heart, her wide-open, ridiculously empathetic heart, surged at the tremble of his lower lip. He was trying to keep it together, but obviously something was wrong. How could Livvie's accident tie in to one of Emma's dogs?

"You can tell me."

He looked down, eyes shining with unshed tears. "Can't."

Emma sat back on her heels as Romeo broke her "stay" command and joined the boy, nudging the kid's arm with his black nose. The retriever settled his muzzle on the boy's lap and stretched his body between them.

"You know, you can't just steal a dog because you want one."

He brushed his cocoa-brown hair off his forehead, scowling and looking just like his uncle. "I know." Matty gave her an indignant huff. "It's not for me." His slim shoulders shrugged, as if stealing for someone else made it okay.

And wasn't I busted for shoplifting granola bars? She reburied the painful memory. "These dogs are trained to help people. They perform special duties for their owners. Did you want one for your mom?"

"No. She's still in the hospital." Matthew ran a black-gloved hand through Romeo's fur and stuck out his lower lip. "It's my uncle's birthday."

Counting back, Emma realized that Livvie had been in the hospital at least a week, if not longer. These days, that meant something serious. Emma splayed her fingers in the soft fur of Romeo's neck. Jackson had joined the military right after graduation, so they hadn't celebrated his nineteenth birthday together. Matthew's sadness seemed tinged with fear.

"Uncle Jackson doesn't sleep. He was in Afghanistan." A

single tear escaped Matthew's eye. "You said that you train dogs to help with nightmares. My uncle wakes up thinking he's under attack." Matthew pet Romeo in quick, urgent strokes, his expression pleading as he finally met her waiting gaze. "Do you have a dog that can stop them? Can you help?"

Emma's eyes welled, but she tamped down her emotions. Livvie in the hospital and Jackson with PTSD? She wanted to help, but how? "Matthew, I am so sorry about your uncle, and your mom. But you can't steal an animal. It's wrong, no matter how good your intention is."

"I've got money." He pulled a wadded twenty-dollar bill from his camouflage pants' pocket. "I was going to put it in the kennel. Your brochure said that you accept donations."

Not a thief—completely.

She had a standard spiel she gave the schools, but the program required personal training. "I help the owner choose the right dog for them. As I recall, your uncle didn't seem interested in a dog." Not even if it was free.

"I have to do it," Matthew mumbled. "He says nothing is wrong, but I hear him yelling—every night."

Emma had to call Jackson. It was the right thing to do. No matter how much she didn't want to make that phone call, it had to be done. Maybe if Jackson understood that his nephew was concerned, he'd see that there was help available—but her hands were tied. And given their history, he might not want to accept anything from her, anyway. "That isn't how the program works."

Matthew sat cross-legged, his back against Romeo's metal crate, Romeo by his side. "If I give him a dog as a present, he can't say no. You can't return a birthday gift."

Not an option. "Can we call your mom?" Surely Livvie would remember her despite the passage of time.

He shook his head without meeting her eyes. "She's in a coma. The hospital says kids can't be in the ICU. I just want her to come home—we watch *Wheel of Fortune* and she always guesses the word."

Could things be any worse for this kid? Was Livvie's accident the reason Jackson was back in Kingston?

Emma put her hand on his arm. "Matthew, let's call your uncle. Where is he?" She didn't know where Livvie lived, but she assumed that Jackson was staying at their house. For how long?

Matthew shot upward, his small body tense. "No!" Romeo's alert expression swiveled from her to Matty and back.

Emma reached for him as he edged away from the crate ready to make a run for it.

"Don't do it, Matthew." Desperate to think of a way to make him stay, she said, "If you run, I'll be forced to call the police instead of your uncle."

His stubborn chin jerked upward. "I'd rather go to jail. Uncle Jackson is going to kill me."

• • •

Jackson was in his sister's garage working on a kinked bicycle chain when the old green phone hanging on the wall rang.

He wiped his hands on a towel. Could be Livvie's doctors, or the insurance company who seemed to think they knew better than the doctor what care his sister needed, the bureaucratic jerks. He'd had to jump through hoops to get basic medications approved.

He picked up the receiver. "Hardy residence."

"Is this Jackson Hardy?" asked the voice of a young-sounding woman.

"Sure is." Dogs barked in the background. His neck tingled and his body tensed. The way she said his name reminded him of Em. His old girlfriend had been on his mind ever since setting foot in Kingston...well, before then, if you counted his dreams.

"This is Emma Mercer. I have Matthew here with me."

Jackson sat up as if pulled by a string. Emma—his Emma—had Matty? The kid was supposed to be in the house completing a book report. At eleven, Matthew insisted he didn't need to be attached to Jackson's side. But what did he know about kids?

Stretching the cord so that he could see through the garage window to the back door of Livvie's house, he scanned the yard for Matty. The small deck, the table and chairs, the green lawn. No Matty.

He sank his hip against the old plywood countertop. Emma Mercer? He'd imagined her in some big city, working as a doctor or an attorney. She'd been so focused on higher education and giving back. "Is he okay? Give me the address—I can leave right now."

"Don't rush. We're at Heart to Heart Dog Kennel." She rattled off an address not too far down the road. Emma paused, the phone muffled as if she was listening to someone, possibly Matty, before getting back on the line. "We can talk when you get here. We'll be in the yard."

Jackson's gut told him Matthew wasn't in danger, which meant his nephew had disobeyed. A dog kennel? He hated to be too strict, because he didn't know Livvie's style of parenting. He knew the military, where you did as you were told or faced NJP, or worse. The Marines referred to non-judicial punishment as being ninja punched, as it could be the officer's choice of reprimand.

Jackson stripped off his coveralls, grabbed the keys to his borrowed motorcycle, and locked the garage. His old high school buddy now owned the auto shop they used to work at, and he'd set Jackson up with loaner vehicles for as long as Jackson needed them.

Within five minutes he was driving down a gravel road. Washington pines lined the strip on either side, creating natural shade against the summer sun. He went slow enough to hear the buzz of the beetles and smell freshly mown grass from the quarter acre of lawn to his right as the line of trees ended.

The dirt lane led directly to a rambling house where a faded silver SUV was parked. A chain link fence surrounded the large yard and enclosed a single-story garage—the same pale yellow as the rancher. It hadn't changed a bit. The only thing different was the light blue sign with black paws painted around the edges below the garage's three ventilation windows reading: HEART TO HEART DOG KENNEL.

Eight dogs raced around the yard, ranging in size from a tiny yipper with designer fur to a giant wolfhound. Jackson parked his cycle next to the SUV as a woman left the garage with her hand on Matty's shoulder.

It clicked into place, the feeling at the auditorium. Emma had been the dog trainer from the school. He hadn't paid much attention to her at the time, too worried that Matty might fail English.

His belly knotted as the reality of Emma rocked the dream version aside. Thick auburn hair that used to fall over his face when she'd lean down to kiss him, freckles dusting her nose. Her lean physique had filled into just-right curves in her knee-length khaki shorts.

His gaze dropped to his nephew, who bravely lifted his face toward Jackson.

God, the kid looked so much like Livvie it hurt, and the reason he'd come back to Kingston rushed over him. Why was he dressed in camo? Matthew's dark brown hair waved past his ears. He needed a haircut already—Jackson added it to his mental to-do list.

He walked to the fence, his stomach tight. "Hi."

"Hi." Emma smiled in cautious greeting. "How have you been, Jackson?"

He stuffed his hands into his pockets. Would she tell him to take Matty and get off her property? They hadn't parted on the best of terms, and he swallowed as he remembered the tears in her eyes as they'd sat on their driftwood log overlooking the bay. He'd broken up with her for her own good—knowing that if they stayed together, neither one of them would have left Kingston.

And now, here they both were.

She watched him warily.

"Things could be better," he said. "You remember Livvie?"

Emma's chin hiked as if he'd insulted her. She'd been in foster care for a brief time before coming to live with her great aunt, and she knew that his parents had been killed in a mudslide off Snoqualmie Pass. Secrets they'd shared with nobody else their senior year in high school.

"I remember your sister."

Matty watched him and Emma. "You guys know each other?"

Before Emma could call him out in front of Matty, Jackson said, "It was a long time ago." He faced Emma. "I'm home on leave with Matty until Livvie gets out of the hospital."

Compassion flickered across her face. "I'm really sorry."

His eyes burned, and he turned away from her toward his nephew, on the other side of the fence with Emma and the dogs.

She opened the gate and let Jackson into the yard, her posture guarded. She didn't offer her hand, and a hug would have been awkward. He looked at Matty. "What's going on?"

Matthew's face flushed, and he shifted from one sneaker to the next. "Uncle Jackson—"

"We've invited you here to pick out your birthday present," Emma interjected, her hand resting between Matthew's narrow shoulder blades.

Matthew seemed to get a burst of hope as he looked up at Emma.

As Jackson assimilated what Emma had said, he knew he had to draw the line. Livvie was not into pets, never had been. The last thing she'd need if—no, *when*—she came home from the hospital would be another responsibility.

Matty had been on him about a dog ever since school got out, and he figured the kid was trying to pull a fast one. "Matty, we talked about this yesterday. You are *not* getting a dog."

Chapter Three

Emma watched Jackson tuck his hands into the pockets of his classic button-up Levi's, the denim following the muscles along his lean thighs, riding low on his unbelted hips. To avoid shaking hers in greeting? The snub hurt. They used to be so close, but as he'd just told Matty, that was a long time ago.

His black T-shirt was plain, his short light brown hair buzzed military style, his piercing green eyes softened by concern for his nephew.

"Emma has special dogs." Matthew glanced at Romeo, lying down behind her. "They help with stuff."

Jackson pulled sunglasses from his T-shirt pocket. "Stuff. You have to be specific with your word choices if you want me to understand."

"*War* stuff." Matthew studied the grass below his feet. Princess, a pretty Maltese with a pink bow, raced after the wire-haired terrier three times her size. Pedro's tongue waggled as he circled the chain-link-fenced yard.

Jackson's expression clouded. "I'm fine. *We* are fine." He fixed his eyes on Emma and settled the black sunglasses on his head. "Sorry he wasted your time, Em, but we'll be going."

Emma stepped forward, catching Matthew by the shoulder so he wouldn't leave. "It's no problem, really. I can help—"

But he had turned, giving her his broad back, the T-shirt stretched tight across his muscles.

Matthew's lower lip jutted out in a pout as he asked Jackson, "Will you just listen?"

"No. Dogs." Jackson looked at him as if he might be hard of hearing. "We don't know what's going to happen in the future." He pulled his hands free from his pockets, walking to where Matthew stood, head bowed. Jackson ruffled Matthew's shaggy brown hair. "Right? I'm here only until Livvie gets better."

The dogs she trained didn't require a stable home life. Sometimes the dog was simply on loan for a short time until the need for the service animal was over. She knew he was in the military but not what branch. "On leave from where?"

"Marines."

Matthew had said Afghanistan. What had Jackson seen? She cleared her throat. "Are you staying here in Kingston?"

"Yes."

She realized that he was putting up a shield against her. Clipped and polite tones, not really looking at her. Fair or not, it made her angry. "Not far from here?"

"No."

Well, no wonder Matthew was at his wit's end. Talking to Jackson was like scraping the last of the peanut butter out of the jar with your finger.

"The dog doesn't need to be permanent," she said.

"No dog." Jackson looked at her with impatience.

Emma realized there was a lot going on here that she didn't understand or know about. However, if Jackson was indeed suffering from PTSD, then one of her dogs *could* help.

Even on a temporary basis, if the man would just give her a chance to explain. He'd always been stubborn once he got an idea in his head.

Jackson scuffed his black motorcycle boot against the green lawn. "Matty. I'm trying, here."

Matthew curled his hand into a fist, his cheeks rosy with anger. "I am too. You won't listen!"

Jackson put his back to Emma, so he was facing Matthew. "I'm listening."

Inhaling, Matthew studied his uncle as if to make sure. Unclenched his hand. "Emma trains dogs to help with bad dreams. I know that you are here only because Mom is in the hospital, but we are family, Uncle Jackson. Mom would want you to get better."

"She'll be home soon." Jackson scowled.

"It's been almost three weeks and she's still not awake," Matty said, his voice hitching.

"I know she's in a coma, but what happened?" Emma looked from one Hardy to the other. It had to have been catastrophic.

"A very bad car accident." Jackson answered her with contained anguish in each syllable, then turned his gaze on Matthew. "The doctor said this is best for her right now, and we need to stay positive. Your mom will come home."

Rocked by this news, Emma looked out to the yard and her dogs. Romeo, the lover of the group, now cuddled with Lulu the beagle. Bandit, her retriever-shepherd mix, panted in the shade of a cherry tree with Sweetie, the golden Chihuahua, curled up next to him. Cinnamon the Pomeranian chased butterflies beneath the lilac bushes while Princess and Pedro did another lap around the yard. Zelda had found a forever home without completing the training. She returned to Matty and Jackson, feeling their pain in an awful situation.

These two could use the unconditional love her animals

offered, even on loan. She'd get Jackson aside to ask about Livvie and to see what she could do.

"I'm sure they're real special." Jackson touched the wide gap of skin between the end of Matthew's shirt sleeve and his wrist. "And real expensive."

"I can help pay," Matthew insisted.

"How, Matthew? I don't think paper routes even exist anymore. And I can tell you right now that not getting your book report finished today will cost you."

Matthew's chin trembled. "The dog isn't for me. It's for you."

"Stubborn kid." He scratched at the light stubble along his jaw as if just now realizing what Matthew had on. "Is that an old Halloween costume?"

Emma cleared her throat, hoping Matthew would get the hint. He didn't have to confess to breaking into her kennel.

"I was going to bring you a dog home as a surprise." He pulled the crumpled twenty-dollar bill free from his pocket.

"Did you take that from your piggy bank?" Jackson's voice was calm, but Emma noticed the way his jaw clenched.

"Yeah," Matthew said. "You gave it to me for taking out the garbage all week."

"I told you to keep that money for something special." He put his arms behind his back, triceps flexing.

"Your birthday *is* special."

"No way is twenty bucks enough for this kind of dog, which you had to know, considering all the research you put into it." Jackson grimaced. "Did Emma know you were coming?"

Oh, no. Emma skirted around Jackson to stand next to Matthew. "I think I have a solution that might fit everybody."

"I'm not sure I want to hear it." Jackson folded his arms over his broad chest. "Seems to me that Matthew was planning on helping himself to a dog without your permission. Is that correct?"

Emma wished she could ease the situation. She understood there were reasons for boundaries and laws—she just felt there was a lot of room for gray in all the black and white of the world. Thankfully, her great aunt Pepita had believed the same.

"Yes, sir." Matthew swallowed and bravely met his uncle's gaze. "I was going to leave my money in the kennel."

Jackson's demeanor remained unyielding. "You could have left a million dollars and it would still be stealing—taking something without permission."

"But—"

Emma coughed into her fist. "We were in the process of working out a deal when we called you."

"What deal?" Jackson shifted toward her, drawing Romeo's attention. Her retriever-mutt mix sat up with a chuffing noise, his head under her right hand.

"A trade." Emma took the offered affection and returned it with a scratch behind the ears. "I know a lot about post-traumatic stress disorder," she told Jackson.

"So?" He kept his expression neutral, his arms still crossed—shutting her out.

She swallowed. "PTSD."

Jackson scrubbed his palm over the top bristles of his hair. "That's a catchphrase used by two-bit shrinks who don't know what else to do."

"That is not exactly true. There have been many studies done—programs to help war veterans." *Two-bit shrink*?

"What does that mean?" Matthew asked, looking from her to Jackson.

"Two-bits. Means a quarter. Twenty-five cents." He didn't stop looking at her as he explained that he felt the advice that came from therapists was worth only a quarter. "And with most of them, even that is too much," he concluded.

"Hey!" Emma said. Lulu leaned against her left calf to stare up at Jackson with dark brown beagle eyes. "I have my master's in psychology, and I am close to finishing my doctorate."

He shrugged as if the years of school and hardship meant nothing, and her temper brought heat to her cheeks.

"Well, that attitude is why I prefer to work with four-legged clients rather than the two-legged variety." She dug her fingers into the fur at Romeo's neck and narrowed her eyes at Jackson.

Matthew understood *that* just fine and laughed.

Jackson gave him a look that quieted him right down.

"I'm fine. Period. So, there will be no trading. What Matthew did was wrong, and there will be consequences at home. Unless you'd like to press charges?"

Matthew's eyes rounded in surprise as he stared at his uncle. She wondered how well the two knew each other.

Emma forged ahead with her offer. "My plan was to trade the price of the dog out in labor. I need an extra pair of hands this summer. Cleaning the kennels, helping walk the dogs. I understand that Matthew is what, ten?" She guessed, having no clue. She'd been so focused on a career that she'd pushed aside stirrings for more.

"I'm eleven!" Matthew bounced up on his toes, silently pleading with his uncle.

"Sorry. Eleven. I won't let him drive the truck or anything, but I could use a pooper scooper." She expected a *yuck*, but Matthew grinned.

Jackson mulled that over, rubbing his chin with his thumb and forefinger. "We aren't getting a dog. I can't promise the summer, because Livvie could be out and home within a month." He searched her face, and she wondered what he saw—the baby crow's-feet? The ten extra pounds? "Would you consider letting him work a couple days in lieu of calling the cops?"

Emma wasn't the kind to rat—but maybe time around the kennel would show Jackson that she wasn't a two-bit anything and could offer a real solution. He had to start with acknowledging the trauma.

"I'm at the kennel on Mondays, Wednesdays, and Fridays," she said. Tuesdays and Thursdays she was at the shelter downtown. Her weekends were split between training classes or the dogs, with any spare minute spent with Aunt Pepita or her thesis. "Let's try it out. See how we fit—but it would be work." She had zero time to be a babysitter.

Jackson frowned at Matthew. "It's a generous offer."

"I want to, Uncle Jackson."

"We have a deal, then." Jackson reached out to shake Emma's hand, his expression hooded. There was a time when she'd known just what he was thinking by the way he looked at her. "Thanks for working this out with us."

"You're welcome." His hand was big, encompassing hers, and she saw a trace of motor oil under the thumbnail. Her palm warmed, and she quickly yanked her hand back. Her mind tried to fit this Jackson Hardy over the one she'd loved in high school. The two men didn't merge. Ten years had passed since then, and a lot had changed, for both of them. "Please, let me know if I can help with Livvie."

"She's at Swedish Hospital in Seattle. Head trauma. One of her good friends is a nurse there, so she has people sitting with her and checking in all the time. The doc suggested a normal routine for Matty, but now that school is out, we visit every other day—the nurses won't always let him in, but we've gotten past them once or twice."

Emma looked to Matthew, who kept petting Romeo. Poor kid.

"Yeah. Every time I hope she'll be awake, but she isn't. Not yet." Matty turned to Jackson. "I can really work with

Emma?"

"Yes." Jackson stepped back. "But I meant what I said, no dog."

Matthew's shoulders slumped.

Emma stopped herself from telling Matthew that things would work out. Truth was, they didn't always work out how you imagined. There was no guarantee that, even with therapy, Jackson would stop having nightmares, or that Livvie would heal without needing further treatment, or that a dog would be the answer. Truth was, sometimes you didn't wind up with your first true love.

"Can we start day after tomorrow, on Wednesday?" Emma asked. "Matthew, with your help, I've got some agility games I'd like to try."

"Agility?"

"Running, jumping, sliding."

"The dogs slide?" Matthew reached down to pet Cinnamon, who'd left the shade to see what was going on. "Even Romeo?"

The golden retriever barked and wagged his tail.

"He's not very graceful, but he likes to have fun." She lifted her left foot. "Kind of like me." She looked at Jackson, who used to tease her about it even as he'd guided her across the floor. "I've got two left feet, but I love to dance."

• • •

Jackson remembered quite clearly the feel of Emma in his arms.

He watched, amazed at how easily she chatted with Matthew in a real conversation about something other than Spiderman. In the last two weeks that he and his nephew had been living together, that was all Matty cared about—aside from his mom, of course, which was a constant underlying worry. Spidey books, the movies—the kid's room was covered in posters.

What had Matty been thinking? Breaking into Emma's kennel. Taking money from his piggy bank. Leaving the house without permission. Jackson wasn't cut out for parenthood, so Livvie had to get better before he messed something up.

"Did you hear that, Uncle Jackson?" Matty asked, his voice rising with excitement. "We're going to teach the dogs to slide!"

Jackson squinted against the warm sun, regretting his derisive comments—he wasn't surprised at all that Emma had her master's degree, though he didn't understand why she had a kennel. He owed her an apology, maybe more than one. It was a good idea to keep Matty's mind off of his mother. "How is sliding useful?"

"Funny story, but true," Emma said, her hazel eyes bright. A dog, part shepherd, brought a tennis ball over, and she took it while talking, not minding the spit. She lobbed it, and the brown and tan tail wagged before the canine darted after the yellow ball. "Hurry, Bandit!"

Emma wiped her hand on the butt of her shorts, ignoring the barking all around them. Bandit, huh? Maybe some retriever, if the tail was a clue. He'd thought service dogs had to have designer pedigrees, but hers looked like average mutts.

"An ESTD—emotional support therapy dog—was on a flight with a woman who suffered from terrible anxiety. Well, there were some problems with the plane, whatever." She paused as Bandit brought the yellow ball back. She took it and threw it across the yard. This time all eight of the dogs chased after it. "The plane stops, but they can't get to the regular terminal. They have to use the chutes to exit the aircraft." She used her hand to make a downward motion. Matthew's eyes were huge in his face.

"A slide from the plane?" Matthew asked.

"Yes," Emma said. "So, the woman is prepared to go down, I mean, she's anxious, but she's got her dog. Thing is"—Emma paused to hold first his gaze, then Matthew's, then his again—"the dog is terrified and can't get down. Well, the woman starts getting hysterical, and the dog is howling, and it's just a mess. Instead of calming the situation, the dog added to the problem. So I try to get a little slide training in." She nodded with satisfaction. "Because you never know."

Emma's smile animated her face, and she went from pretty to beautiful. Not that Jackson was noticing.

"What happened?" Matthew inched closer to Jackson and looked up to him for reassurance. "How did they get down?"

"They had to blindfold the dog, and the only one who could hold her was her owner." Emma sighed happily. "The dog can be a best friend as well as a partner. Working together as a team."

Jackson didn't need a best friend. He needed his nephew taken care of until his sister was on the mend. Then it was back to the grind for another ten years until retirement. He noticed the oil beneath his thumbnail and wiped it off with the edge of his black T-shirt. As fourth generation military, the Marine Corp had his loyalty.

Bandit dropped the ball at Jackson's feet. He nudged it toward Matthew. Romeo scooped it up and ran off, the dogs all running after him. Emma laughed. "You snooze, you lose. Never a dull moment around here."

Jackson turned at the sound of a vehicle crunching slowly up the pine-shaded driveway. A green and blue minibus parked next to his bike. A whooshing sound indicated the door was opening as the bus hydraulically lowered.

Emma waved at the driver as an older woman, so wrinkled she could be eighty or a hundred, got off the last stair, leaning on a bright purple cane. Dyed-orange hair that matched the slash of lipstick across her mouth was in direct competition with her cherry red sundress and purple sneakers.

Jackson grinned, remembering the spunky woman with great fondness. She probably didn't have the same regard for him, and his grin faded.

"Aunt Pepita!" Emma walked toward the fence separating the yard from the driveway and stopped at the gate. The dogs rushed around in circles, yipping and barking hellos and the wolfhound emerged from the bushes, a yellow petal stuck to his head.

This was not the time to try to talk with Emma. Dang it, it was his birthday, Jackson thought, and he didn't want to spend it punishing Matthew. "Come on, Matty. We need to get going." The knowledge that he would get to see Emma again in just a few days lightened something heavy inside.

Emma pulled her attention away from her aunt, who listed slightly as she made her way toward the bright blue front door of the rancher. The old house was huge, especially compared to the three-bedroom Craftsman Livvie owned.

The bus left with a two-honk salute, and Emma whipped a card from the front pocket of her light-blue polo. Her fingers were long and slender, he noticed, her nails short and unpainted. No wedding ring, but that didn't mean anything. "Here's my number—house phone on the top, cell below. Nine is fine?"

"We'll see you then." He cleared his throat, aware of her subtle floral perfume. "Matthew?"

His nephew straightened and looked directly at Emma in a way that made Jackson proud. "I'm sorry about...you know, earlier." He pointed to the kennel with one hand, the other petting a golden retriever mix Jackson thought she'd called Romeo.

"You made it right," Emma said with a decisive nod. "I

look forward to getting to know you better, Matthew." She turned to him with a smile so genuine Jackson couldn't help but smile back and wish that things were different. "Happy birthday."

"Thanks."

She opened the gate and eyed his motorcycle, careful to keep the dogs on the other side of the fence as the three of them left the yard. "Do you want me to drive Matthew home?"

Jackson reached down to the side compartment and pulled out a small, open-faced helmet that he handed to Matty. "No, we've got this. Do you like to ride, Emma?"

"I've never been on a motorcycle." She tucked her hands in her pockets.

He took that as a "no, thanks." He'd learned overseas. "There's nothing like it."

Matthew climbed onto the back seat. "Especially when we go fast."

Jackson pierced Matty with a "be quiet" look and swung his leg over the leather seat.

"Well, see you later then." Emma hesitated as if she wanted to say more but shrugged instead and followed the path her aunt had taken to the house.

Jackson watched her go, noticing the curve of her hips, long legs that he knew for a fact looked great in a bikini. "See you."

What a day. It had started with an email from his commander, wishing him a happy birthday and telling him to hurry back; his unit needed their best sniper. Livvie's vitals hadn't changed, which was a good thing, and now his nephew had tried to steal him a birthday gift for nightmares he didn't have—from the one woman he still dreamed about. *Oorah*.

"I'm hungry, Uncle Jackson." Matthew slid on his helmet.

"Then let's get something to eat." He put on his helmet,

too. "Tell you what. It's my birthday. No more talk about dogs, okay? Let's go to the Winged Pig for burgers."

"Yes!" Matthew thrust his fist into the air with a cry of victory.

"But, dude, you've got to change into something that fits. What made you think you could break into Emma's kennel wearing camo that shows more skin than it covers?"

Chapter Four

Jackson stopped at the house so that they could each get cleaned up before his birthday dinner.

The three-bedroom was painted brick red with a brown roof and beige trim. Nothing fancy, but his sister had done a great job of making it a home. Military brats, they'd learned to be neat because you might be moving at the drop of a hat.

"Wash behind your ears," he told Matty, closing the front door behind them.

Matty scuffed his way down the hall as if dragging a twenty-pound weight tied to his ankle. "La-ame!"

Jackson recognized himself in the stubborn set of Matthew's shoulders. "And hurry so we get the good table." Right by the window with the best view of the pier.

"Race you." Matty ran the rest of the way to his room, his pout forgotten.

Goofy kid. Jackson stepped into the spare bedroom and went straight to the closet for a clean polo. He edged aside his service uniform, choosing the dark blue shirt over the gray. Time to do laundry again, he noted. Only two shirts left.

He unlaced his motorcycle boots, then kicked them off. Dressed in plaid shorts, leather sandals. *Good to go.*

Jackson stopped to study a collage of pictures in a three-photo horizontal frame on the dresser. He and Livvie as kids, Matty's baby picture in the center, and he, Livvie, and Matty from Christmas two years ago when he'd flown them to Fort Lauderdale where they'd spent a week being tourists and hitting the beaches.

They Skyped occasionally, and he sent postcards, occasionally. Livvie was his next of kin and he was hers in any emergency. Like this one.

His eyes stung as he recalled her laughing face just last month when they'd Skyped for her birthday. He'd asked her what she wanted, and she said he could send her a hot, single guy to come clean out her garage. Next call was from the cops, and then Bonnie, her best friend who had Matty, but she couldn't keep the boy. Jackson had flown out of Afghanistan within the week on emergency leave.

He centered the picture on the dresser.

"Uncle Jackson, are you ready yet?"

Jackson poked his head out into the hall from his bedroom. The home was cozy with a beige patterned carpet. Driftwood frames lined local beach pictures on the walls. Livvie's career as a dental hygienist gave her weekends off to be with Matty and a steady income that provided a roof over their heads.

Jackson had gifted Livvie the down payment without batting an eye, joking that he just wanted a couch to crash on when he came by. He didn't realize he'd need his own room and prayed that his sis recovered completely, and quickly. "Yeah, Matty. What's taking you so long?" He sauntered out of the room like he had nothing better to do.

Matthew, dressed in shorts, sneakers, and a red T-shirt that actually fit, ran toward him with his head down, a football tackle. He moved to the side, caught Matty around the waist, picked him up, and dropped him on the fluffy blue couch in the middle of the living room.

"He-ey!" Matthew, laughing, bounced off the cushions. "I just let you win 'cause it's your birthday."

"Nice." Jackson walked to the phone, pressed play on the answering machine, and waited for it to start as he rummaged for the keys to the truck under the pile of junk mail on the table.

It was Mitch. "Hi, Jackson. Hi, Matty. Just wanted to wish Jackson a happy birthday." Mitch started singing in a high-pitched voice, the guys at the auto shop doo-wopping in the background.

Jackson hit stop and headed toward the door, keys in hand. "Come on, Matty. Good thing Mitch knows how to do an oil change, because singin' won't be how he makes his millions."

"Funny...not."

He locked up and followed Matthew down the front steps.

"Why are we taking the truck?" Matthew asked as they passed the parked motorcycle for the five-year-old royal blue Dodge Ram.

"It might be late when we come home. I don't trust anybody else on the road after dark, you know that." He loved the motorcycle but wasn't blind to the added risk at night.

Matty climbed up to the cab and buckled in. "Are you still mad at me?"

"I am *not* mad at you."

Jackson started the truck with a rumble that sounded like it might need a new muffler sooner than later. He'd fix it up for Mitch as payback for the loan of the vehicles.

"Promise?"

"Promise." He left the dirt driveway and signaled onto the road, leaving the hills and winding down to the beach.

Seattle was just a thirty-minute ferry ride away and had all the glitz of a big city but the baggage, too. Swedish was the best neurological hospital in the country, which made the traffic and congestion a fair trade, to his way of thinking. Livvie deserved the best.

Kingston retained a small-town charm despite the proximity to the Emerald City. Here, he and Matty liked fishing off the pier, and at low tide, they searched for starfish in an array of brilliant colors.

He couldn't believe Matthew had tried to *liberate* a dog from Emma's kennel! So what if Jackson didn't sleep much? He grabbed a few hours here and there, a habit left over from active duty. When you did sleep, you had one eye open, or you risked never waking up.

The Marine doc had warned him about PTSD, but Jackson never dwelled on what had happened on the front. No time. No desire. No need.

Matty rubbed his tummy. "I want a cheeseburger and zucchini fries."

"Who eats zucchini?" It was a joke they played every time they went to the Winged Pig. Jackson ended up eating half of the order, dipped in ranch dressing. Freaking delicious.

"Do you want birthday cake, Uncle Jackson?"

"No cake."

"Do you want me to get the waitress to sing to you?"

"Do you want me to double your pages to read tomorrow?"

Matthew laughed. "I'm glad you're here, Uncle Jackson."

"Me, too, Matty."

Later, after a thick, juicy burger with blue cheese, mushrooms, and a double side of zucchini fries, they parked at the pier and walked down to the beach to watch the moon over the Cascade Mountains. White peaks of snow, even in summer, instead of the flat, dry desert of the Middle East.

He felt a pull toward his men, but Livvie and Matty were his priorities.

"I guess we should get home," Jackson said. What would Emma do if he called her tonight? Her business card burned a hole next to his wallet.

Matty shrugged. "Can we watch a movie?"

"What do you want to see?" He pulled his keys from his front pocket.

"I don't know. Emma is nice."

"Where did that come from?" He ruffled Matty's wavy hair as they walked back to the truck. It was like the kid read his mind.

"She could've been real mad at me, but she wasn't. I didn't want her to call you, though." Matty climbed into the passenger seat.

"Good thing she did."

Matthew snickered. "I told her to call the cops instead. You were going to kill me." He shuddered, his cheeks shadowed in the dark.

"That would explain the worried look on her face when I picked you up." Jackson reached over and lightly pushed Matty's arm. And the way Matthew had dressed for his breaking and entering? She could have called child protective services. They were *both* lucky Emma was a nice woman.

Matthew laughed and rubbed his skinny biceps.

Emma'd always had deep compassion for others, and he knew her offer of assistance toward Livvie was sincere. What could she do? What could any of them do? His sister had to heal on her own. If only he could take on that burden.

They rode home in companionable silence, and Jackson parked in front. They climbed the steps to the home, and Jackson stretched his tight shoulders—he was used to more physical activity. Maybe he'd buy weights for Livvie's garage now that he'd cleaned it out.

"You pick the movie." All in all, a good ending to his birthday. "We can go early to see your mom tomorrow, and watch the fish guys toss the snapper at the market."

Matty went inside. "Okay. Can we bring Mom flowers?"

"You know they aren't allowed in ICU." Matty's small face pinched together, and Jackson pulled him close. "But we can text Bonnie in the morning and see about some plastic ones, or silk?"

"Okay." Matty pushed back from Jackson, trying to be tough. The tubes and machines were scary to him as an adult, so it was easy to imagine what it would be like for Matty. Livvie's hospital room was kept sterile, and there was no room for personal items like get well cards or pictures.

"Bonnie says that people sometimes remember things from when they are in a coma. It's important that we tell your mom how much we love her."

"Okaaay." His tone, on the verge of tears, suggested a permanent subject change as he shuffled into the kitchen to make microwave popcorn, filling the house with the scent of butter.

Jackson cracked open a locally made beer. He rarely drank, and never to excess, but sometimes the amber malt just tasted good. "Spiderman? Again?"

"It's my favorite!"

"Fine." Jackson didn't really care what they watched. This time with Matty was special, and he promised himself he'd be better about staying in touch once Livvie came home. He didn't let himself think about any of the negative outcomes of her accident and the coma.

Fighting for liberty, training with his marine unit, was all-encompassing. Being a soldier required a man's full attention or he risked losing not only his own life but those of his team.

Spiderman was a one-man show, a hero who ended up winning the day but losing the girl. Jackson could relate. At eighteen, he'd met the perfect woman, but the timing wasn't right. Ten years later and it still wasn't right. Seeing Emma after all this time had dredged up memories of love, but that was all they were. Memories best packed away again.

"Can we watch one more?" Matthew settled next to him on the big L-shaped couch.

Jackson must have dozed through most of the first movie. "How many Spidermans did they make?" They could stay like this forever. Two dudes just hanging out and enjoying some cinematic miracles where the good guys got to win. In real life that was not always the case.

Drowsy, he scooted his back against the couch, bunching a pillow under his head to get cozy as he fought the weight of his eyelids. He liked the warm comfort of the television in the background, tethering him to the here and now. Matty against his side.

His eyes closed. Just for a second.

A barrage of gunfire sounded from the right, and Jackson peeked over the embankment, his rifle at his side. Hot sun beat down. The desert amplified heat, making the corners of Jackson's mouth crack and bleed.

He brought his canteen to his lips and sipped. The lukewarm water did little to quench his thirst, but he forced it down. Dehydration killed, his captain said. You mess up? You risk the safety of the unit. Brothers-in-arms, teammates.

Jackson's brothers were the ten men in a six-foot by ten-foot hole they shared, sniping the enemy before they got close. Remi, from his right, handed him a fresh canteen.

"Your turn for shut-eye."

"No. I'll stay." He stared out at the desert. Gold and gritty sand. Smoke from oil fires in the distance.

"Captain's orders," Remi drawled. "Thirty minutes."

Jackson, head down, made his way across the hard-baked dirt to the tent and crawled in, asleep before fully inside.

A bomb exploded next to the tent, shrapnel tore back the canvas sheet and splintered the poles.

Jackson startled awake and grabbed his throbbing leg. Shit. He looked at the rip in his camo. The flesh wound, cauterized by the shot. No blood.

I'm fine. He turned to look at the others sleeping. God, not sleeping. That kid from Iowa, half his body gone. Not screaming. Dead.

Dead.

Remi came running toward the tent for Jackson. "You okay?"

He nodded, his mouth so damn dry. "Iowa. Hansen?" He shook his head and pointed to the blood-filled cot.

Another shrill whistle signaled incoming mortar, and Remi forced Jackson down, underneath the bodies of their brothers. He fought against the gore, the rising bile in his throat.

God, no—get up. Get up!

"Uncle Jackson. Wake up!"

Jackson pulled himself from the rubble, the thunderous bombs reverberating in his ears, making his head throb.

"It's fine, I'm fine." His voice was scratchy and gruff. The desert. He moistened his mouth with a dry tongue, expecting the taste of blood, but there was none.

Matthew pushed against his chest, his face red with anger.

Jackson blinked in surprise. "Hey. What did you do that for?"

"Emma's dogs can help you."

"I just told you, Matty. I'm fine." *I can handle this.*

• • •

The dogs Emma chose for the Emotional Support Therapy Program had to be compassionate in nature, smart, and empathetic.

Tonight, all eight were in the house as she and Aunt Pepita watched another romantic comedy. Her aunt loved the movies, knowing good and well she'd get a happy ending after the roller coaster of laughter and tears.

They'd watched a lot of them after Jackson had left her for the Marines. How was it that seeing him again could bring back all of those emotions? She'd grieved, healed, and *moved on* in the last decade, for heaven's sake. And yet... she slammed the door on those memories and went to the kitchen.

"Ice cream, Aunt Pepita?" Emma called.

Emma wore flannel pajama bottoms and a T-shirt, her feet bare. The summer was cool at night, shaded by the mountainous trees. If you breathed really deep, you could smell Puget Sound through the open, screened windows.

"We still have peanut butter chocolate?"

Emma opened the freezer. "Yep. And chocolate chip mint, too."

The shuffling sound of her aunt's slippers preceded her to the kitchen. "I want a scoop of each." She wrapped a thin purple paisley robe around her ample frame, tying it at the waist as she entered.

"I love that about you." Emma laughed softly and took down two bowls.

Pepita Mercer was Emma's great aunt on her dad's side. Emma had never met Nick Mercer, but Aunt Pep brought him to life with pictures and memories.

Emma fixed the ice cream, and they sat down at the end of the table opposite each other. Pepita reached for the stack of paper napkins she'd filched from the local coffee shop and handed some to Emma before tucking one over the front of her sweatshirt.

"I'm going to donate the twenty-five dollars I won at beach bingo to Heart to Heart." Pep tugged at the lucky green shamrock posts in her ears.

"Keep it. We have enough for this month. Besides, you'll need a stake for your trip to the casino next week." The senior center organized themed mini-vacations throughout the year.

Pepita spooned ice cream into her mouth and closed her eyes, making a humming noise of contentment. "Did you hear back about the grant money?"

"No. Not yet." If the new kennel proposal was rejected again, she was tempted to hire someone experienced in grant writing—which also cost money. But she could do so much more if only she had the land. Just last week, Cindy had turned away two dogs because their no-kill shelter was full.

"How many did you send out?"

"Twelve, and we've had a half dozen rejections, at least." Emma let the cool chocolate melt on her tongue. "Professor Collard called today. I have an appointment with him first thing in the morning."

"About?"

"I'm assuming my last report on sleep apnea."

Pepita zeroed in on her over the table. "Don't think I'm so old that I didn't recognize Jackson Hardy out there today. That man has always had a nice tush."

"Aunt Pepita!" Though, if forced under oath, she would have to agree. She'd learned her lesson the hard way with Jackson, and it had left a scar.

"Is he back in town to stay?"

"No, so forget any matchmaking ideas. He's in the Marines, but poor Livvie was in a car accident. Jackson is taking care of Matthew, his nephew."

"Cute kid. I saw him from the bus." Pepita's brow furrowed as she hunched over her bowl. "Too bad about his sister. Well, if anybody can help them through a tough time, it is you."

"It can't be me." She hadn't told Pep about Jackson not even noticing her last week at the school because, dang it, it had stung—but *that* was the emotion she needed to remember, not the warmth in his green eyes as he'd taken her hand in thanks. "Jackson has his hands full," she said, taking another creamy bite. "Matty tried to steal Romeo today."

Pepita gestured with her spoon, flicking small droplets of chocolate to the table. "What? Why? For his mom?"

Emma was careful to compartmentalize her emotions. "No, she's in a coma at Swedish, and Jackson, here to take care of Matty, is having PTSD episodes that he doesn't remember."

"Why didn't Matty talk to you about it rather than break into the kennel? I'm assuming he saw you at school or something."

"Last week, at Kingston Middle." She knew what it was like to have nothing around you under your control, to be in the center of a tornado as your world twirled and tumbled. "His plan was to leave a twenty and give Jackson the dog so that he would be forced to accept it and, thereby, get help."

"Not a bad plan," Pep said. "You can't give back a birthday gift."

"Poor kid is grasping at straws." Matty couldn't do anything for his mom, and Jackson had his own issues. "Thought I was going to have a heart attack when I came home to find the lock jimmied open on the kennel."

"The dogs are fine," her aunt said with a dismissive wave. "It's you I worry about. Juggling your business with finishing up school. Maybe you should take a break from the kennel and tie up the loose ends. You've spent years, and you are *so* close."

Emma winced. Not normally the kind to drag her feet,

she'd discovered while doing research for her doctorate on dog-human relationships that animals were excellent alternative medicine for many behavior disorders, including agoraphobia. Her mother had suffered terribly, and her fear of leaving the house had ultimately caused her early death.

"I'm not giving up," Emma said. "I study when I can." There was a growing need for service dogs. Instead of finishing her doctorate, she'd started a viable business that needed to expand in order to turn a profit.

The lot next to this one was for sale—if only she had a spare hundred grand. That was so far out of her reach it might as well have been a million. "It isn't just the degree." Tension rose like a tide, and Emma took a deep breath. Calm. *Center.* "It's the internship afterward, then the year or two of practice under a mentor, before I can get my certification."

"Doctor Mercer has a nice ring," Pepita declared.

Emma held her hand to the thumping pulse at the base of her throat. "It is overwhelming." Matthew's attempt to break Romeo out of the kennel had released a torrent of memories that wouldn't go back to their assigned crates, not only of high school but her upbringing. She swirled her spoon around the empty bowl. "What if a therapy dog could have helped Mom?"

"Oh, sweetie. You have *got* to let it go. Your mom, bless her soul, was afraid of her own shadow."

"I know—now." Years of therapy later.

Pep peered over the frames of her orange glasses. "Your poor mother didn't have your strength."

Emma had been raised indoors, taught to be cautious of everything from the UPS driver (who might kidnap her and sell her to bad men), to beautiful lilies (poisonous if somehow mixed with water or a pot of coffee), yet she never questioned her mother's love.

By the time her mom had gone to the doctor for severe

stomach pain, the cancer had spread from her ovaries to her breasts. She never did come home. And Emma was put in foster care at twelve. The two years that followed became a fight for survival.

Judge McDaniel, who knew her from her juvie cases (once for running away, once for shoplifting) had pleaded with her to think of someone to contact or else she risked becoming a long-term ward of the state. Two months later, Aunt Pepita had made a home for her fourteen-year-old great niece, although it had taken years before Emma trusted that she was safe.

Jackson had shown her what it meant to love another person romantically, wholeheartedly—and on the flip side, the heartache when they let you down.

Pepita tapped her spoon against Emma's ceramic bowl to get Emma's attention. "You are a woman with a lot to offer. You have the ability to help other people with anxiety disorders because of who *you* are, and that includes how you grew up."

They'd had this conversation a dozen times and then, like now, her aunt's words soothed old hurts. "Thank you."

Pep released a dramatic sigh. "Though I wouldn't mind some little ones running around the place."

Emma bristled. "We have eight under the table right now." Her hands were full with the dogs' training regimen and growing client list—a family had to wait, and she was okay if that family was of the canine variety.

"You know what I mean. And you aren't getting any younger."

"I am not even thirty yet." Emma already felt as if there weren't enough precious hours to get everything accomplished.

Pepita rinsed the bowls and put them in the dishwasher. "And not that you asked my advice, but if a certain hottie comes asking you to go for a ride on his motorcycle, I'd say yes."

"Jackson Hardy is the last person on this earth that I would go anywhere with." He'd shown her love but then snatched it away.

Pepita leaned back against the kitchen sink with her arms crossed. "Are you holding a grudge? I thought you said you were over him. If that were true, you wouldn't mind offering to help him out. He's a soldier, Emma, in need of assistance."

"He doesn't think anything is wrong. Stubborn as always." Emma shook her head. "I am *so* over him. And I am helping him out, by the way. Matty will be working off his 'crime' at the kennel with me."

"Oh, that's good. You can talk to Matty, then, or rather, listen, which is what you are so wonderful at doing. Especially to me. I'm sorry if I nagged, dear."

Emma smiled at her aunt. Wild orange-ish red hair curled in all directions, and she matched her clothes by vibrant colors rather than patterns. She nagged because she cared. "You're pretty wonderful."

Her wrinkled cheeks flushed. "Oh, stop. Now, let's take these beasts out to the kennel and get them ready for bed. Come!"

At the magic word, all eight dogs exploded from beneath the long table and headed toward the back door and the treat jar. They knew the routine.

Thanks to her aunt, Emma's dreams that night were filled with a green-eyed hottie in jeans on a motorcycle, and Lulu riding in a sidecar wearing sunglasses and an aviator scarf. Emma wore Jackson's football jersey and watched from the bleachers.

Chapter Five

During the summer, Seattle was lush and green because of the rain and the mountains, and the three months of summer were pure heaven on earth.

Everything seemed to be in colorful, fragrant bloom. Tuesday morning Emma walked into Professor Collard's office at the University of Washington on the Seattle campus with the brightness of the season lifting her step.

He wasn't at his desk, so she waited in the hall and scanned her email on her phone. Nothing from the shelter that required her attention. She'd called Swedish Hospital but they couldn't give her any information on Livvie Hardy. Her role, if anything, would be support for Jackson and Matthew—they were supposed to come by tomorrow morning. What would it be like, having Jackson around?

"Emma!"

She looked up at the familiar deep voice of her professor. From London twenty years ago, he retained an English accent and had a penchant for vests. Bright blue eyes glittered at her from beneath black brows, and he had a full head of black hair.

"Professor Collard, how are you?"

"Come in, come in." He lifted a coffee mug in the deep purple university color, a *W* in gold. "Needed to refuel." He gestured to the upholstered chair for guests on the other side of his desk for her, while he went around to his black leather seat. "Did you want coffee or tea?"

"I'm fine." The sooner she was finished here, the sooner she could return to her job at the shelter.

He swiveled toward her and set his mug on the desktop. "Emma." Professor Collard stared at her intently.

She had the first inkling that this might not be about the paper she'd turned in. Yes, it had been slightly rushed, but her facts were correct and… "Yes?"

"You have been working on your thesis for over a year now."

Her cheeks heated.

"We have had students take longer, but my concern is that this program is for students who are serious about getting their doctorate."

She squirmed beneath the weight of his scrutiny. "I am serious, Professor."

He pulled her printed assignment from a folder on the corner of his desk with her name on it and handed it to her. "I am used to receiving pristine reports. Occasionally, one will come in with a coffee stain." He flipped over her work and she cringed, wishing she could sink into the floor.

"Yours is the first I've ever gotten with a paw print on the back."

"I am so sorry," she began, remembering when she'd dropped the pages beneath her desk. It was small, so possibly Sweetie or Cinnamon.

He cut her off with a disappointed head shake. "If you can't get the rough draft of your thesis to me, minus paw prints or stains of any kind, by September first, then I will consider your withdrawal from the program."

Stunned, Emma bit the inside of her cheek to keep from shedding the tears burning her eyes.

"You have an empathetic gift, Emma, that I find remarkable. I think you will be a wonderful doctor. But what is this about?" He jabbed his finger against her paper. "It is not professional and suggests that you are not taking this seriously."

"I have a kennel where I train emotional support therapy dogs. It started small, with my work on anxiety, and dogs, and the next thing I knew, I had eight." She shrugged.

He sat back and rubbed his chin, blue eyes searching her mind as if to discover her doubts.

"I didn't mean to start an ESD business, but I love it. I'm not the only person to work while finishing their schooling, right?"

"Correct." He studied her then leaned forward, his elbows scattering papers. "Do you want to be a doctor, Emma, or a dog trainer?" He held up his hand without waiting for her to answer. "You think about it, because I have people on a waiting list for this doctorate program. I would hate for you not to finish your studies here." He fiddled with a button on his vest. "Rough draft to me by the first of September." He gave her a nod of dismissal, and she blinked, getting to her feet.

"Uh, I'll be in touch."

"I hope so, Emma. The world needs doctors who care."

She left, not bothering to look at the beauty around her as she drove onto the ferry from Seattle to Kingston, shaken to her core. The rest of the day she spent putting together all of her published articles. How close was she to finishing?

Wednesday morning, Emma was outside with the dogs in the yard by nine. She had a mug of dark roast coffee in one hand and a giant chewy bone in the other. King, part wolfhound, all the way huge, weighed in at a hundred pounds and needed encouragement to take part in the exercises. "Fetch!"

Bandit was the smartest of the lot. Part German shepherd and part golden retriever, he was a puzzle solver who liked the mind games. Romeo needed some finesse with his skills, but his innate kindness—as proved two days ago, with Matthew— showed that he was a good fit.

Emma was all about the heart, hence the name of her kennel.

The rumble of a motorcycle sounded along the gravel driveway, and the dogs all stood at attention. And then, in some doggy code she'd never understand, they decided that the newcomer was a friend. Their ferocious barks turned into welcoming growls as Jackson and Matthew came into view.

They parked and, thanks to her aunt and her dreams of him, her gaze dropped to Jackson's butt. She immediately lifted her eyes and hoped her cheeks weren't flushed. If he noticed her blush, she'd blame it on being outside and exercising, though she hadn't done anything more strenuous than lift her coffee mug and throw a dog bone.

Matthew, dressed in jean shorts, a blue T-shirt, and sneakers, waved. He pulled a baseball cap from his back pocket and shoved it over his helmet hair.

Jackson hooked his thumb at Matthew. "Sure you're ready to spend the day with my criminal in training?"

"Uncle Jackson!" Matthew gave him the stink-eye.

Not unlike Pepita and me.

"I'm ready to get some help around here," Emma said. "I checked the child labor laws, and so long as I let you drink from the hose every two hours and give you a thirty-minute lunch break, we're good."

Matthew's shoulders slumped. "Great. You think you're

funny, too."

Emma laughed. "I'm not?" She opened the gate. Jackson stayed on the other side of the fence, indicating he was going to leave but wanted a word.

"I checked you out online."

"You did?" But he knew her... "And?"

"Masters at the University of Washington?"

She lifted her purple mug with the team logo.

"In the doctorate program for psychology." He nodded as if impressed. "Project coordinator at Kingston Animal Shelter."

"Part-time. I find my ESD candidates there. It's a win-win."

"You have this kennel?"

"I am applying for grants to enlarge it—too many dogs get lost because there isn't enough room at the shelter."

"Your house didn't pop when I ran the sex offender search," he said, deadpan.

She hoped he was joking. "You did *that*?" She shook her head, used to being the good guy.

"Can't be too careful. My sister is fond of her kid."

"He is a cutie." She said a silent prayer for Livvie, that she was healing, and glanced at Matthew, who ran with the bone in his hand, held high. The dogs followed as if he were the Pied Piper.

"You were supposed to leave after graduating from Kingston High," Jackson rumbled low.

Emma froze, surprised that he'd gone there. She'd been willing to start fresh and not bring up their history, because it had been so long ago.

He tugged at his jaw and held her gaze. Seconds passed and she was powerless to look away as he said, "I almost called you." It was as if he had to pull the whispered words from his mouth.

She gripped her mug tight, having no choice but to witness his reluctant confession. If he hadn't been forced into seeing her, he wouldn't have. There would have been no phone call to see how she'd been. No offer of friendship. He'd cut her out of his life. Her words in response were clipped. "Ten years ago, or yesterday?"

He winced. "And many times in between."

And like that, Emma suddenly knew that her teenaged broken heart had healed. Whether or not he'd wanted to call didn't matter—what mattered was the present. Seeing Jackson at the school had brought up the past, which is where their love story belonged.

Matty raced by, the dogs on his heels. Emma took a centering breath and let it out slowly. "Ancient history. I hardly remember that time." She changed the subject before it could get more awkward. "How is Livvie?"

"No change." He gripped the fence. "That's supposed to be good news."

"With head trauma, complete sedation allows rest for healing." She'd reached out to one of her colleagues who specialized in treating patients with physical injuries to find out what might be done. As frustrating as waiting was, they had to do it.

Emma touched the top of his hand and offered a supportive smile. "I'll feed Matty lunch. Give him a real water bottle. Can I bring him home? We should be done by four-ish."

"I was thinking I'd stop by."

Concern? Worry? He had so much going on that she offered before thinking of the consequences. "Come around 12:30 for chicken salad sandwiches, and you can catch the glamour of dog training." She looked down at his boots. "You might need a hose to rinse off afterward. I wasn't kidding about a pooper scooper. Eight dogs, what can you do?"

He cracked a smile. "I'll try to get away. I'm helping out a buddy today. Thanks, Emma. Have Matty call me if he needs anything. It's good to keep him busy."

He pulled away from the chain link and walked away. She dragged her gaze up from his back pockets. The man was made for denim.

She finished her coffee and set the mug by the gate. "You ready, Matty? Now, this first part of the day isn't so fun." She led him inside the garage and handed him a pair of latex gloves and a pooper scooper with a small shovel. She also put on gloves and grabbed a heavy duty black bag. "Let's go."

He wrinkled his nose but didn't complain, and they walked through the front yard and the acreage out back. She pointed to the property next door, all wild foliage on the other side of her chain link fence. "Someday I want to buy that lot, too."

"What will you do with it?"

"Make a bigger kennel and training center."

"Why don't you do it now?"

"Money." She rubbed her fingers together.

"Yeah, Mom tells me all the time that she's not made of money."

Emma laughed. "How are things going, living with your uncle?"

"He doesn't make good pancakes like Mom, but he tries his best. We like to watch Spiderman movies," he told her. "Well," he grinned, "I like Spiderman. Uncle Jackson doesn't care."

"My aunt and I watch romantic comedies. We love laughing."

"My mom reads romance novels." He scrunched his nose. "Yuck. Lots of kissing and stuff on the covers. But she bought me comic books at the bookstore in Seattle. That was cool." He looked over the grass. "Yesterday we went to see Mom in the hospital. Aunt Bonnie was there—she's not my real aunt, you know, but my fake aunt—and she says that Mom is just the same, which everyone thinks is good, but I don't get it."

He sounded very doubtful and very scared. Her heart thumped painfully. She knew how that felt, to have an ill mother. "I remember your mom," she said. "She was so pretty in high school, with long brown hair and big brown eyes. Like yours. She used to take pictures."

"She does, still," Matty said. "She likes the mountains best. Her favorite photos are on the walls in our house."

Emma kept her voice even-toned. "Did you get to sit with her for a while yesterday?"

He nodded, his face pale. "I have to wash up really good and can stay only a minute." He glanced up at Emma, sorrow and confusion in his brown eyes. "She doesn't look like my mom."

Her emotions squeezed tight, but she remained calm for Matty. "Because of the machines?"

"There's a tube to make her breathe until her head is better. The doctors had to shave her hair." He shrugged but kept his eye on her for her reaction.

"Hair grows back," she said. "Maybe she'll like it short after this."

"Maybe." They took a few more steps in the grass. "Aunt Bonnie says that she will look cute in hats."

It seemed like hopeful conversation, which was important for everyone. "Well, I am here if you ever want to talk, okay? You're welcome to play with the dogs, so long as you check with your uncle, and me, first."

"I wish my mom liked dogs." He kicked at the bag with the toe of his sneaker. "Do you think one could help her get better? Maybe Cinnamon—she's small. We could sneak her into the hospital."

"How about we don't break any more rules for a while?"

She smiled to show she was teasing. "Your mom has you, Matty. I bet you she won't stop giving you hugs once she's better."

He grinned at that. "She used to do it all the time."

Jackson had been great at hugs, too. Maybe it ran in their family. She hoped to God that Matty never had to experience the loss of his mother the way she had.

She and Matty worked quietly for a time, scanning, scooping, and bagging at a comfortable pace. And then, not unexpectedly, he asked, "So, is it, uh...normal, for Uncle Jackson to not remember his bad dreams?"

"Yes." She walked a few more paces over the mowed lawn. They'd cleaned up the area well, but she wasn't ready to go in just yet. She tied the bag. "Oftentimes when we have nightmares, our mind thinks it can protect us from the danger, or bad feelings, brought on from the dream. So, we don't remember it when we wake up."

He frowned.

"It's normal to resist the feelings we get during a nightmare, so the mind and body collaborate—the brain erases the memories, and the body stays awake and fights the idea of sleep..."

"Even if he's, well, shouting?"

"Yes." She swatted at a bee that buzzed past her nose. "It's not unlike sleepwalking. Did you ever do that?"

He pulled his baseball cap from his head and stared at her as if she might be pulling his leg. "Is that for real?"

"Sure is. My mom told me that I used to walk in my sleep. I liked to go to the refrigerator." She rubbed her stomach.

"Do you still?" He scratched behind his ear before putting his hat back on.

"No. I guess I outgrew it." She shrugged. "Sometimes things go away over time." *Time helps, but not always.*

"It's getting worse. Uncle Jackson doesn't sleep very often. When he does, I don't wanna wake him up, you know? But he might end up having scary dreams. I looked it up on the internet. A person has to have five hours of sleep a night, or they could go *crazy.*"

She put her hand on his skinny shoulder. "Matthew, what your uncle has gone through is a little different."

"He wakes up and says he's fine."

She'd witnessed Jackson Hardy deny anything was wrong—how to make him understand? "I can try to talk to him later on about it, okay? Because we used to be friends"— she cleared her throat—"he might listen to me." *Or he might tell me to mind my own business.*

"I wish I had a cell phone." Matthew ducked his head, the bill of his baseball cap casting a shadow along the green grass.

"Why?"

"So I could videotape him. Then he'd have to believe me."

"Oh, that's probably not a good idea." *It was a great idea, but she'd hate for Matthew to be in trouble.* But she would definitely talk to Jackson in private. He probably didn't realize how scared it made Matthew to see the one person he was counting on out of control.

She doubted Jackson Hardy would ever harm a hair on Matthew's head, no matter how upset. Still. "Why don't you give me a call the next time he's having a nightmare? You shouldn't wake him, Matty. But if it is bad, then I can be there for you." She shaded her eyes from the sun. "I don't live far— call me."

Matthew exhaled so hard his shoulders bowed forward. "I just want him to get better."

Matty probably felt like he could help fix some of what was happening with Jackson, whereas his mother was out of his control. "I'm here to help."

"I'll call," he said decisively. "If Uncle Jackson shouts again. Sometimes he stays awake all night, so he doesn't sleep. Drinks Red Bull. *Yuck*."

Yuck was right. "Once I'm there, then I can sit with you and we can talk about all the different options for easing PTSD. It doesn't have to be with the support dogs. I'm a psychologist, too. Okay?"

Relief eased his stiff spine, and his slight body relaxed. "Thanks, Emma."

"You are very welcome." She prayed it would be a good start toward Jackson's recovery. Matty was relying on him.

• • •

Jackson wiped the motor oil from his hands and stared at the shiny black BMW. It had been a heck of a job, but it was done. He turned to Mitch and checked the time. Just after twelve.

"Hey, do you mind if I duck out? I want to see how Matthew's doing." Emma had been very cool to invite him to lunch. Seeing her the other day had sparked dormant feelings that, on top of everything else, he had no time for.

"Can't believe he tried to steal you a dog for your birthday." Mitch finished washing his hands in the sink and grabbed a paper towel. "A boy needs a pal to hang out with."

"Well, that's just it, right?" Jackson paused, thinking of a foggy future where his sister might need even more help once she'd come home from the hospital. "Who's going to take care of them?"

He remembered the other night when Matthew had woken him, saying he'd had a bad dream. It wasn't like he was hurting anybody, for Pete's sake. He just had to make it through the next few weeks until Livvie was better, and then he'd be back with his unit, and things would return to normal—well, Afghanistan normal.

His means of coping with the desert memories was to bury them deeper in the sand. His means of coping with his sister, helpless in a hospital bed? Well, that was new, and he had to figure it out.

"Say hi to Emma for me, will you? I see her now and then around town. She's as pretty as ever, all that red hair." Mitch leaned against the counter.

Jackson, hit with a pang of jealousy, was tempted to tell his pal to back off. After his stupidity this morning, saying he'd thought about calling, for the *last ten years*, well, he wouldn't be surprised if the Mercer house was on lockdown, with him on the outside. He gritted his teeth. "Sure."

Jackson waved and left the shop. The bike roared to life beneath him, and he drove toward Heart to Heart Dog Kennel.

If he remembered correctly, Aunt Pepita made amazing chicken salad sandwiches, and he hoped she didn't add arsenic to his. When would Emma have time to be in the kitchen? Girl was smarter than Einstein and truly kind, and yeah, pretty.

He parked in front of the house, and Matthew ran around the side lawn to greet him. The dogs were in the fenced part of the yard away from the rancher.

"Hey! Emma said you might come. We're spitting watermelon seeds—Aunt Pepita is winning. She's got a space between her teeth." Matthew tapped his front tooth. "Pretty cool, huh?"

Jackson chuckled. "Pretty cool."

Matthew raced ahead, and Jackson rounded the back of the house, then stopped in surprise. The front was nice. Well-kept. Seventies rancher, long driveway. Garage to the side, with a chain-link-fenced lawn. Just as he remembered.

But the backyard was spectacular—like something in a city garden. About twenty yards away, a fountain that had to be six feet across with a stone cherub in the center spewed water into the air that landed in the basin below.

To his left, a bramble patch of blackberries was woven against a trellis. He recognized tomato plants, zucchini, and pumpkin in the garden beyond. Birdhouses nestled in pine trees or attached to wooden poles attracted blue jays and sparrows that darted back and forth. Butterflies fluttered around the tall lupines and sweet peas. Two fat orange felines lounged with flicking tails on the back porch.

He turned to walk up the three wooden steps to the screened back porch, where a picnic table with a red and white checked cloth was loaded down with sliced melon, a platter of sandwiches, a bowl of potato chips, and a pitcher of iced tea.

"Jackson! Welcome."

"Looks like I arrived just in time," he said, his stomach growling at the homey display. He patted his flat belly.

The wrinkled woman with bright orange hair and glasses stood from the picnic bench she'd been sitting on. "Come here, Jackson. What do you think of the backyard? I started planting and just couldn't stop. Retirement blessed me with a green thumb."

He stepped forward, and the old woman pulled him into a hug. "It's so nice to see you again," he said against her poof of hair.

She leaned back, one gnarled hand on his shoulder for balance, gesturing to the long wooden bench with her other. "Have a seat. Is tea okay? I can get you water or put on a pot of coffee."

Emma nudged open the back kitchen door with her hip, holding a plastic tray with plates, silverware, and cups.

She saw him, and her pink mouth stretched into a welcoming smile, her guileless face the sweetest thing he'd seen in a very long time. Emma hadn't changed in that she was still kind, still beautiful, and still not for him.

"Hey," she said. "I was hoping you'd make it. Your nephew is a champion in the yard-cleaning department."

Nice. He looked at Matthew, who shrugged as if shy but was obviously pleased.

"I promised him some fun this afternoon." She stood before Jackson, and he knew her to be five feet, eight inches to his even six feet. "I thought we'd reinforce what I've been going over with the dogs—some simple hand controls."

"How is that an ESTD thing?" he asked, straddling the bench. He hadn't forgotten her passion as she'd shared the story about the woman on the plane.

"It's not just for that. Who doesn't like a trained dog?" She set the tray down and offered him silverware wrapped in a cloth napkin. "Stay, sit, roll over. Do the dishes."

"I can see how that last command would be a winner." He ruffled the bristles of his hair. "Do you place all the dogs you train?"

"So far, yes. Our longest trainee is Lulu. Beagles are not as popular a breed as they once were." She held up her hand. "Don't get me started on the designer dog craze. It's always been around, but thanks to the internet, styles go viral. Next thing you know, the shelter is filled with Chihuahuas—after the Taco Bell commercials, remember? And then everybody wanted a Pomeranian when Boo pictures went viral on Facebook."

She looked ready to take up the fight. Champion for the underdog, literally. Seemed she'd grown up since their orphan days. Him, too.

"The problem is that I don't have enough space to grow Heart to Heart Kennel. I'd love to have a no-kill dog shelter where I can take in hundreds of dogs, make sure they find good homes." Like she was already doing, but on a larger scale, he thought.

Aunt Pepita stirred sugar into her tea. "Our Emma is going to have her own practice for *people* someday, too."

"Pep," Emma said with a warning expression. "Not if I don't get my thesis done." She turned to Jackson. "My professor is turning up the heat. But enough about that. Are you hungry?"

He shifted on the bench seat, gesturing to the food. "This spread looks amazing."

Pepita sipped her tea, nodding with satisfaction. "Just a little something. Emma reminded me that you liked my chicken salad. I am so sorry about your sister. But we sure are glad to know your nephew. Did you ever get married, Jackson?"

Jackson poured icy cold tea into a glass. "No." He set the pitcher down on the table and nodded to Emma. "Can I pour you some?"

"No, I already have one somewhere…" Emma looked around and then reached across to the porch railing and picked up her glass of tea, cubes of ice clinking. "There."

"Emma was Matty's age, well, a few years older, when she came to live with me." Pepita gave him a knowing look over the top of her orange-framed glasses. "Kids are resilient, and no matter what happens, you just love him, and he'll be okay."

"Well, the hospital is doing all they can to make sure Livvie is on the mend." He appreciated that neither woman pried with further questions, as if sensing that he was on the edge and didn't have answers. Jackson breathed in. He'd forgotten how nice it could be, sittin' on the back porch and enjoying the summer sun—sitting next to a beautiful auburn-haired girl.

Emma handed him a paper plate. "Help yourself." She called out to the yard where Matthew was petting one of the orange cats. "Lunch is ready, Matty."

He ran up the wooden steps to the screened back porch, more at ease than Jackson had seen since the accident. Fresh air and sunshine were just what the doctor ordered—for them both.

"You can wash over there," Emma said, pointing to the large tub sink at the far end of the deck. "More lemonade, Matthew?"

"Yes, please," he said, turning on the water and using the bar of soap without any hints from Jackson. He dried his hands on a paper towel and then sat on the bench next to Aunt Pepita.

Jackson felt the brush of Emma's arm as she reached across his shoulder to refill Matty's plastic tumbler. Her sweet perfume blended with the flowers in the garden, her body mere inches away.

His attraction roared to life. She'd always been in his heart, but she'd made it very clear this morning that the past was just that—ancient history.

The casual banter at the picnic table was easy to flow in and out of as they all ate watermelon and chicken salad with chilled green peas. Matthew was eating without complaint. *Weird kid.* Jackson had learned to eat anything and be grateful for it, but veggies still weren't his first choice.

Emma reached for her drink and accidentally bumped his elbow. Cool tea spilled onto the table between them. "Oops, sorry, Jackson! Did I get you?"

"No." He wouldn't have minded if she had doused him. Her reddish-brown hair had streaks of gold in the shaded light of the covered porch, and her skin, lightly freckled, seemed soft. Jackson quickly pulled his gaze away from her rosy lower lip and bit into his sandwich.

"Uncle Jackson," Matthew said from across a bowl of watermelon. "Sometimes Emma takes the dogs to the park at the beach. Isn't that cool?"

"It is." He swallowed and dabbed at his mouth, turning to Emma. "Do you take all eight dogs at once?"

She shook her head, her hazel eyes bright. "I'm not that brave. My max is four at a time, though usually fewer. I was wondering if Monday I could bring Matthew with me? He'd be a big help with the leashes."

Jackson's first response was to say no. They couldn't get embroiled in Emma's world—they didn't belong. She was smart, a shrink. He was a high school graduate with sharpshooter skills destined for military life. The past was not always the past.

He knew the scent of her skin, had memorized the texture of her hair. "Friends" would never be enough, not when Emma made him want it all. She always had. So much so, it was scary.

He was sure she'd be long gone by now, kicking Kingston's dust off her heels, but she hadn't even left for college.

Even so, he was headed back overseas in a few weeks.

Emma nudged him with her arm and winked, long auburn lashes fluttering, and he remembered her "butterfly" kisses against his cheek. "You can check my driving record. Nothing spotty."

He cleared his thick throat. "What makes you think I didn't do that already?" It had been part of the public record when he'd searched, not even a parking ticket.

"Really, Jackson?" Emma took a drink of tea.

The table quieted as three sets of eyes turned to him, waiting.

"Fine. Next week you can go to the dog park with Emma. But I gotta say, Matty, this doesn't feel much like a punishment."

Chapter Six

After lunch was over, Pepita volunteered to do dishes. Matty asked Jackson to stay for a while, and Emma turned to Jackson with a daring grin. "Want to see what my dogs can do?"

"I'm curious," he said. "It looks like you've built something pretty great here." Matty darted down the stairs of the porch to the grass.

"If you have the afternoon free?" Emma wasn't sure what Jackson was doing with his days, and she'd hate to impose.

"Yeah. I took a month of leave so I can be here with Matty and help Livvie. I've been filling in at Mitch's auto shop in exchange for use of the truck and bike." He went down the wooden stairs, his boots on the lawn. "Mitch says to tell you hi."

"Same." She'd seen Mitch around Kingston, but she didn't really socialize unless it was something to do with her pups. They headed to the chain link fence that separated the lawn with the dogs' yard and the shaded field where she had some agility equipment set up: an adjustable slide, a crawling tube, and various bales of hay for climbing and jumping.

Matthew twisted his baseball cap backward on his head. "This is a way better playset than I ever had."

"I never had one." Her mom's fear of leaving the apartment had included a fear of public spaces, which meant that while Emma could look at the park across the street, she wasn't allowed to play in it.

"No swings or anything?" Matthew asked in disbelief. He looked to Jackson as if she had to be joking, but Jackson knew. He'd been the first and only man she'd ever opened up to about those dark times.

Jackson put his hand on her shoulder and squeezed.

She quickly moved away from his offer of comfort. "I survived. Anyway, it was fun putting this together." She'd talked to a couple of dog trainers to get an idea of what would be beneficial. "You might meet Sawyer Rivera—he's a high-ranking dog trainer in Seattle."

"What does that mean?" Matty scooped up a tennis ball from the grass.

"He's the best. I persuaded him to add our shelter to his roster, and he promised that if I get this grant, he'll help me with the optimal design for my shelter."

They strolled past two different-sized barrels. "These are for jumping. But it's not all about physical activities," she said. "I want the dogs to use their *brains* to problem solve." She pointed to the three-foot-high maze she'd built with changeable gates so she could switch the tracks. "I'm working with some of the dogs, Pedro and Bandit, on how to communicate via flashes of light, like Morse code, but way simpler."

"What's that?" Matty tossed the ball up in the air and caught it.

Emma sighed, reaching back into her own mind for an easy explanation. "Back in the way old days, before the internet and telephone..."

Matthew laughed. "The *really* old days."

"People communicated through telegraph, signals carried by light or sound in a short code. You could ask your uncle about it, I bet. They probably still use it in the military."

"A secret code?" He glanced at Jackson.

Jackson snagged the ball from the air when Matty tossed it again. "I'm not telling. It's secret for a reason, bud."

"Hey!" Matty laughed but wasn't actually upset. "When can we start?"

"Soon as we finish going over the equipment." She showed him the plastic slide that could be adjusted to different heights. "Even Cinnamon can go down it."

"It's like they're training to be in the circus," Jackson said. Now that he had the yellow ball, he didn't seem to know what to do with it.

"A little." She handed Matty a metal clicker the size of his pinky and offered one to Jackson, who shook his head.

"We use these in training—you can keep this one. We click to affirm a correct behavior instead of verbal communication, for folks who might not be able to speak clearly. Like someone who has suffered a stroke that affected their speech."

"Okay." Matty studied the clicker, holding it carefully.

"Romeo is the newest, and he likes you, so he might try to suck up. You have to be firm, and if you give him an order to stay, he has to stay, or he won't be able to participate."

Matthew nodded with a serious expression. "Got it."

Emma headed toward the kennel. "All right then. Let's wake them up from nap time."

Matthew snickered and stuck his hands in his front shorts' pockets. "Nap time. Dogs don't need naps."

"Of course they do," Emma said, sharing a smile with Jackson. "It's hard work, being an Emotional Support

Therapy Dog. There are different types of dogs, just like there are different kinds of people." She patted her heart. "These guys feel emotions for others at a deeper level. It's called empathy. Like when Romeo laid his nose on your leg last week. He felt you were sad."

Matthew put his hand over his own heart.

"That was his way of sharing your sadness and offering comfort in the best way he knew how."

Jackson stayed with them, listening. That was something she'd always liked about him—he never had to be the center of what was going on.

She opened the door to the air-conditioned kennel and turned on the lights. The pups *woofed* in greeting. "Show time! Jackson, do you mind doing the heavy lifting? We've got to create a maze with the bales of hay."

"Nope." He brushed a hair back from her temple in a gesture that he might have done a long time ago. "Once things are set up, I can go on a slushie run."

Jackson's soft touch made Emma shiver despite the heat.

"Yes!" Matty said. "Blue raspberry."

She looked at the boy and shook her head. "Your lips will be blue for days."

"I don't care." He rubbed his tummy. "It tastes soooo good."

She smiled at Jackson. "Do they still have cola flavor?"

"Oh yeah. That used to be your favorite."

"Good memory."

"I haven't forgotten anything about you, Emma Mercer."

She gently pushed him toward the hay bales before she did something stupid like confess that she remembered him, too. Chocolate or vanilla? Jackson was vanilla. Beach or mountains? He was beach.

Emma or the military? He'd chosen the Marines.

Now he effortlessly lugged the hay from the garage

outside, and she had to pull her focus from Jackson to the dogs, who waited patiently to start their games.

"Okay..." Deep breath in, deep exhale. "Let's start on the end with Romeo."

• • •

Jackson had been gone for less than an hour on a slushie run and now had a carrier stashed in a small cooler to keep the treats from melting.

He rode down the long, shaded drive to the yellow rancher at the end, listening to Pearl Jam. They'd had a great time at lunch and setting up the agility course. Jackson realized that Emma was in her element, training these dogs with firm boundaries and lots of treats. She had an easy way with Matty that Jackson liked, and he could see her with a houseful of kids in addition to her beloved dogs.

He parked, pulled the keys from the motorcycle's ignition, and stuffed them into his front jeans' pocket. Emma and Matthew were in the far field with the dogs. He spied Pepita, sitting on a bale of hay as she gave orders to the mutts. It looked like chaos.

He picked up the small cooler and let himself in the gate, carefully closing it behind him. Watching his step, as warned—eight dogs, what could you do—he made his way to the group.

Bandit kept his eye on Jackson, though he didn't leave the other dogs. They didn't rush around him as he walked up. Too busy playing. Or was this work?

Pepita blew an old-fashioned metal whistle. The shrill blast made everyone freeze, including Matthew, who had dirt on his knees, a bruise on his cheek, and a grin on his face.

The women greeted him with smiles, but the attention was focused on the game.

Pepita tooted the whistle, and they all crawled forward. She blew it again, and they stopped.

"Pedro, you were last. Come." Emma snapped her fingers and the dog joined Lulu, King, and Romeo next to Pepita's bale of hay. Pedro lowered his head as if in shame and gave a low *woof.*

"What's he saying?" Jackson asked Emma.

Emma had pulled her auburn hair back into a ponytail. "He wants to play again. Pedro is a sore loser. Matthew, however, is a champ. The dogs love that he's in the game."

The Chihuahua inched forward along the trampled grass without the whistle.

Emma pointed and snapped her fingers. "Sweetie, I saw that. Come."

Sweetie, tail between his legs, joined them on the sidelines. Bandit barked, and the dogs stilled. Readied.

"Is he the boss?" Jackson asked. The dog had a lean, muscled body, and the tail reminded him a bit of his own childhood dog. Goldie. He hadn't thought about Goldie in years.

"Bandit? He thinks he is," Emma answered with a shake of her head. "But I get to be the boss." Jackson thought she made a very sexy team captain.

Pepita gave the signal and Matthew, Cinnamon, Bandit, and Princess all crawled forward. She blew it again, and they all froze in place, except for Cinnamon, who took three extra steps.

Emma snapped her fingers. "Come on, Cinnamon. Next time."

The Pomeranian lifted her head regally as she took her spot next to Romeo, who gave her a sympathetic lick.

Matthew was out, then Princess, which made Bandit the winner. The dog seemed to know it, too, and ran directly to Pepita, who pulled a bone the size of a chicken drumstick from her skirt pocket.

Bandit took his prize to the shade beneath the cherry tree. Pepita got up and presented each of the dogs on the side the same treat, and when she came to Matthew, she handed over a wrapped Twizzlers stick.

"You played well, Matthew, but Bandit is a Freeze whiz. Wins every time."

Matthew accepted the candy with a thank-you.

Jackson handed out the cups of slushie—blue for Matty, cola for the rest of them. "Having fun?"

"Oh yeah."

He didn't bring up the book report due, but he knew Matty would get to it. They had it on the calendar in the kitchen.

Matthew offered the licorice to Jackson. "Want a bite?"

"No." He'd lost his sweet tooth about the time he discovered girls and acne, and then there was Emma, just the right amount of sweet. "Thanks. Nice bruise."

"I was chasing Romeo and hit the maze."

Emma looked at him with an apologetic shrug. "We put some ice on it."

"No worries. Part of running with the dogs." He scuffed his boot along the grass. "Well, uh, thanks again for today, but we should get going." Jackson didn't want to, and that was a problem. He wanted to suggest pizza and movies—maybe another game of tag, to prolong the camaraderie.

"Next Monday, the dog park on the beach. Bring a swimsuit, a towel. Can you swim, Matthew?" Emma was asking his nephew while looking over his head at Jackson.

"Yes," Matthew said. "Mom made sure I had lessons."

"Livvie and I grew up swimming in pools all over the world." He looked at Matty. "Your mama was part fish." He regretted that his parents weren't alive to see their grandson. An ache lingered, but he pushed fear for his sister aside. He had to have faith that she would be okay.

Bandit, done with his treat, sauntered toward Jackson and Matthew and nudged Matthew's hand with his long brown nose before doing the same to Jackson.

"No more treats." Jackson showed his hands.

"He's saying hi. Pet me," Matthew said, giving the dog a scratch behind the ear.

Jackson dropped to one knee to look the dog in the eyes. "Congratulations on the win, boy." He used both hands to give Bandit a good rub across the back before standing up again. "We had a golden retriever growing up."

"You did?" Matthew asked. "What was his name?"

"Goldie. Your mom got to name him; otherwise it would've been something cool, like Maximillian. Or Thor."

Emma and Pepita laughed while Matthew nodded. "Mom is such a girl."

"Hey," Emma said. "Nothing wrong with girls."

"Goldie's a silly name."

"Who do you think names the dogs around here?" Emma asked, pointing between Pepita and herself.

"But you're different." Matthew finished his licorice and shoved the wrapper in his pocket. Jackson made a note to check all pockets before doing laundry. "You're a professional."

Pepita stood and brushed golden straw from the back of her shin-length skirt, sucking the last bit of frozen cola from the cup. "Thank you, Jackson. That was just right." She lifted the whistle to her mouth.

The dogs watched. Waiting. Bodies tensed and at the ready.

Pepita blew three times, and the dogs raced for the garage like greyhounds on a track. Jackson looked at Emma. What the hell?

"Dinnertime," Emma said, holding up her whistle. "A

trained dog is a happy dog, for everybody."

"I believe you," Jackson said with a drawn-out drawl. "I just saw Bandit win a game of freeze tag."

Emma laughed. Matthew raced behind the dogs and Pepita and left Jackson to walk next to Emma.

She smelled like warm sunshine and fresh-mowed grass. Did she ever make time to go down to the beach like they used to? "Thank you for the maze and the slushie." She shook the mostly empty cup. "Matthew really did great today," she said.

"Thanks for not calling the cops on him." He glanced at her sideways. Her long legs kept stride.

"Ah, he just wanted to get something special for you." Her sweet voice told him that she'd forgiven any trespass. "For your birthday. How was it?"

"We went out for burgers." He shoved his hands in his pockets, fighting the ridiculous notion to touch her hand. "That was plenty good enough for me." He'd had birthdays pass forgotten in a desert where he was grateful to be alive.

She put her fingers against his arm, the skin warm. His gaze lifted to her face. Would her mouth be as soft, her kiss taste like cola?

"How's Livvie doing? Matty and I talked a little bit today about his mom and…" She let her words trail before saying, "I am happy to talk to you, and Matty, if you need someone to listen."

Was she being a friend, or offering her professional services? His shoulders tightened as they walked in tandem. "We're fine."

"I know that you're dealing with a lot right now, and I'm just letting you know you aren't alone."

"Thanks."

"If you don't want to talk me because of, well, high school"—he sensed she was holding back an eye roll—"I can recommend someone else. Another counselor." She snuck a peek at him. "I know an amazing psychologist who deals with PTSD."

The friendliness he'd been feeling evaporated, and Jackson stopped walking, waiting until she looked right at him. He lowered his voice, determined to get his point across. "There is nothing wrong with me, got it? I don't want to 'talk' to somebody. I'm going back to Afghanistan in two weeks." Their command expected a batch of new recruits at the end of the month, and he needed to be there to make sure they were trained right.

Livvie had to get better. If she didn't, he would have to rethink his game plan. He would have serious questions for the doctors when he went to visit his sister tomorrow.

Emma's hazel eyes narrowed, and her smile faded. She stepped back and lifted her chin, creating an additional barrier between them. "Matty is afraid. He's worried that you, his sole custodian, might not be okay. I'm sorry if that messes up your timeline, *Captain* Hardy."

Chapter Seven

Friday morning, Jackson dropped Matty off with Hunter, his friend from school. He met the mom and exchanged phone numbers, something Matty swore was normal and okay, before catching the ferry to Seattle and the hospital to visit Livvie and get some answers.

His nephew was torn between swimming or visiting his mom in the hospital—where most times, he wasn't allowed to see Livvie. Jackson promised him that if there were any change, he'd come right back and get Matty.

All night, he'd rehashed his harsh words to Emma—he'd pushed back because he felt cornered. He didn't have the time to deal with supposed nightmares.

What if Livvie wasn't better within the month? He could take a longer leave, maybe, but the thought of his men on patrol without him didn't sit right.

The hardest question to ask was, what if Livvie never got better?

Jackson entered the hospital and took the elevator up to the ICU. His sister was alone in her room, hooked up to the ventilator and IV bags. Her eyes were closed with purple bruises beneath them. Her mouth was the same pale color as her skin. A sob caught in his chest as he sat at her side, covering her fragile hand with his calloused one.

When their parents died, they'd had only each other. "I love you, sis." He bowed his head, begging her to wake up. To come back from wherever she was behind the bandages on her head. "We need you."

The *blip* of the machines was ceaseless.

He'd done some research on medically induced coma patients and how some came back with memories of their loved ones. Some came back with brain damage. Some didn't wake up at all. His eyes burned as he stared at Livvie, willing her to feel his love for her. "And Matty—Liv, you are a rockstar mom. You've done a great job. He misses you. Loves you."

Her hand beneath his twitched.

"I hope you're taking the time you need to heal in there, Liv." Emma's words came back about him having his own timeline…seeing Livvie now, so helpless in the hospital bed, he knew that he was kidding himself.

Two weeks. Even if she woke up today, she'd need therapy. His parents had left them too soon, and they used to dream about having more time together as a family. Yes, his unit needed him, but his sister did, too.

He'd send off the email to his commander when he got back requesting an extension. Bracing his shoulders, Jackson listed new priorities. His family came first even if it meant having to retrain the new recruits after he rejoined his men. Those lives were also his responsibility, and he didn't take that lightly.

• • •

The next day, Jackson watched Matthew reading a book on the creation of Spiderman from the window of his sister's garage. His nephew sprawled on a lounger in the backyard, feet bare.

The school said one book a week, a single page report per book—didn't matter what subject. At first it had been a struggle to get Matty to read, but it was getting easier for them both as his nephew accepted the new routine.

Jackson counted the screws in a small box and wrote the number down on a scrap of paper. Not that Livvie would ever utilize this as a shop, but at least she had room to park whatever car she might buy, along with their bicycles.

Matthew hadn't heard Jackson's warning to Emma when they'd left Heart to Heart Dog Kennel the other day, and Emma hadn't given anything away as she'd waved goodbye with a promise to see them on Monday.

Why did he want to call her so badly?

Emma was kindness personified. The girl who'd overcome a tragic childhood had become a woman of integrity. Her passion for wanting to save the dogs—all of them—made him want to pitch in and start building. That she trained them to comfort others, as she had a special gift, was the perfect choice. He'd been an idiot to think she'd live in the big city—she didn't want that. Had she ever?

Maybe it had been an excuse, his excuse.

She made him wish for things...like picnics and barbecues.

"Don't go there." Jackson shook his head, shut the drawer, and pulled his smartphone from his back pocket.

He powered it on and slid down the list of contacts, his eye on Matthew. Both feet stretched out in front of him, the open book on his lap as he snacked on carrot sticks. *Weird kid.*

He pressed Emma's number and listened to the phone

ring. She answered on the third trill. "Hello?"

"Hey, Em, it's Jackson."

Silence. Then. "How are you?"

He didn't blame her for being cautious after his outburst. "All right. I wanted to let you know I've decided to extend my family leave for another month. Means I'll go back around the first of August."

"I see. Any change with Livvie?"

"Nah." His throat ached, and he coughed. "But even if she was woken up tomorrow she'd need time."

"I don't know how things work in the military—will you be okay?"

"I have personal time saved up. Three months paid emergency leave before I have to worry about that. Benefit of working for the government. It ain't all glory," he joked.

"Thank you for calling to let me know," she said in stiff tones.

His apology was next on the tip of his tongue when she said, "I know you didn't plan on a family, well, kids, but Matty seems like a good boy. He's going to need you, Jackson. I'm glad you're there."

"I'm sor—"

"I have to go. Bye."

Jackson's stomach tightened, and the responsibility that was drilled into a Marine from the second you set foot in boot camp weighed down on him. His team, his duties, his country.

Instead of diving down that rabbit hole, Jackson thought of Matty. Not Matthew as a cute and chubby baby, or as an energetic toddler or smart six-year-old, but Matthew now. Big eyes in a youthful face, growing like a weed.

"Screw it." Jackson closed the garage door with a snap of the bolt. He knew how to be a damn good soldier, but no one had trained him to be a good father figure. "Matty, how 'bout some pizza? You're never gonna bulk up if you keep eating those carrots."

. . .

Emma and Pepita followed the short trail from the SUV to the bay, each carrying a bag of stale bread. They'd done this ever since Emma had moved here from Atlanta. Their spot had a long wooden bench, perfect for viewing the distant Cascade Mountains, and a seawall between the park and beach where the gulls perched.

Maybe because Emma hadn't been allowed outside while growing up, she loved the outdoors now, especially the water. Rivers, lakes, the ocean or bay, the movement and sound soothed her soul.

Her aunt made her way down the path, leaning on her cane. The floral print summer dress had large front pockets, and she wore red flip-flops on her feet. Aunt Pepita sank down on the bench and lifted her purple toenails from her afternoon pedicure, a white flower on each big toe.

"You should have come with me," Pepita said. "My treat, for all you do."

"I don't have time for manicures or pedicures," Emma said, her own toenails naked. She sat down, too. "And polish with my job is a waste."

"A woman should take time to feel pretty—not that you need any help, with those cheekbones," Pepita declared. "It's nice to be pampered."

Emma breathed in the salty air from the bay and opened the brown paper bag of bread scraps. Seagulls gathered on the old seawall in front of them, separating the park area from the sand below. "I know, fill the spirit as well as the mind and body. I got my hair trimmed yesterday. Does that count?"

"How would I know? It's always in a ponytail or stuffed

in a hat." Pepita tossed breadcrumbs on the wall. A seagull squawked to keep the other gulls away and tapped it up in its orange beak.

This was her happy place. The waves on the beach, the smell of salt and fish, the cool air from the mountains. It never mattered how hot the day had been, evenings were perfect.

At fourteen, Emma's arrival at the rancher had been culture shock. She was raised in downtown Atlanta, and the expanse of nature around the yellow house had seemed daunting. Her aunt had welcomed her great niece with warm hugs, long walks, and lots of unconditional love.

Emma rolled a few crumbs of bread between her fingers to make the piece bigger. "You remember Lucky Charm?"

Pep had granted Emma access to her bookshelves, the back porch, and the ever-present pitcher of iced tea. Her aunt had won her over forever when they'd found a stray dog, matted and filthy. Emma knew her aunt would never agree to keep the mutt, but instead, Pepita had gotten out her herbal shampoo and a hose. After a spirited discussion and multiple trips to the thesaurus for the word lucky, they'd decided to name her Lucky Charm.

"She was the first." Her aunt grinned. "Little did I know that rescuing one would lead to converting the garage into a kennel. And possibly a whole new training shelter! The dogs are great, but you need to find someone to love." Pepita tended to be one-tracked.

"I have no time right now, Aunt Pep." Matty being so great made the idea of family and kids somewhat appealing in the far distant future. But now that Professor Collard had essentially put her on probation for her doctorate? "Romance has to wait."

"I think you should give Jackson another chance."

She whirled on the bench. "Are you kidding me?" He'd left her for the Marines. "He is career military. Nothing has changed about him in the last ten years."

"A lot has changed, for you both."

"I'm not that love-struck girl anymore, thank God."

"He's a hottie."

"So you keep saying." Jackson was cute, no—handsome. Cute was for babies and puppies, and there was nothing cute about Jackson's muscled physique.

"The problem is," Pepita continued, throwing a crumb to a large gull. "All of your schooling has given you this ideal of what being in love should be."

Did Aunt Pep have a point? She'd learned in her psych classes that love was often confused for other emotions that didn't usually stand the test of time. Sexual desire, lust, jealousy—just to name a few.

"I've had boyfriends. You make me sound like a nun, and that is not the case." She'd dated, but her focus had always been on a higher prize. Grades, scholarships, starting her own business, getting her degree, and always saving the pups.

"Love makes you do stupid things, but you can't help it." Pep sighed, sounding wistful. "I may not have had a great marriage, or children, but I did love." Pepita emptied the first of the bags and then crumpled the paper. "Yes, I did."

"You could fall in love again." Her aunt had a full dating life. "What about Harold, your casino partner?"

"Ha. He's all right," Pep said. "Funny, which helps pass the time on those long bus rides."

"Speaking of casino trips, do you have everything you need for the one coming up? I can't believe you'll be gone for a whole week."

"There's a thousand-dollar jackpot! Got to pack my gold hoops."

"Right." Trust her aunt to think about the good luck first. "But I was actually talking about your medicines for the week. Do we need to make a stop at the pharmacy?"

"Nope. Got it all taken care of."

She loved her aunt's independent spirit. Opening a second bag of bread scraps, Emma turned toward the pier. "Hey, that looks like Matthew." Her nape tickled as she spied the taller figure behind him. "And Jackson."

"Where?" Pepita arched her neck and shifted on the bench.

"Coming out of the pizza place." He'd sure been mad at her, for crossing the line—but what were they? Friends—not really. He'd once finished her sentences for her.

She didn't blame him for reacting when she'd brought up his nightmares— he didn't understand how they affected Matthew. If he would just listen, she'd explain the situation could be temporary. Bandit seemed taken with Jackson, and the man had surprised the heck out of her when he'd dropped down to really give the dog a thorough petting.

She'd assumed, because of his vehemence against having one, that something had changed and he no longer liked dogs, but that wasn't the case. It was Livvie. Jackson thought he was protecting his sister and didn't realize that the dog could come back to her kennel.

Matthew and Jackson looked in unison toward the beach.

Emma lifted a hand with bread in it to wave, and a seagull swooped in the air and snatched it from her fingers. Pepita screeched in surprise while Emma pulled her hand to her chest, laughing. "That's what I get for not paying attention."

Matthew raced down the pier and jumped the two feet into the sand below. He scrambled up and over the seawall like a fiddler crab. "Are you all right, Emma? Aunt Pepita?"

"Yes," Emma said, still laughing.

Her aunt splayed her palm across her heart. "Like to scare me to death."

Jackson followed the path from the pier to the beach and joined them a minute later. "Sneaky bird," he observed.

"Can't trust a seagull," Emma agreed. "My fault." She scooted over on the bench to make room for Jackson as if it were the most natural thing in the world.

Matthew was up on the seawall, shooing the gulls away and balancing on the two-foot cement block. She remembered doing the same thing, always waiting for Pepita to tell her no, but her aunt gave her the freedom to trust herself. And if she fell? A hug, a bandage, and advice to try again.

Jackson sat down, and Emma became acutely aware of him as a man. Not Matthew's uncle, or a potential client, not the ghost of her high school crush, but someone who stirred her senses in the now. His jeans brushed her bare thigh, and she wished for a moment that she'd worn longer shorts. Though for the weather, her tank top and sandals had to be more comfortable than his jeans, boots, and T-shirt.

She pulled her gaze from his muscled arm and the edges of a tattoo peeking beneath the armband. He caught her looking and smiled.

Blushing, the curse of the redhead, she said, "What's that tattoo?"

He scrubbed his hand over the inch-long bristles on the side of his head. "Ah. First tatt after joining the Marines. Had to be an American eagle, complete with flag. Not very imaginative."

A teensy part of Emma hoped to see it someday. "I still don't have any tattoos."

"Does that sound like regret? We can fix that, you know." He pointed to the Inked Inc. neon sign a block down Main Street.

"No thanks." She didn't like needles. "What were you guys doing?"

"Pizza. Fabio's by the slice, that way we each get what we want. Can't believe that kid likes green peppers."

Emma laughed. "Fabio's has been around forever.

Remember the garlic knots?"

"We'd order a dozen and split them," Jackson said. His smile dipped as if he didn't want to go there.

Garlic kisses used to be one of her favorites. This summer would be torture if everything became a memory of how *they* used to be.

Matthew raced headlong down the wall, seagulls flying in front of him.

"He's got so much energy." Jackson crossed his arms and stretched his legs out in front of him. "Thanks again for the other day. That's all Matty talks about. Drove me nuts with that clicker thing. We went to the library before dinner, and he picked out a book on golden retrievers instead of Spiderman."

"Wow," Emma said. "The dogs beat out Spidey?"

"I know." He uncrossed his arms and looked at her. "Sorry about my attitude. It's just that things are, well, complicated."

Pepita got up and walked the empty bags to the trash can at the end of the pier, leaving Emma alone with Jackson. Matthew chased after Pepita, talking a mile a minute about his new book.

Emma kept her voice low, her eyes on his. "Thank you for the apology. But I just wanted you to know that I am here to listen."

His expression closed down, his face an impassable mask.

She hurried to reach him before he completely shut her out. "Remember that Aunt Pepita was there for me, after my mom died." He winced, his jaw tight.

"She listened to a very lost teenager. I remember how safe I felt, being able to share things. Matthew has opened up to me, and I'm offering to be that shoulder for him. I'm a psychologist. There are tools I can teach him to cope with change and conflict. With your permission, of course."

Jackson sat forward, his elbows on his knees, his hands in

fists. After a few minutes, he said, "So long as you don't try to fix me, then I agree. I can pay you."

She bit her lip but held his gaze. Stubborn man. "Not necessary. I like having him help at the kennel."

"We don't take handouts, doctor."

"I am *not* a doctor. Yet." *Maybe never.* She sat back, her eyes on her aunt and Matthew, who were walking back. Slowly. *Thank you, Aunt Pepita.* "I'm just about done with school, but then I have to intern, and mentor, and basically—" She clamped her mouth shut before she overshared her fears that she'd fail.

He straightened and looked into her eyes. She opened her heart, urging him to see that she wanted to help him. That was all.

A seagull flew between them to land on the beach, snagging a crumb of bread out of the sand and flapping its wings before taking off again.

The emotional connection was broken, and she sighed. "I want only what's best for Matthew." *And for you.* Her heart ached at the suffering he was burying just to get through each day.

"I believe that." His mouth twitched. "That's the only thing keeping me from telling you to take a hike."

"Jackson!" She sank her elbow into his side.

Matthew and Pepita strolled up.

"Uncle Jackson, let's get ice cream, please? I ate two pieces of pizza." He rubbed his flat tummy. "I'm still hungry."

Jackson leaned forward and wiped pizza sauce from the corner of Matthew's mouth with the pad of his thumb. "Okay."

"Want to come?" Matthew asked Emma and Pepita.

Jackson started in surprise.

"No," Emma inserted smoothly before her aunt, who was a sucker for ice cream, agreed. "We have to get back to the dogs."

The two Hardy guys left, headed toward Main Street and The Happy Cow, the quaint ice cream parlor with fourteen flavors of homemade creamy goodness.

Emma watched them go, Matthew practically skipping in his hurry for a cone and Jackson's confident stride as he checked the street for traffic before they crossed. Her insides tingled. She looked out at the bay and made a wish as the sun's rays glittered atop the water. *Please take away this attraction to Jackson Hardy.*

He was, as she used to say in high school, a hot mess—she had the credentials to know.

Chapter Eight

The following Monday, Jackson showed up with Matthew right at 9:00 a.m. Emma hadn't been certain he would still come, and she hadn't called to make sure. They were trying to figure out their relationship, which was familiar but new.

She'd dropped Pepita off earlier at the senior center, wishing her luck and slipping her an extra hundred-dollar bill for just in case.

Dressed in army green cargo shorts—for the pockets— and a tan T-shirt with tan Converse, Emma was ready to call the dogs for a ride. Not sure if she'd have help, she'd already gotten them out of their kennels, and they now raced around the yard, barking their good mornings to Matthew and Jackson.

Matthew, in shorts, sneakers and a gray tee, carried a backpack over his shoulder. "Hi Emma! Got my stuff."

"Stuff?" Jackson asked.

"Sorry." Matthew tossed a *busted* look at his uncle. "I got my swimsuit and towel."

"Close enough," Jackson said with a short chuckle. He

looked at Emma. "Morning."

"Hi." She waited, following his lead. Would he be chatty? Or head off to wherever he was going today without any conversation?

"Listen." He put his hands behind his back as he waited on the other side of the chain link fence. "I was wondering if we could talk after?"

Emma nodded. "Of course." She wasn't sure she should extend the offer, but what did it hurt? If part of what held Jackson back was a lack of trust, then maybe he needed to spend more time with her. He could rest easy, knowing that she had Matthew's best interest at heart. "My aunt is out of town for the week, so I'll have the house to myself. If you're up for dinner, I can cook."

Matthew nodded, bobbing up and down on his toes to show his answer.

Jackson hesitated. "Yes. Great. I can bring wine. Dessert?"

"I make a mean lasagna, so whatever you think goes with Italian."

"Okay. Cannoli?"

"Perfect." They looked at each other and then away. Emma's pulse raced, and she hoped she hadn't made a mistake by inviting him back into her home. Her sanctuary.

"Bye, Matty. Be good."

"See ya, Uncle Jackson. Lame." He dropped his backpack by the fence and entered the yard with the dogs, who greeted him like a long-lost friend.

Jackson left with a halfhearted wave. "Lame?" He said over his shoulder, "I used to be cool, you know."

Emma knew that for a fact. "Oh, yes. I remember."

Matty rolled his eyes and took off around the yard with the dogs. His happy shouts, as he ran, brought a grin to her face. He finally joined her at the fence, his cheeks flushed from his sprint. The dogs jumped around him excitedly. Kids and pups went together like peanut butter ice cream and chocolate syrup.

"How's it going, Matthew? Did your uncle have nightmares over the weekend?"

"Nope." Matthew pulled his water bottle from the side pocket of his backpack and twisted the cap to take a drink. "It's like he's afraid to fall asleep. He won't sit comfortable on the couch. Drinks a ton of coffee."

Not healthy, but Jackson was coping. "So, do you like lasagna?"

"Yep. Mom used to make it. With bread and salad. I love salad." He rubbed his tummy.

"You do?"

"Uncle Jackson says I'm weird."

She laughed—not many kids admitted to being a fan of veggies. "Romeo likes lettuce. I guess we all have our little quirks. That's what makes us interesting." Emma stopped before she went into a lecture he probably didn't want to hear. "Are you ready?"

Matthew's eyes brimmed with excitement. "Now? Yes!" He quickly returned his water bottle.

Emma blew twice on the training whistle. The rowdy dogs lined up at the fence, backs to the driveway as they faced her. Bandit's tail swiped the chain link. Matthew stood at her left side.

"Who gets to go?"

"Since I have your help today, I want to take the four bigger dogs. Romeo, Bandit, King, and Pedro." Romeo *woofed*, waving a front paw.

"I have my clicker." Matthew patted his back pocket.

"Perfect." She called the four small dogs to join her, using the motion to stay once they were at her feet. Then she clipped leashes onto the four big dogs' harnesses and handed the leads to Matthew. "They have to stay with you." She lifted her palm, making longer eye contact with King. "Stay."

The smaller pups trotted behind her when she whistled for them, walking in a single line. She crated them in the air-conditioned kennel with an extra treat. "I promise just you four will go next time." They didn't seem to mind as they gnawed on their chicken-flavored rawhide strips.

Emma closed and locked the kennel door, returning to Matthew. Pedro, Bandit, King, and Romeo all remained in sitting position, canine expressions hopeful—they loved going for rides. "Looking good, guys." She pulled kibble from her pocket to reward them. "To the SUV!"

Matthew opened the side door, allowing Pedro and Bandit to climb in the back seat, making room in the rear hatch for King and Romeo. Emma checked her supply tote for her special treats, kibble locked in a paper bag with a few pieces of bacon for different flavor, water, collapsible bowls, and the whistle, before getting into the driver's seat. Matthew belted up. "What are we going to do first?"

"We've got a ball and a Frisbee," she said. "The idea is to get them acclimatized with other dogs and for them to listen to the whistle signals, no matter what else is going on around them."

"They can't be distracted," Matthew said.

"Correct. If the dog is going to pass the American Kennel Club's Good Citizen test, there are ten requirements they have to follow. Bandit and Pedro are more advanced, which is good because Romeo and King can learn by watching them. Remember Zelda, at school? She was sweet, and we found the perfect home for her without a certificate."

"What was wrong with her?"

"Nothing was wrong. Zelda was too excited to sit still during the tests."

"I don't like tests either."

She pulled a piece of paper from one of her many pockets and handed it to Matthew. "If they don't pass, they don't get to be certified as service dogs, or emotional support *therapy* dogs, which means they can't go into *all* public places with their owner." Emma started the SUV and headed downtown. "We're going to work on the first three items today."

Matthew scanned the list, his forehead scrunched in concentration. "Dogs don't get paid," he said with all of the surety of an eleven year old.

"What are they going to do with money?" Emma countered. "These dogs get paid in what they want most: love and companionship."

"How do you know that?" Matthew sounded as if he needed to be convinced.

"Because I went to school and learned all about it." Emma glanced in the side mirrors, appreciating the light traffic of Kingston compared to Seattle. Midmorning during the week meant they had the road leading down from the hill to themselves. "Animal behavior science."

"That's a real thing?" His brown eyes challenged her for the truth.

"Sure is."

"But you studied people too, Uncle Jackson said. You're a shrink."

Was Matthew deliberately trying to get under her skin? She exhaled and bit back a smart remark. "I'm a *psychologist*."

"Why aren't you a vet if you like dogs so much?" His knobby knees bounced as he waited for her answer.

"I like people too, I really do. It's just that sometimes," she hesitated, "sometimes I feel for the person who is hurting so much that it upsets me." Emma slowed for a stop sign, braked, and then pressed on the gas pedal. "One of my old boyfriends in college suggested pet therapy, and it was a good fit."

"You had a boyfriend?"

"Yes. You don't have to look so surprised, Matthew." Emma wasn't sure how to take his shocked expression. "I've had a few." *Including your uncle.*

"Why didn't you marry them?"

"Now you're starting to sound like Aunt Pepita." She pulled into a parking spot by the dog park. "I never found someone who made me want to get married." She'd learned that if she was thinking about her studies while the guy buying her a burger was trying to impress her, it was best not to go on a second date.

He stuck out his lower lip before finally giving her a nod. "Makes sense."

"Yeah? Then can you do me a favor and explain it to my aunt?" She glanced at him and grinned. "Aunt Pepita has two boyfriends."

"She does? What do they do?"

"Go dancing. To the movies."

"I don't like to dance, and you said you aren't very good." He spoke matter-of-factly. "If you want to go to the movies, I'll go with you. But you have to buy the tickets. And the popcorn."

"Thanks. I'll keep that in mind." She turned off the engine, and the dogs paced back and forth, excited for an outing. "All right, one of the things that we need to expect from our animals is that they properly exit the car. We don't want them so excited that they jump out and knock us over or run into the street and get hurt."

Matthew's eyes widened, his hand hovering over the latch on the passenger door. "What do we do?"

"They've been trained to stay with the verbal command, but I also want them to respond to the whistle. Dogs need to know verbal first and then the whistle. We use a clicker sometimes for this, too. Come on, watch me open the back door."

There was no traffic in the parking lot, and she and Matthew faced the rear window. Bandit and Pedro both sat expectantly—neither dog jumped on the glass.

She held up her hand, palm out, in the nonverbal command for stay. "I make sure they both see me."

Matthew nodded, his studious gaze going from her to the dogs and back.

"Next, I open the door." Emma stood close enough to stop the dogs in case of an emergency, but she was confident that these two would obey and not run loose into the street.

"Stay," she said, maintaining eye contact.

They sat, waiting, eyes on her.

"Stay." She blew once on the whistle.

They waited. She felt their mounting excitement, but they didn't break the command.

"Up." She reached into her pocket of treats for bacon-infused kibble and gave one to each.

She blew once on the whistle, which was the command for sit.

Both sat back, their ears high and proud.

"Good!" She gave them each another piece of kibble before reaching for their leashes. "Up!" Tails wagging, they each stood in the back. She blew the whistle twice for them to stay, and then she stepped two paces backward. Three short blasts of the whistle and then she said, "Jump."

They each did, landing close to her feet and staying at her side, away from the open expanse of pavement. She led them to the sidewalk and handed the leashes to Matthew. She blew the whistle once and the dogs sat.

"You have control of them now, but hold their leashes while I get the other two dogs, one at a time. Romeo is a little better at it than King, believe it or not, even though he is newer."

"What am I supposed to do?"

"Hold them. If they move from their sitting position, repeat the verbal command to stay. If they don't listen, then we will work on that command together, in the park."

The dog park at the beach was segregated into sections of fenced area for large dogs and then another for small pups. It gave Emma a chance to get her pets mingling with strangers and new dogs in a positive way.

She opened the side door to greet Romeo. "Sit." The dog wore a perpetual smile, but this was not playtime. "Stay."

His body wiggled against wanting to follow the command and wanting to get out of the car and into the park. His nose lifted as he smelled the other dogs, and his tail thumped against the seat.

But—he sat. And stayed. Which was progress. "Very good boy," she said, leaning in to check his leash before stepping back and saying, "Jump."

He landed on the sidewalk and started toward the dog park, but she said, "Stay." Romeo strained against the leash but then released a huff of breath and sat down with a low growl in his chest, his eyes darting from her, to the park, to Matthew, and back to her.

"Good boy."

Matthew laughed. "He didn't want to."

"No. But he did, and that's what we want to encourage." She treated Romeo's behavior with a piece of kibble. Shoulders back, she returned her attention to King. "Your turn, Big Stuff."

King barked once, announcing he wanted out, before jumping down from the seat to the sidewalk.

"No, King. Let's try it again." Emma got the wolfhound back in the car, closed the door, and then walked next to Matthew to pet Romeo while talking to Bandit and Pedro. She ignored King. "Good dogs. We have to teach King how to wait his turn."

Romeo whined and tore his attention from the dog park to the closed door of the SUV, where King had his nose pressed against the glass. King barked. *"Woof!"*

She shook her head. "Sit."

He did.

By the time she opened the door again, King was sitting, but panting heavily. "Good boy. Now stay." She held her palm up. His furry limbs quivered with impatience, and he scooted to the edge, his ears at attention. They had to master the verbal commands before she could even think about the whistle for him.

"Jump."

This time, King was aware of his body, and her body, as he landed next to her on the sidewalk. "Good boy!" She scratched behind his ears and under his muzzle, giving him three pieces of bacon kibble.

Romeo nudged King with his nose, staying seated.

"Improvement," Emma said, smiling. "Matthew, how are Bandit and Pedro?"

"They didn't move an inch," he reported.

"Give them a treat. Thanks, Matthew. I couldn't do this without you." He really was a great kid. Jackson had scored in the nephew department.

• • •

Jackson watched Emma and Matthew from a spot on the pier, his eyes tracking Emma's auburn ponytail. He'd called the insurance company about a disputed claim for Livvie, then did some research on what he'd need to do if he had to stay longer than an extra month.

He'd called Bonnie, who said there had been no change in his sister's condition. At this point, the doctors had decided to slowly reduce some of Livvie's medication, keeping her under to see how she would respond. They specifically were worried about the wound in her head that they'd tried to fix with laser surgery. Nothing to do but continue to pray and wait.

So, being hungry for fish tacos—the best place was on the pier by the dog park—he figured, why not bring them all lunch?

He wasn't spying but satisfying his curiosity. *Uh huh.*

He picked up three orders of fish tacos with *pico de gallo* on the side and a bag of homemade tortilla chips, then walked the half mile or so from the pier to the enclosed dog park.

They were temporarily out of his line of vision, and Jackson was tempted to turn back before Emma, or Matthew, saw him. He wanted to tell Emma that he did trust her with his nephew, that she could talk to Matty, if that helped him with his feelings about his mom.

There was nobody he trusted more when it came to emotions. Feelings.

He crossed the parking lot and heard Emma whistle for the commands before he saw them at the very far end. Two little dogs were yipping and yapping in the small dog park separated by a fence. Not Emma's dogs, though. Pedro, Bandit, Romeo, and King all sat at attention as Matthew stopped before each one and held out his hand for a shake, then brought their paw up, as if checking out the nails. Strange.

Emma saw him and waved. "Hey, Jackson!" She wore army-green shorts loaded down with leashes and bags in the cargo pockets. Water bottles? Sneakers the same shade as her shirt.

He leaned his forearms against the top of the fence, the bag of tacos dangling from his fingers. "You guys hungry? I brought lunch."

Matthew finished with the last dog and looked at his

uncle with a grin. "I'm starving."

"Join us?" Emma invited, unlatching the inner gate. "Matthew, you can release the dogs with four whistles."

Matty gave a burst of four with the metal whistle, and the dogs bolted forward as if freed from an invisible tether. Jackson walked into the enclosed space, holding the bag high. "Impressive."

"That smells delicious." Emma eyed the bag approvingly. "The Greasy Fish?"

"None better." Jackson followed her to a picnic table she'd commandeered for the dogs and their accessories. They had the large dog park to themselves. "You got the run of the place?"

"Yeah, there was a dog here bigger than King. A Newf, New…" Matthew looked at Emma for help.

"Newfoundland. About two years old and full of energy." Emma cleared a space so they could all sit. Matthew took the same side of the bench as Jackson, so they faced Emma.

The dogs sniffed him hello before taking off at breakneck speed around the park and along the beach area. Hard-packed sand made it easy for them to run and play tag with the low-tide surf.

"Anyway, him and King went nose to nose. I was worried they would fight, but Emma gave King the command to sit, and he did—the bigger dog snuffled him all over. Slobber and everything."

A smile twitched at the corner of Emma's mouth.

"Nice," Jackson said, imagining the amount of saliva a Newfoundland had. Maybe worse than a Saint Bernard. "You want to wash up before we eat?"

"We did already. There's a hose by the tree." Matthew rubbed his hands together. "Fish tacos?"

Emma took a plastic bottle from her side pocket and passed it to Matthew. "This too, please. Hand sanitizer never hurt anybody."

Matthew didn't complain before squirting some into his palm. She did the same and offered it to Jackson.

"Sure," Jackson said. "Of course you'd be prepared. I wouldn't be surprised if you had a first aid kit somewhere in your pockets."

Emma's smile widened as she lifted a white box with a red cross on the front from a canvas bag. "No room in these shorts. I've got duct tape, super glue, safety pins, scissors, a pocket knife, and some rope."

"You should have been a Girl Scout," Jackson teased.

"Right." A glimpse of something dark crossed her expression but then was gone as she told Matty, "Aunt Pepita taught me about the wilderness. My mom didn't do camping."

Jackson opened the paper bag and handed out tacos. "I didn't mean to bring it up." His mind flashed to Emma roasting marshmallows over a campfire, her slender body silhouetted by the leaping flames against dark shadows.

"It's okay. It's not a secret." She snagged a tortilla chip.

"We should go, when Mom is out of the hospital," Matty said.

"It's been a while since I've slept outside," Emma said.

"We sleep in a tent!" Matthew quickly reassured her. "That way bugs don't get you. Or bears."

Chuckling, Jackson ducked his head and bit into a taco. Emma's auburn hair, hazel eyes, and freckles across her nose seemed the same—he used to kiss those freckles until she laughed. She was the kind of woman who imprinted herself on a guy so nobody else would do. He'd dated, of course, but he'd kept his heart off-limits.

She spooned the chunky salsa onto her taco and brought it to her mouth, sinking her teeth into the soft flour tortilla.

Matthew devoured both of his tacos without saying another word, then looked up in confusion. "Who do I ask to be excused? My boss, or my uncle?"

"Boss," he said.

"Uncle," she said.

Jackson wiped his mouth with a paper napkin. "You're excused."

"You can change into your swimsuit if you want to get in the water." Emma pointed to the wooden building that housed bathrooms and a changing area in the park. "It's important not to overdo the lessons. Let's have some fun. Don't go past your knees with the dogs, though, okay?"

Matty nodded.

"We'll watch from here." She studied Jackson. "Too bad you didn't bring your suit."

"It's all good. I didn't intend to barge in on your party." Would she swim? Seeing Emma in a swimsuit the rest of the afternoon might be worth hanging around for.

"We've finished the training for the day."

"I should head back to the house," he said, hearing the regret in his voice. "But I'll see you tonight. Thanks a lot, Emma."

She bagged the taco trash and got up to walk it to the garbage can. "Thank *you*—lunch was a great surprise. Way better than the granola bars and fruit I'd packed. It's such a gorgeous day; it really is too bad you have to leave."

Matthew came out of the bathroom in his swim trunks and bare feet, walking past the picnic table toward the beach but stopping to face Jackson.

"Can you stay, Uncle Jackson?"

Emma studied Jackson's attire as if mentally stripping him down. "You could roll up those jeans and toss the stick around. Matthew is almost as quick as Bandit."

Matthew said, "Hey!" His face had healthy color, his narrow shoulders brown from the summer sun. "Come on. It'll be fun."

Matty took off at a run, joining in with the dogs who greeted him with barks, woofs, and licks.

"Why not?" Jackson asked out loud. "I could use a little fun." He sat down on the bench and slipped off his boots, wadding his socks up and shoving them inside. He rolled up his jeans and took off his T-shirt. "You got sunscreen in there?"

"You bet. The spray kind. So just put your arms out and twirl."

He chuckled, sucking in his breath as the cool spray hit his bare skin. "You going in?"

"Right behind you."

She nodded toward the water and turned around, lifting her shirt over her head and slipping her shoes off by hooking the toes to the heel of the opposite shoe. She hadn't bothered with socks. She wore a tankini swim top and kept her shorts on.

Jackson swallowed his disappointment that she wasn't wearing a skimpy two-piece and followed her to where she'd joined Matty at the water's edge. Her figure had curves it didn't use to have, and he wondered what she must think of him, after all this time.

Bandit brought him a piece of driftwood that was covered in black barnacles, seaweed streaming from one side. Disgusting, smelly, but perfect for a dog.

Jackson tugged the piece from Bandit's mouth and tossed the stick down the beach. "This is dog paradise."

Matthew and Romeo were knee-deep in the water, splashing in the waves. Emma and King stood back, watching while Pedro raced from Bandit to Romeo to Emma and King then back again.

"Everybody should sleep well tonight," she said.

Jackson retrieved the driftwood and threw it up high. "That would be nice. I can't tell you the last time I had a good night's sleep." He regretted the sentence as soon as the words spilled from his lips. *That's what I get for being too relaxed. Watch it, Hardy.*

He felt Emma's eyes on his back. Instead of admiring his Marine-lean muscled torso, she was opening her mouth as if to dispense advice.

Matthew thought he had problems with nightmares, which was the reason they were all at the dog park to begin with. Jackson stopped mid-throw, looked back over his shoulder and said, "Keep your advice to yourself, Doc. I'm fine."

Chapter Nine

The old kitchen smelled like garlic and tomato sauce, and Emma's stomach growled. Appliances from the eighties, the last time Pep had them redone, still worked just fine. Painted white, three windows allowed plenty of light, and there was loads of counter space.

Emma hummed as she set the table, her feet bare, her damp hair up in a bun at the back of her head. She'd chosen a light-yellow sundress with orange flowers and reminded herself that she didn't need to look pretty—the Hardys had both seen her in the mud. But she swiped copper shadow on her lids anyway and ran a hint of gloss over her lips.

Lemonade, iced tea. A big ceramic bowl of salad made with veggies right from their garden. Cucumbers, tomatoes, carrots, and romaine lettuce. Buttermilk ranch dressing. She surveyed the table, looking for anything she might have missed.

"Salt and pepper," she said aloud, swiveling on her toes and heading to the cupboard.

A knock sounded at the front door, and her pulse jumped.

Jackson had surprised her earlier, taking off his boots to play in the surf with the dogs that afternoon. A nice surprise, watching him and Matthew on the sandy beach.

A nicer surprise, watching the muscle on Jackson's rock-hard physique as he tossed a stick to Bandit, the eagle tattoo in flight with each flex of his biceps. She'd watched him years ago, playing football, swimming, hiking. She'd known every inch of his body by touch. Was there anything as bittersweet as a first love?

His slip about not sleeping well made her certain that her choice to let him know her better was the right one. Building trust took time. There was no way for her to help without that foundation.

Another knock sounded, louder this time. Emma made for the living room, the four pups trotting behind her. Cinnamon kept looking up and back at her, as if wondering who it could be. They rarely had visitors.

Princess nipped at Lulu, who had stepped on her paw, and Lulu barked once. "That did not sound like an apology, Lulu," Emma said, reaching for the round brass door handle.

The Hardys stood on the other side of the screen door, a bottle of wine in Jackson's hand and a bouquet of flowers in Matthew's.

"What a wonderful treat!" The simple joy she felt as she let them in was a reminder that it had been too long since she'd had company over. Friends mattered, but between school and work and the kennel, her best friends were her dogs, besides her aunt. Who'd been the last person to stop by? She couldn't even remember—maybe Sawyer.

"We could smell dinner from the driveway," Jackson said. "It's been a long time since I've had homemade lasagna."

"It was fun, putting it together." She shooed the dogs out of the way. "Come on, pups, let them in."

Matthew handed her the flowers, a multicolored bouquet

wrapped in green tissue paper, so he could pick up Cinnamon, who wiggled happily as she licked his chin.

Jackson, seeing her arms full of flowers, lifted the bottle of wine. "Is there anything you can't do?"

Pleased, she said, "That list is too long to even get started on." The foyer led into the living room, which held a television and a couch, two recliners, and a bookshelf stuffed with romance novels and magazines. Jackson knew to go right, down the short hallway leading to the huge kitchen, which had a door to the back porch and yard.

Was it company that made her tummy tingle with anticipation, or was it specifically Jackson? Emma couldn't banish his broad shoulders and muscled torso from her mind. She gripped the bouquet so tight the plastic wrap crinkled.

Jackson put the wine on the counter next to the large white double sinks. "I brought a burgundy, to go with the Italian theme."

"Perfect," Emma said. "Though I'm not much of an expert." She enjoyed a glass with dinner now and again but preferred tea.

"Me either." He skimmed his palm over the top of his short hair. "I asked the guy at the grocery store."

"Did you pick these tomatoes?" Matthew set Cinnamon down on the floor, so he could examine the kitchen table. "I love tomatoes." He patted his stomach.

Emma turned to Matthew. "Yes, from the garden. The plants are loaded! Maybe we could gather them after dinner? You could take some home. If I remember correctly, you're the weird kid who likes salad." Emma moved the flowers to one hand and offered a high five with the other.

"Yep," he said proudly, smacking her palm with his. "I've even got Uncle Jackson eating zucchini."

"Deep fried," Jackson clarified. "Manly veggies."

"Well, do you mind using those man-skills to open the

wine?" She pointed to the drawer next to the sink. "We have an old-fashioned corkscrew, so it takes some muscle."

Jackson's grin made his green eyes darken to jade and her stomach twist. Oh no, she thought. But then she countered with, why not? This was just an innocent dinner between friends.

Neighbors.

It's lasagna, for heaven's sake. Nothing serious.

Jackson pulled the drawer open, digging through the odds and ends until he found the silver wine opener that predated the kitchen appliances. "Got it."

Emma turned to Matthew, who was studying the ceramic pots of herbs she and her aunt grew under the window. "I added some of the parsley and basil to our salad."

"Yum."

"Matty, Matty, Matty." Jackson popped the cork from the bottle. "Wineglasses?"

"Cupboard to the left." Emma checked the clock, put the salt and pepper shaker on the table, and asked, "Matthew, what would you like to drink? Tea, lemonade? Or iced water?"

"Lemonade, please."

She poured the tart yellow beverage into a glass over ice. "We have about fifteen minutes before dinner's ready. Want to sit outside on the back patio? Or on the couch in the living room?"

"I've never seen your house," Matthew said. "It's as big as a castle."

She remembered worrying that she'd get lost in it when she'd first moved here. "Then follow me, and I'll give you the ten-cent tour."

"What does that mean?" he asked, squinting up at her. His nose had gotten pink today despite the sunscreen she'd slathered on him.

"It means that it's a cheap thrill, not too exciting, but I'll do my best. We need to put some aloe from the garden on your poor nose later. Sorry about that." Emma handed Matthew the lemonade and accepted the wineglass from Jackson. Their fingers touched, and she smiled her thanks. "Coming?"

He'd once had free reign of the place, though they'd spent most of their time outdoors. "I wouldn't miss it," Jackson said, sipping as he followed her and Matthew from the kitchen.

"This is the bathroom, and down this hall are two bedrooms and my office." The rancher gave "sprawling" a new meaning. Emma gestured to the other side. "Aunt Pepita has her own rooms down that hall. Hopefully, she's winning big," she said with her fingers crossed.

"I've always loved this place," Jackson said, his breath warm behind her. "Doesn't look this big from the outside."

Matthew followed her and Jackson as they walked down the carpeted hall. She opened the office door and flipped on the light.

"This is where I study and get the paperwork done for the kennel." She'd painted the walls pale blue and the molding and doors bright white. Her desk was a golden oak, and the beige carpeted floor was covered with all sizes of dog beds. "See those bins? Full of leashes, harnesses, treats. Anything you might want for a dog."

"This is so cool." Matthew checked out the books on the shelves—her library contained information on various dog breeds.

She pointed to the shelves on the other side of the desk. "You can borrow one if you want, Matthew."

"Save me a trip to the library," Jackson said, his interest in the space evident as he looked around. "This used to be a sewing room, didn't it?"

"Yeah." Emma glanced up at him. He remembered.

"Sewing is one of those things I never mastered. This is a much better use for the room."

She headed out to the hall, making sure that Matty was following before she turned off the light and shut the door.

"And the next room here is a spare bedroom." She opened the door but didn't bother with a switch. The room was brown on brown; comfortable, but never used.

The guys were on her heels as she reached her bedroom suite.

She had a cushy oversized chair by the window that was perfect for reading in the morning light, and a round glass-topped table in easy reach. Her closet hid a multitude of shorts, T-shirts, and sneakers, and her double-sized bed had a pale blue down comforter and lots of big pillows. The twin bed Jackson might recall had been replaced the summer he'd left. A bookcase took up one wall, floor to ceiling, crammed with memorabilia and books.

Emma spied a sock under the bed and casually kicked it out of view.

"It's cozy," Jackson said. He looked at the yearbooks on her bookshelves. "Good old Kingston High," he said with a rumble. "Do you mind?" He brought his graduating year out with a forefinger and set his wineglass on the shelf.

"Not at all. Matty, your uncle was on the football team. I'm sure there are pictures." She was glad now that she hadn't tossed out the yearbook from their senior year along with the mattress.

"I want to see!"

"Give me a sec." Jackson opened to the back and the senior pictures. He sat on the floor cross-legged, and Matthew hovered behind him.

"Is that you, Uncle Jackson? You had long hair." Matty looked from the picture to Jackson in disbelief. "Where's Mom?"

"She was two years ahead of us," Emma said. "Maybe you can ask her, later, if she has a yearbook."

"I liked my long hair, but I joined the Marines right after graduation. It's a family tradition." Jackson surveyed the pages and rubbed his short cut. "Shaved my head in boot camp and never looked back."

"Does that mean I have to be a Marine?" Matthew's brows furrowed as he eyed his uncle expectantly.

"Grandpa was Air Force, and your grandma was in the Army. Your mom was in the ROTC in high school before deciding to be a dental hygienist...but you, Matty, can be whatever you want."

Matthew's shoulders lowered in relief. "I want to play basketball."

"You keep growing and you'll be tall enough, that's for sure," Jackson said.

"Is that Emma?" Matthew looked from her senior photo to her. "You look the same. Let's see yours, Uncle Jackson." Matty tapped the picture of Jackson in his senior cap with a gold tassel and snickered. "Is that you? In the funny hat?"

"Graduation cap—you'll have to wear one, too, someday," Jackson said. He turned the page, and his face paled before he snapped the book closed, rising in a fluid motion.

"Not if I have to wear a dress." Matthew perused her shelves, stopping at her shell collection. "Can I look at these, Emma?"

"Sure." Emma watched Matthew carefully pull out the jar filled with sea glass and sand dollars. What had Jackson seen that had bothered him so much?

Jackson slid the yearbook back into its spot but placed a photo of the two of them kissing under a disco ball on the shelf next to his wineglass. God, they'd been so young. Awkward silence filled the air between them.

"That was taken at the Harvest Dance, remember?"

She'd been so shy, a bookworm, and wild Jackson had asked her to the dance—they'd become inseparable. Livvie was mostly gone at college, so Jackson had spent his time with her and Aunt Pep.

"First dance of the school year. I got lucky finding you." He picked up his glass but left the photo.

At the time she thought she'd been the lucky one.

He must have seen something cross her face, because Jackson inched closer to her, his upper arm almost touching hers. "I thought I was doing the right thing." Jackson tipped her chin up to look into her eyes. "I'm sorry."

"Don't be." She stared at the diplomas on her walls, the certificates of achievement. Would she have accomplished so much if Jackson had stayed in Kingston, or would they have gotten married, had kids, and grown to hate each other? He'd never asked her to go with him. Would she have?

"You have a lot to be proud of, Emma."

She shrugged, seeing Professor Collard's disappointed blue eyes in her mind instead. "I guess so. I have my paper to finish, and then two years of working under a psychologist to look forward to." Emma took a drink.

Jackson shivered in mock horror. "I'd rather march twenty miles a day in the desert than go back to school."

Emma arched her brow. "You are saving the world in your own way, Jackson. I am very proud of you."

He touched his glass to hers. "Not everybody feels that way."

"I won't go into politics, but you are a soldier representing our country and putting your life on the line so that I can have my opinion. That is worth a thank-you." She lifted her glass and sipped.

His eyes warmed, and her toes tingled.

His hand on her back surprised her with the gentleness of the touch. "You are so smart, Emma. You could do anything.

Why psychology?"

"In going to therapy myself, searching for answers, I decided I wanted to help others with mental health issues. It's pretty common, I think."

He shifted his wine to his left hand, pocketing his right. "You're not common, Emma. I think you're pretty special."

His compliment made her blush, and she quipped, "Crazy, maybe."

"You don't look crazy. I've seen crazy."

She grinned. "Then I guess it worked. See? Worth every penny of that twenty-five cents." Emma elbowed him, not wanting things to get too heavy.

"Ouch." He swirled the wine in his glass. "I'm sorry about that remark."

"Apologies accepted. Now, let's stop poking at the past."

He put his hand on her waist, and the heat of his fingers traveled down her skin. "Deal. Tell me about the EST dogs. I get your degree, but I don't understand the kennel."

She sipped the deep red burgundy, letting the oaky flavor linger on her tongue. "Dogs offer unconditional love, no matter what. Bad breath, bad hair day, mismatched tennis shoes. The dogs I pick tend to be empathic. They can tap into their owner's feelings. In some cases, fending off an anxiety attack before it happens."

"Anxiety?"

"Sometimes people can be overwhelmed by situations or emotions and feel like things are outside of their control." She tipped her head toward Matty, playing with Cinnamon and the sock her dog had dragged back out from under the bed. "Like, Livvie's accident."

She kept her insights about his PTSD to herself for now. He needed time to open up to her. They had the summer, from the sound of it. Before he went back to his reality, putting his life on the line in the military.

Their conversation was interrupted by the fire alarm going off in the kitchen.

Jackson was out the door and down the hall before she could process what was happening.

Matty, wide-eyed, looked at her, and she held out her hand with a laugh. "I guess the lasagna's done."

• • •

Jackson rescued the lasagna, which hadn't burned, and turned off the smoke alarm.

Emma, cheeks rosy as she laughed, said, "What happened?"

He pointed to a burned cube of cheese on the heating element inside the oven. "Cheese spill. Dinner is saved." He bowed and put the hot dish in the center of the table.

"My hero." Emma refilled both their wineglasses and topped off Matthew's lemonade, her pretty pale-yellow sundress swirling around her knees. She opened the silver package of garlic bread, steaming hot from the oven.

His stomach rumbled.

"I heard that, Uncle Jackson," Matthew giggled, his hand over his mouth.

"Sorry." But damn, it smelled good, better than anything he'd had in a very long time.

"Don't be." Emma took off the mitts and hung them on clips next to the oven. "We worked hard today. We all deserve a feast."

Jackson heard the slightest hitch to her tone that let him know she was still trying to find her balance after their conversation in her bedroom. She'd kept that picture of them tucked away in the yearbook. He'd read the back inscription. *Love always, Emma and Jackson.* Being here did bring back memories, and not all of them were sad. Jackson had even found himself singing in the shower.

Emma cut the lasagna into squares. "May I serve you?"

Matty nodded, his eyes on the cheese dripping over the spatula as she lifted a piece and put it on his plate.

Jackson's mouth watered as he held his plate in place. Two squares. He grinned at Matthew. Ha.

Matty rolled his eyes.

Emma passed the bread and salad.

Jackson drizzled buttermilk ranch dressing over the greens. "We don't eat this well at home," he said.

"I doubt that you eat only takeout," she said.

"True," Jackson said. "But my culinary talents stop at Cheesy Hamburger Helper."

"It's good, too," Matthew said.

"I bet it is." Emma nodded at them with satisfaction, her pink lips lifted in a warm smile. "I'm so glad you're here for dinner."

The funny note in her voice was gone, and Jackson could tell that she meant it.

They ate in silence—well, between oohs and ahs—before finishing the first round. Matthew ate a second piece, and Jackson barely completed a third. His mind was willing, his mouth salivating, but his belly was stuffed like a turkey at Thanksgiving.

"Don't forget you brought cannoli for dessert." She noticed his expression and laughed. "Later. I figured we could sit on the porch and watch the cats chase butterflies. Let the food settle."

Jackson wasn't ready to call it a night, so he gladly agreed.

"More wine?" he asked, pointing to her empty glass.

"No, thanks. I'm too full to put anything else in my stomach." She patted her tummy.

Matthew had one more piece of garlic bread. "This is soooo good."

"We had a busy day." Emma leaned back, pushing her hair away from her face. "I bet the big dogs are still napping."

"Can we go play with them?" Matthew asked, hopping up with boyhood energy.

She laughed softly. "How can you move? Tell you what. Give me fifteen minutes to digest on the back porch, in the shade, and then I'll think about it. I'm on pasta overload."

Matthew got up from his chair and went around the table to give Emma a hug. "Thanks for dinner, Emma."

Jackson wished he had the freedom to hug Emma like that. But they were just becoming friends, of a sort. Nothing in the past, but all in the now.

She waved away his offer to do the dishes, got up, and opened the back door. The trees provided shade, making the evening pleasant. "It'll stay light out until nine," Emma said. "I love summer."

Twin orange cats sat on the edge of the fountain, lazily swishing their fluffy tails. Matty raced down the steps to pet them, and they didn't seem to mind the extra attention he lavished on ear scratches.

Emma sat on the back steps, her dress barely covering her knees. Freckled, he noticed before quickly glancing away. She tucked her bare feet out of sight as he took a seat next to her on the step.

Matty, as if he hadn't just eaten half an Italian restaurant, ran after the squirrels at the feeder.

"This is paradise," Jackson said. He lifted his face to breathe in the pine-scented air, which held a hint of ocean. So different from the barren Middle East, the constant stench of burning oil, the weight of a rifle strapped over his shoulder. It was nice to relax his guard. Sit with a pretty woman. An intelligent woman who made a very tasty lasagna.

"I count my blessings every single day." She folded her hands in her lap, glancing at him before looking out at the fountain.

"You're a very good cook."

"I follow the recipe," she said. "I'm not creative enough to come up with something original."

"Why do I doubt that?" Creativity showed in the Heart to Heart Dog Kennel design, in creating a business outside the norm, in training the dogs to use a slide, for Pete's sake.

"It's true." She tapped his knee, the gesture nervous. "I'm not complaining. I mean, why screw up a perfectly good lasagna by tweaking it?"

"No complaints here. In fact, I insist on dish duty."

Emma smoothed the hem of her dress and watched the cat pounce after a water droplet that landed outside the fountain. "Dishes will take me two minutes."

He leaned his elbow back on the top stair. "You have a magic wand?"

"I have a dishwasher." She looked over her freckled nose at him, daring him to argue.

"Me too." He pointed to where his nephew tossed pebbles into the fountain. "Matty."

"I heard that!"

Jackson laughed and lowered his voice. "It's been an adjustment learning how to run a household with a boy. He's forgiven a lot of frozen pizzas."

Emma smiled gently at him, this time resting her whole palm on his knee. He'd worn shorts, so she touched skin. She pulled her hand back quickly, as if burned. Jackson liked the warmth of her fingers, her feminine touch, and wished she'd keep it there.

"He loves you very much," she said in a hushed tone. "How are things going with Livvie?"

Jackson's shoulders tightened at the reminder that this was not his life—not really. "No change, Bonnie says. They're doing some neurological tests this week." He cleared his throat. "I got an email from my commander this morning asking me to reconsider my leave."

Emma's head whipped around, her hair flying to smack him in the face, her hazel eyes wide. He jerked backward with a laugh.

"Sorry," she said, pretty cheeks pink with embarrassment. "What did you say? I mean, what will you do?"

"What could I say?" He looked at Matty, doing somersaults in the grass. "Livvie isn't better yet, and Matty has nowhere to go."

"They can't fire you?"

"Technically, according to the family emergency leave policy, I can take up to twelve weeks before I would be expected to return to active duty. But I hate to let my commander down." Their unit worked as a team. *Remi, Shockley, Scotts, McMahn.*

"That's understandable." Her voice was rich in compassion—she was a natural listener. "And a lot of pressure for you."

He scratched at the stubble along his jaw as Matty ran across the expanse of green lawn and launched into a triple somersault.

"Probably." He smiled at her, counting the freckles across her nose. Fifteen, maybe. "I'm good at what I do."

"Which is what?" She smoothed an auburn lock from her cheek.

He lifted his finger and thumb as if his hand were a gun. "Sniper."

Would she pull away? Some women didn't like guns. Soldiers kept this country free, and he was proud to be one, just like the generations of Hardy men before him.

She'd said she was proud of him—did she mean it? Her forearm brushed his leg, and her throat turned a deep shade of rose as she held his gaze. *Sweet. She wouldn't say what she didn't mean.*

He tilted to the right, wanting to touch her mouth with his. Sample a quick taste of Emma to add to his memories. Her lips slightly parted, the pulse at the hollow of her throat sped, her eyes dilated. They were so close to a kiss that all he had to do was move his head forward...

She stood abruptly, smoothing the yellow fabric down over her hip with an eye toward Matty, racing around the fountain. "I'll get dessert."

Jackson snapped back. Was she inviting him inside?

"I'll help."

She held the door open for him, and he followed her. The instant they were out of sight, she launched herself at him, wrapping her arms around him to hold him tight—he couldn't have broken free if he'd wanted to.

And he didn't.

He buried his hands in her soft, soft hair and cupped her head so that he could study Emma and memorize each new line and freckle. He gently brought the pads of his thumbs to her smooth jaw and plump pink lower lip. Her eyes, swiped with copper, glittered sensually as she absorbed his touch. Auburn lashes at half-mast as she relaxed into him.

He dropped one arm to her hip to balance her, the other still cradling her head as he lowered his mouth. She lifted to him, their lips whispering across each other's mouths before crashing together like surf against the sand.

She tasted different but the same. It was meeting his other half, something he'd been missing and suddenly needed more than his next breath.

"Em."

"Jackson." Her words were hot against his lips and brought the embers of desire flaming bright.

She entwined her fingers behind his neck and pressed in to him.

He clasped her tight, feeling the warmth of her feminine curves, the temptation she offered.

The smack of sneakers up the porch steps made them break away like guilty teenagers.

Jackson's chest heaved. They weren't that anymore.

Em's eyes flashed, the pulse at her neck fast as a hummingbird's.

"Emma," Matty asked, innocently entering the kitchen. "Can I have some lemonade?"

"Sure, hon. I was just getting the cannoli out. Are you ready for dessert?" Emma turned her back to him, and Jackson detected a tremor in her voice.

Jackson knew then that he'd never be over Emma Mercer, not if he lived to be a thousand.

Chapter Ten

That night, Jackson and Matthew put on Captain America instead of Spiderman for a change of pace.

The evening at Emma's had ended with picking tomatoes off the vine and sharing cannoli. If he could just forget about the kiss in her kitchen, then things would be fine. But instead, that intense attraction had flared again while they'd done the dishes! He sat back against the couch, running the scene over in his head.

He'd handed her a dish from the running stream of water, and she'd accepted it to stack in the dishwasher. His wet, slick hand against her warm fingers. *Zing*. Foolish as it was, there had been a spark of attraction that had flared so brightly he'd almost dropped the plate. But it was not okay for him to touch her soft and floral-scented skin. He'd hurt her before, and he couldn't ever forgive himself if he did it again.

"Popcorn?" Matthew asked from the kitchen pantry.

"No. Thanks." How did the kid have room for more food? Not that he was complaining, but he figured it was a good thing Matthew was in shorts for the summer. He'd need longer pants come September. Jackson would take Matty shopping for school clothes so Livvie didn't have to worry about it.

Jackson washed his face and changed into loose pajama pants and a sleep T-shirt. He caught sight of his blue uniform hanging in the closet. It seemed to call to him. His commander needed him back. Body taut, he walked toward the open closet, touching the fabric of the uniform, the stripes and pins and commendations he'd earned for bravery.

What he remembered—when he allowed himself to think on it—was artillery fire, brave men fighting for their country in a desert war that stretched the boundaries of courage and skill. You survived, you were lucky. He'd been lucky. *So far.*

Others had not been.

He slammed the closet door, shut off the light to his bedroom, and rejoined Matthew on the couch.

"Here, Uncle Jackson. Want some?" Matty, in Pokémon pajama bottoms that were showing some ankle, handed him the bowl.

Out of reflex, Jackson scooped a small handful and chomped a few kernels as he sat back and fluffed the cushions. "Hit play, Matty. Let's watch the good guys win."

Sure, superheroes were fake, but it was nice to know when you started the movie that they would end up on top.

In an actual battle, you had no damn clue.

Eyes heavy, he relaxed, thinking of how great Emma had felt in his arms. How right she'd fit against him. They'd been magic together, and he knew they could be again—but he couldn't do it. Wanted to, oh yeah, but he had to stay away from her warm body. She knew how to kiss him. Emma.

Gunshots peppered the sand around camp. Mortar fire singed his nostrils. The stench of blood tainted the hot desert air. Good guys. They were supposed to be the good guys, fighting for freedom.

The enemy used the dry terrain to their benefit, their robes blending in with the sand and making them impossible to see.

Remi crawled up next to him behind the sandbags, keeping his head down as the enemy fired round after round into the American compound.

"Shockley's been hit," Remi said, sweat dripping down the side of his face.

"Dead?"

"Soon."

No point in calling for a helicopter, then, he surmised. "Anybody else?"

"They're trying to destroy the howitzer."

They'd put false intel out that this compound had a new weapon in order to draw the faction out to the east. Here they were, but air support was not. "We'll counter with snipers." He was used to being bait—thrived on the anticipation as he watched the enemy fall into their trap. Nobody in his unit was supposed to die, but that was war, wasn't it? Taking chances with your life.

It was what they did.

He aimed his scope over the sandbags and sighted the sniper to the left. There! He got off a round, and his enemy went down. Problem was, there were always more.

Remi dove as a grenade lobbed over the sandbags—too close. Smoke filled the foxhole. Remi's left side jerked as if shaken by an invisible hand, and blood pooled beneath Jackson's feet.

Not Remi, he whispered. Not Remi.

"Uncle Jackson!"

Jackson woke and tried to orient himself. He sat up, feeling the nub of the couch cushions beneath the pads of his fingers, tasting popcorn instead of blood, hearing the sounds of gunfire—from the television. Not in Afghanistan. Not in battle.

On the couch.

His pulse raced and sweat poured down his back, his temples, and he swiped his hand over his face.

It was bad. *So bad.* His body shook, and he swallowed past the dry knot lodged in his throat. *Remi from Louisiana.*

"Uncle."

He heard the sound of Matthew leaving, heading toward the kitchen. Heard the faucet being turned on and his nephew getting a glass from the cupboard.

Jackson wanted to get up, to shake off the pain-filled memories, but he seemed glued to the couch and couldn't free his mind of the blood. The screams. The dry desert air that stung his nose.

"Here." Matthew's brown eyes were impossibly wide. "Have some water."

He accepted the glass with trembling fingers. Sipped. Pounded the sounds and smells and horror back behind the wall he'd built. He'd been vigilant against them, but tonight's dinner had been so normal that he'd made the mistake of relaxing his guard.

"My fault," he whispered, taking another small drink of the water, unable to meet Matty's gaze. "My fault." Iowa. Remi, or Shockley? Or letting down his guard?

He breathed in and out, as the Marine doc had taught him to do.

Jackson, so focused on getting home to his nephew, had told the guy everything he wanted to hear.

So he could be with Matthew.

It was normal to have a few bad dreams. He realized they freaked Matty out, and so he'd tried real hard to keep from a deep sleep. Pots of coffee, high-octane energy drinks, tea.

He knew how to rest with one eye open, usually.

Damn lasagna and cannoli and a pretty girl—he'd been fooled into complacency.

"Uncle Jackson." Matty took the water from his loose grip. "Are you okay?"

"Yeah," Jackson said with a weak nod. "Fine." His voice sounded odd to his own ears.

He settled back against the couch, his feet planted firmly on the floor, his forearms resting on his knees. When he finally looked at Matthew, his nephew was staring at him with determination.

"What?" Jackson asked, his sense of trepidation returning.

"I want you to call Emma." Matthew's chin jutted forward.

"No." Jackson closed his eyes.

"She can help."

"No." He scrubbed a palm down his face. "Just a dream, Matty. That's all."

"How long do you think you were sleeping for?"

"What?" Jackson opened his eyes and focused on Matthew. "I dozed off for a few minutes."

"No, Uncle Jackson." Matthew's stubborn chin quivered. "You slept like that for an hour."

Jackson felt the scowl forming on his face as he looked at Matthew. "You timed me?"

Matthew held up Jackson's smartphone, his hand shaking. "I have it on video."

Jackson's body tensed as if waiting to be hit. Betrayal ate its way up his throat. His nephew had videoed him sleeping? *Calm down, Jackson.* "Why would you do that?"

"Because you won't believe me!" Matthew shouted, tears in his brown eyes, his small chin square with courage as he faced him down.

Jackson rose from the couch, anger in every movement. "You just want a dog."

"That is not true. You know it isn't."

It took all of his self-control to keep from verbally lashing out.

"I'm worried about you," Matthew said, holding his ground.

"I'm fine." His jaw clenched.

"You don't have to suffer."

"Suffer? Matty, you don't know what it was like over there—and God willing, you won't ever have to know." He stood, stretching to his full height, his arms behind his back. "Why didn't you wake me up?"

"I tried."

"So, you used my phone?"

"I needed you to see for yourself." Matthew shook the phone for Jackson to take. "You say you don't have nightmares, but you do."

Tempted to smash the device underfoot, Jackson took it, furious. "Go to bed, Matty. We will talk about this in the morning."

He felt too raw, too violated, to be fair.

Matthew stared at him from the corner of the couch, uncertainty in every bone of his body. "I should have called Emma."

He didn't want his nephew to be afraid of him, for heaven's sake. Right now, he couldn't trust himself not to shout. "*Now*."

Matthew skittered off the couch and ran down the hall to his room, where he slammed the door to show his protest.

Jackson stared at the phone, then closed his eyes, asking

for the strength to actually see what his nephew saw. Despite how badly Jackson had wanted to shield him from the horrors of war, it hadn't happened.

He pressed play. Him, sleeping, muttering as his arms were drawn up to his chest.

Just sleeping. Odd, to watch something that you don't remember. What was the big freaking deal?

Then his eyes twitched—his hands lifted to his chest in fists. The fury on his sleeping face sent a cold shiver down his spine as he watched the video play.

"Get down, Remi!" What had been a whisper in his dream had been a shout from where he'd been sleeping on the couch.

His cheeks flushed a dark crimson, his body taut—watching himself made his stomach churn, but he made himself look. For the whole hour. Then he sat abruptly on the floor, his legs crossed, his strength gone.

No wonder Matthew was scared.

Jackson had been fighting sleep, thinking he was fine. Handling things okay—but things were not *fine*. How to fix this messed up situation, his way?

He'd start sleeping in his room, and no more dozing on the couch, so Matty wouldn't have to hear. He just had to hang on another month, and then he'd be back in the Marines where nobody got any damn sleep.

God, from watching this video, he was in no shape to take care of anybody. He thought of Emma, her calm demeanor, her sweetness.

If he found out that she was behind the video... He forced a breath, from the soles of his feet to his aching head. *Call Emma.*

She was the last person he could drag into this mess. She was overwhelmed with work and school, but she would help because she cared, but then he would have to leave her all over again.

Pressing play, he watched the video again and knew he had to take some sort of action. Forcing himself to face the issue head on, he powered up the laptop and did a search on PTSD.

• • •

After how fast Jackson and Matthew had left last night, Emma was surprised when Jackson called her the next morning. "Hello," she answered, sitting down at the kitchen table.

She never, *never*, never should have kissed Jackson Hardy. Handsome soldier, a man of integrity, hardened by war, but kind and loving toward his family. A dangerous combination for any woman, especially one who'd loved him once before.

She'd thrown herself into his arms after that heated look he'd given her on the porch, and he'd felt so good. But it had taken her an hour of scrubbing out the kennels to find her emotional balance before bed, all to have it disrupted by his starring role in her dreams.

"Morning." Jackson's gruff voice relayed his anger. She heard an undertone of fear. A hint of vulnerability.

She braced herself. Was it Livvie? Had something happened overnight to his sister? Or Matty?

"What's going on?" she asked in a very calm tone.

"I want to talk to you. Can I come over?"

"Sure. I don't need to be at the shelter until this afternoon. I've got coffee on."

"This isn't a social visit."

Okay. The tone conveyed anger, and the only other time he'd been angry had to do with his PTSD. "All right. I'll see you soon." She ended the call and quickly got up from the kitchen table.

The dogs, all eight of them, *woof*ed as she raced from the kitchen, her hair flying behind her. Getting dressed would be good, something professional. Emma needed the reminder that she couldn't be the woman he'd kissed in the kitchen.

Opening the closet, she shoved hangers back and forth on the rack looking for something that would convey the right message—strictly business—but she didn't own black because it showed the dog hair the worst. Princess joined her in the closet, tugging on a bootlace.

"Cargo shorts, brown. Cargo shorts, khaki. Cargo shorts, tan. Oh wait, cargo shorts—army green. Oh, here's a pair in navy blue." *Pathetic.*

Cinnamon joined Princess in the shoe pile and Pedro barked.

"Out!" she announced, shooing the fur babies forward. King sprawled across her bed with Lulu at his side.

Finally choosing dark brown shorts, a tan polo, and brown half boots, Emma stuck her hair in a ponytail, but then took it out, letting it fall to her shoulders. Brushed her teeth—no coffee breath—and then left her bedroom, the animals following her. She paced her office. *Not a social visit.*

Emma pulled an article from her shelf on PTSD that she'd found for dog training, scanning it for useful information. She made a copy for Jackson.

Ten minutes later, Jackson knocked on the door, dressed for a somber occasion in black jeans, black motorcycle boots, and a black T-shirt. She brought him to the living room.

"Hi." She gestured to the couch, which she'd covered with a quilt—good thing, or Jackson would be wearing enough fur for his own coat.

The dogs sensed that it wasn't playtime and greeted Jackson in a subdued manner before she gated them in the kitchen. Bandit and Romeo sat at the gate where they could see, as if eavesdropping.

Emma joined Jackson in the living room. He regarded her from his place on the sofa, his arm across the back, his heel over his opposite knee. Defiant. "Sure you don't want coffee?" she asked.

"No." He dropped his phone on the stack of magazines in the middle of the table. "Did you tell Matty to video me?"

Not to do with Livvie. Emma took a centering breath and sat on the chair next to the couch. She remembered the conversation as she and Matty had cleaned the yard. "Matthew had shared with me that you didn't believe you were having debilitating nightmares."

Jackson's green eyes went dark with anger. "Yes or no?"

Would Matty be in trouble? "No, I did not." She kept her voice even. "But he feels powerless. You told me that you were fine," she said in a gentle, non-accusing way. "Handling it, as I recall." She nodded, encouraging him to speak.

She now understood the phrase "glaring daggers"—Jackson's razor-sharp expression left her flayed and stinging. His muscled jaw clenched as he exuded fury.

Bandit whined across the gate separating the dogs from the living room. "I asked him to call me when you were having another episode, if he was afraid. I could be there to help you." She kept her hands folded over her knee so that she didn't offer comfort to Jackson.

"He said he should have called you." He drummed his fingers over his kneecap.

"Did you watch the video?" She searched his face.

Jackson emanated controlled anger, every muscle tense as he watched her from the couch. "Yes."

"You don't have to show it to anybody else." She waited a few seconds before adding, "It allowed Matthew to be proactive. He's very concerned."

"Have you seen this?" Jackson's chin angled sharply toward her.

"Of course not." She gentled her voice. "How could I have?"

"Going behind my back doesn't seem to be a problem for you." Jackson leaned forward, bracing his forearms on his legs as he stared at Emma.

"Jackson, that's not true. In fact, I asked your permission to talk with Matthew."

She scooted to the edge of her chair, her knees an inch from his, looking into Jackson's eyes. "Matty wants your nightmares to stop and is asking for assistance. He can't do anything about Livvie being in the hospital, but with you, there is something he can try." He looked at her with such a crushed, vulnerable expression that her breath caught. This was a man used to being in control, in charge, and he didn't know what to do next.

"You can talk to me," she said.

"I don't need a shrink."

Emma winced. "As a friend then."

He jabbed his finger against the coffee table. "I don't want to be friends. I think that kiss yesterday proved we have too much between us for that."

"We agreed to start fresh." Emma studied his stiff posture, the stress lines at the corners of his eyes, indents between his light brown brows. She wished she could kiss those stress marks away, but he was right. There was too much between them for her to offer anything less than her heart—and that, she firmly kept under lock and key.

"How about I just listen? No titles." She spread her arms wide, palms up, her head to the side.

He needed to purge the poison from his subconscious in a healthy way. Meditation, yoga, centered breathing, traditional therapy. Accepting his emotions hurt like a bruise, but she opened herself to him anyway. Afterward, she would go the beach with one of the dogs to release the energy.

"I'm here because I promised Matthew I would get help for my nightmares. Obviously, they're scary to him, but I can't own a dog. I'm going back into the service as soon as Livvie gets home."

She waited.

"It's not fair to her." Jackson met her eyes. "She'll need less responsibility; taking care of Matty will be enough—maybe too much."

When he paused, Emma quickly jumped in to explain. "A dog doesn't have to be a permanent addition to the house. Some are placed in homes for a short time—to assist through rough patches."

Jackson swallowed, his hand fisted on his denim-clad knee.

"Not long-term," she repeated.

"Temporary?" he asked, as if to be very, *very* sure.

"Yes."

He sat back, still scowling, but in thought rather than anger.

After a few minutes he said, "Thing is, I *need* to get back in the service. It's a decent living, with good benefits. It's who I am. I didn't sign up to be a dad. That said, I won't walk away from my family. For the first time since joining the Marines, I don't know what to do."

Emma saw his anguish as he was torn between duty to country or family. How Jackson viewed himself. "One of the first things you ever told me about yourself was that you were fourth generation military."

"I did?"

"Yeah. But when Matty asked if he had to go, you didn't say yes." She curled her hands together in her lap.

"My dad wanted me to enlist," Jackson said. "I owed it to his memory."

How had she not figured that out? She'd gone into

psychology trying to understand her mother's illness. "Your dad would be proud of the man you are, Jackson, even if you were changing oil with Mitch at the auto shop for a living. You are a good man."

Jackson gritted his teeth and dragged his gaze from the coffee table and his phone to Emma. "No, I'm not. You don't understand war." He turned back to the phone. "I didn't realize how bad things were with my nightmares."

She felt his pain, his uncertainty. "Is there any way to further delay your return?"

"I want to go. But now, after seeing this video, what if I'm a detriment to my unit?"

He rubbed his throat, as if it hurt to swallow.

"I'm here, Jackson, if you want to talk."

He reached for her, and she placed her hand in his. "I trust you more than anybody else in my life. *Anybody*. But I can't…share what I saw with you."

Protecting her? "There is nothing about you that would make me think less of you."

Jackson pulled his hand free. He'd witnessed his own mortality, she realized. As a soldier, someone who put his life on the line twenty-four hours a day, there had to be a part of your mind that didn't accept death looming over your shoulder.

"I read that before you're released into civilian life, you have to talk to a psychiatrist. Is there someone you can make an appointment with?"

"Yeah." He leaned forward, his muscled back taut beneath his T-shirt. "The guy that passed me to come home on leave gave me a list of local doctors." Jackson met her gaze, his haunted. "I'm career military, Emma. It's what I do; it's what my family does."

His identity was wrapped in honor, integrity, loyalty—and he was being torn in different directions. "Then let's figure out a way to get you better. In addition to talking to a psychiatrist, I know that we can train one of the dogs to wake you before the onset of a nightmare."

"What's the point, if I'm going to a shrink?"

He sounded low, dejected. She forgave his comment. "Sometimes it takes months to get into a doctor's office, and the dog can help right now. Sleep makes a difference."

"I get some." He glared at the phone with the incriminating evidence.

"Not enough. Trusting that you will be woken before you have a nightmare will allow your body to fully relax."

He said nothing. She hoped he was listening, finally.

"Working in tandem with your doctor as well as one of the dogs can get you into top shape before going back to your unit." Where he'd be creating new fodder for nightmares, she thought, hiding her concern for him behind a patient smile. "Are you ready to move forward?"

"I'm here, aren't I?" Jackson pinched the bridge of his nose. "I was up all night watching videos on PTSD. I get it, but you have to realize that understanding doesn't change a damn thing. I have ten more years until retirement. Then I can fall apart."

"That's not how it works." Emma heard the emotion in her voice and deliberately took a calming breath.

"Then tell me how."

"You choose a dog." She pointed to the pups gathered at the gate. It was not a surprise to her that Bandit was still sitting there, his canine gaze tracking Jackson.

"And?" Jackson wasn't looking; he continued to glare at the phone as if the device was responsible for the upheaval in his life.

"We create a system. I come to your house and we set up monitors. Study your sleep patterns. Train the dog to wake you before you slip into a bad dream."

"You make it sound easy."

"It's what I do." She realized that her desire to help Jackson was braided with desire—period—and warned herself to take care.

His green eyes were a storm of clouded emotion, dulling their usual brightness.

"Matty was really scared. By me." His voice broke, his shoulders hunched forward as if bowed by a great weight. "I'm the one he's supposed to count on, and I didn't listen to him."

"You're listening now," she said, overcome by his sorrow. She blinked and sat up straight. "And before you beat yourself up too badly, remember that you have done a commendable thing, coming home to care for Matthew. I take it that his dad is out of the picture?"

"Yeah."

"You are Matty's uncle, and there are plenty of men out there who would pass off the job of his care to someone else. That's not who you are."

She couldn't stop herself from reaching for him and settled on resting her hand on his knee for a second, the touch as light as a bird before it flew away.

"How do you know that?"

"It's my job to know that." All of her intuition agreed with her professional assessment.

"What do I do, Emma?" His low voice strummed across the few inches separating them.

She leaned over the coffee table, making sure they were eye to eye. "Let's start with getting some sleep."

Chapter Eleven

Emma watched with relief as Jackson allowed his head to fall back against the couch cushion, his eyes at half-mast. She understood that talking about a problem could be the beginning of healing.

She sat forward. "Now, which dog do you see suiting your lifestyle the best?"

They both looked over to the gate. Bandit stared back at them, his gray ears tipped up and alert.

For the first time since he'd showed up at her doorstep, a smile crossed Jackson's face. He unclenched the fist he had over his knee and walked to the gate, where he studied Bandit. He rubbed the back of the dog's neck.

"I guess this one, right, boy?" Jackson opened the gate for Bandit to come through.

Emma, thrilled, didn't see any point in waiting. She jumped up from her chair and hurried across the living room, her boots sinking into the padded carpet. "We can start today. Integrate Bandit into your household."

"We have to be clear with Matthew that this is

temporary." Jackson looked at her, his voice and gaze hard. Tough. "Right?"

"Okay." Emma stuffed her hands into her pockets.

"I don't want his hopes up that we get to keep him."

"I get it."

"You promise you will take him back?"

"Bandit is a service animal in training. You know how I feel about the dogs, Jackson, and if you don't, then, well, you don't know me at all."

"Sorry," Jackson said. "I do know you."

There was no guarantee that the nightmares would go away forever, but the mind was a powerful tool. Jackson never let his brain shut down completely, which meant it was on overdrive. Sleep provided a break from thinking, protecting, guarding.

"I don't mind him being in the room," Jackson said. "But I don't want him on the bed."

"We can set up a crate for Bandit—he needs to sense your changes in breathing—pre-nightmare." She looked from Bandit to Jackson. "But it's nice for him to have his own space, too. A place he knows he can go."

"Sure."

"I've got all that. I'll pack food, a water dish. Toys." She snapped her fingers. "I printed out some material on dog training and PTSD for you. We'll use a clicker to train him to wake you up." Emma walked to her office for the article, talking as she went down the hall. "You know they have special service animal phones to dial 911?"

"I don't need a special phone," Jackson said.

She returned to the living room, the article in hand. "I know. I was just saying. Dogs are so smart, but they feel, too." Emma patted her heart. "And the training is important."

"I feel kind of stupid," Jackson mumbled.

Emma cocked her hip. "Why?" Stupid was so not an

adjective she'd use for Jackson Hardy.

"I need a *pet*." Jackson dragged out the last word. "I should be able to handle this on my own."

Bandit growled his disapproval.

"Jackson," Emma said, her throat tight, "you serve our country. That requires courage and maybe seeing or doing things that you wish you hadn't. I thank you for that. But there *are* consequences."

He waved her gratitude away, focusing on the back of Bandit's head, which came to Jackson's knee.

"I'm serious. And grateful. Coping with what is essentially a completely different life isn't easy, and yet you have not only picked up the reins of your nephew's world but done so with fairly little upheaval. I am not at all surprised that your past comes knocking at night, when you are vulnerable and tired."

"I should be able to deal with it." He looked toward the kitchen full of dogs, his throat bobbing as he swallowed.

"Says who?" Emma yearned to comfort him with a hug, or at least to hold his hand, but her own forbidden feelings made that impossible. Especially now that he'd come to her for help. As a client.

"Me."

"Well, guess what? You're choosing a way to handle it. The truth is that you might never get over your bad dreams, but between therapy and the ESD, you will be on your way to coping without the need for Red Bull."

"I like Red Bull." He paced across the floor. Bandit followed at his heels. "It's like he understands what's going on," Jackson said.

Emma smiled. "Spooky, but in a great way." Her phone *ding*ed, and she read the text from Cindy at the shelter. "When it rains, it pours," she said, looking at Lulu, snuggling in the kitchen with Pedro. "Someone requested Lulu after seeing her picture on the website. I've had her for almost seven months." She'd gotten used to the idea that Lulu might always be around.

"Do you need to go?"

"Not yet, Jackson. Let's get you and Bandit settled first. Tell you what—we can grab the supplies and bring him to your place. I'll stop by after my shift at the shelter to see how you're getting along. We can set up a routine for a better success rate."

"What does that mean?" Jackson crossed his arms, the defiance back in the lift of his chin.

"Well, no caffeine after noon, no alcohol or spicy food."

He scowled.

"Sleep in your bedroom each night. Go to bed at the same time."

"I'm not a child," Jackson said.

As if she wasn't very aware of that fact? He exuded testosterone as if needing to prove who was top dog with each breath. "These are guidelines for what works."

"Matthew has more leeway." His green eyes narrowed, and Emma sensed he was on the verge of changing his mind.

"I'm not saying that you have to do it, just that it helps. You said you trusted me, Jackson."

"Are you going to sleep with me too?" His brow winged upward, and he speared her in place.

Emma's cheeks heated, remembering how they used to have no problem fitting on her old twin bed. She swallowed hard and stuffed her phone into her shorts' pocket. "Not *with* you, with you." She decided right then to call Sawyer, because he had more experience with war veterans than she did. "I don't think—"

"Hell, no." He shook his head. "No way."

Emma watched as Jackson allowed Bandit to lean against his leg, subconsciously taking comfort from the dog.

She knew Bandit could help, but it required time and

training. "You wouldn't have to know that I was even there."

"Because you won't be."

Getting Bandit into the home without specific training wouldn't work. "Jackson, please. We need to come up with a plan."

"What kind of plan?"

"We can choose." She handed him the papers she'd printed on dog training and PTSD.

He took them without reading what they were and rolled them into a tube. "No...never mind."

Her heart sank. "Why?"

"This is way too much." Jackson lifted his hand from the top of Bandit's head. "I'm not ready."

She felt his panic. Anxiety magnified across his handsome features. "For what, Jackson?"

"I need to call the shrink, then we can see—it wouldn't be right to Matty, bringing Bandit home and then asking him to give the dog up."

Emma nodded, seeing right through the ruse but going along with it even though her heart was breaking. What mattered was that Jackson got help, especially since he was going back to his unit overseas. "You're right. That is a good idea."

"Yeah?" He shoved his right hand into his front jeans' pocket and pulled out the keys to his motorcycle. "Listen, I'm sorry that I bothered you."

"It was no bother. It *is* no bother. Maybe ask your psychiatrist about having a dog. Bandit. Just for a while. I will check with Sawyer. He's done this kind of training before. I'll ask him for the least intrusive way to train Bandit to wake you up." She half smiled.

Emma leaned against the wall of the hallway, facing Jackson and the front door, the dogs behind the gate blocking them in the kitchen and watching every word they bantered back and forth.

Bandit sat at Jackson's side, emitting a low rumble from his chest.

"So why don't you go home, call your doctor, and then let's talk again tomorrow or the next day? We will be right here." Emma was proud of herself for not adding any pressure when she wanted to take him by the hand and walk with him as he headed into the unknown.

Just like before, he hadn't trusted her to be his partner.

Jackson backed up toward the door. Bandit looked from her to Jackson in confusion.

She snapped her fingers to her side, and Bandit, reluctantly, tail and ears down, joined her as Jackson closed the door.

Emma watched out the peephole as he practically ran to his bike and sped away.

"Not this time, Bandit." Emma dropped to her knees to look into the dog's brown eyes. "You are a very intuitive pup, aren't you? Jackson needs us. You." She ruffled the fur at his neck. "Good boy."

• • •

Jackson didn't need anybody other than Matthew. God, he'd almost made a huge mistake, bringing Bandit home.

But the dog had made him feel better somehow. What if the nightmares came because he deserved them? What if he deserved the nightmares because of what he'd done in the name of war?

He parked the bike next to his truck and went inside. Matty sat at the small dining room table chowing down on a bowl of cereal, the book on golden retrievers open in front of him.

Jackson poured himself a cup of coffee. "How's the book?"

"Cool. Did you know that golden retrievers are the third most popular pet in America?"

"No."

"Yeah, it's true. Because they're so friendly. And really smart."

Jackson drank from his mug, leaning his butt against the counter as he waited for more from Mr. Encyclopedia.

"They are easy to take care of, and even though they have long hair, all you have to do is brush them."

He waited.

"Bandit is part golden retriever," Matty said in an offhand manner.

The kid was good, Jackson would give him that. "Yeah. I remember Emma telling us that."

Matthew looked up from his bowl of cereal, a droplet of milk on his lower lip. "Did you talk to her?"

"Yes."

"Uncle Jackson!"

"We had a nice conversation."

Matty let his spoon fall against the plastic of the bowl. "And?" His bright eyes and earnest expression made Jackson wish he really was a superhero.

"I'm going to find a psychiatrist today, and if he agrees, we *talked* about getting a dog on a very temporary basis."

Matthew exploded upward from his chair as if launched by a rocket and raced toward Jackson, who barely lifted the mug of hot coffee out of the way in time. Setting it behind him, he enjoyed the hug for a moment before gently taking Matthew by the shoulders.

"Hey, look at me now."

Matty, still grinning, looked up. "Yeah?"

"Temporary, maybe."

"I know, geez. I heard you."

"It's a lot of responsibility. And I'm not saying yes. I'm

saying maybe. You'll have to do your share. I'm not good with the pooper scooper."

"I will, I will."

"I know you will. I'm counting on it."

Jackson nudged Matty toward the table.

Matthew sat and picked up his spoon to chase the little circles around the milk. "I'll take him out and walk him. And I know how to use the whistle. But Bandit is so smart, he will help you." He slurped his cereal. "I know it."

"How did you know I was thinking about Bandit?"

"Duh. He picked you."

"You're a goofy kid, Matty. I love you. Very much. And I'm sorry about the nightmares."

He looked down into the bowl. "It's okay."

Jackson refilled his coffee and sat across from Matthew. "Since I'm doing the psychiatrist hunt, I wondered if you wanted to talk to someone?"

Matty lifted his face, his expression confused. "About what?"

"Your mom. Me. School, heck, whatever you want to talk about."

Matthew quieted but bravely held his gaze. "Is Mom *really* going to come home?"

The coffee he'd been drinking rose up, burning Jackson's throat.

Matthew squeezed his eyes shut as if to avoid crying. "I know that makes me a bad person, not stayin' positive."

"You aren't a bad person." Hell, his parents had died and it had been Livvie who'd been strong and kept them together. "Your mom has so much love inside her that I know she will do whatever she has to in order to come home to you. Being your mom is the best thing in her world; she told me that."

"But what if she's hurt so bad that she can't?" Matty sniffed and scratched the tip of his nose, looking to him for reassurance.

Jackson lowered his head, feeling pulled apart. His nephew needed him here. His unit needed him overseas. "Then we will handle it, bud."

"What about your job?"

"That's just it. Because I've been doing it so long, I'm kind of good at it." He paused, wondering how he'd gotten to be so "good" at war. "And my boss needs me to come back." He shoved his mug an inch forward with his forefinger.

"So you're going back to get shot at?" Matthew's cheeks paled beneath the summer tan.

"It's what I do, Matty. It's what we Hardys have always done." The reason sounded weak when faced with his nephew's legitimate fear of the future.

Matthew pushed his chair back from the table, the legs screeching across the linoleum floor. "Well, I don't like it."

He waited, as if expecting to be punished for saying what he felt out loud. Jackson thought back to what Emma, so earnestly, had told him earlier. "There are no wrong feelings, Matty. Let's just see what happens. I won't leave you alone, okay?"

Matty's lower lip quivered, but damned if the kid didn't square his shoulders.

"Go hop in the shower, and I'll make this phone call."

Matty left the kitchen, head high. Jackson went through the junk drawer beneath the phone in the hall and dug out the stack of paperwork holding the list of doctors' numbers. He hadn't planned on using any of them and had scribbled the number for pizza delivery on the page corner.

He sat down at the kitchen table, avoiding putting his elbow in spilled milk. What he wanted to do was talk to Emma. Tell her what he'd seen. Confess to her what he'd done. She was a damn good listener.

But he couldn't do that—Jackson didn't want to see the desire in her eyes that she had for him turn to shame.

Chapter Twelve

Jackson and Matthew took the Kingston ferry across Puget Sound to Seattle. Standing on deck, they watched the jellyfish blossom in pink florets in the water. Salmon, seagulls, pelicans. Nothing like this in the Middle East. He hunched against a sudden chill.

"See that?" Matthew asked, pointing into the distance. "I bet it's a whale!" Matthew stood on tiptoes, hanging over the rail.

Jackson pulled him back by the collar of his T-shirt. "Careful. Water's too cold for me to dive in and get you."

Matthew grinned. "You would, though."

Snorting, Jackson exhaled and lifted his face to the sun. "Yeah. I would."

The thirty-minute ride ended near Pike Street Market, and Jackson pointed toward the Ferris wheel. "Tell you what, if we have time after the counseling appointment, we can get clam chowder at Ivar's and take a ride on the wheel."

"Really?"

"Sure. It would be fun." In the month that they'd been

together, there had been very little fun. Getting Matty caught up at school so he wasn't held back a grade, worry over Livvie living or dying, figuring out medical insurance, and trying to parent his nephew had taken everything he had. Time spent with Emma had been sunshine in the rain.

They found a spot in a twenty-story parking garage and he reached for his phone, remembering that he'd told Emma he'd be in touch.

Jackson typed a text, and his thumb hovered over the send button. He reread the text for the third time. Like a kid, he thought, wanting to make sure it sounded just right. *At the shrink's office.* No fuss. He sent it and slid his phone in his back pocket.

He'd gotten lucky, getting this appointment the same afternoon—either that, or the guy, Leonard Smith, was a total chump. His receptionist said that there'd been a cancellation, and if he hurried he could have it. Fate?

The military was all about rules meant to keep you fit and alive, but you had to adapt to the situation or wind up with your guts on the sand. Remi used to say you had rules so you could break them.

Remi. Jackson shivered. "Let's go."

The garage let out onto First Avenue, and the office building was on Third. He and Matthew walked up the hill together.

"This is a lot busier than where we live," Matthew said as another taxi whizzed through a yellow traffic light.

"I prefer the quiet."

"'Cause you're old." Matthew snickered.

"Twenty-nine is not old."

"Is too. I'm surprised you can climb this hill."

"You better be careful." He nudged Matthew's skinny arm. "Not to get grounded for the rest of the summer."

Matthew rolled his eyes. "Lame. You always say that."

They reached the tall gray stone and glass office building and went inside the air-conditioned lobby. A bank of elevators was to the right, and a long desk with a receptionist and a series of phones was to the left.

Marble floors shone in the sunlight filtering through the floor-to-ceiling windows.

"Fancy," Matthew whispered. The whisper echoed across the high ceilings and wide expanse of open floor space.

"Maybe our doc isn't such a chump after all."

He'd been given a list of names from Veteran's Services and chose at random. The receptionist, a pretty Asian woman in her mid-thirties, beamed at them from her spot behind the desk. "May I help you?"

Her cultured tones matched the richness of the wood trim and velvet curtains. Jackson cleared his throat, wishing he'd done more than put on a clean polo shirt. His black jeans were very underdressed for the building, and Matty looked like a street urchin out of *Scrooged*.

Oh well, he thought, striding toward her, his head high. "Hi. Jackson Hardy to see Dr. Leonard Smith."

Matthew was stuck to his side much like Bandit had been earlier.

"Welcome. I'll phone upstairs to let them know you're here. Take the elevators to the tenth floor."

"Thank you," Jackson said with a nod.

They turned and walked across the expanse of marble tile, the soles of their shoes making the occasional squeak.

Once they were in the elevator, Matty burst out laughing. "Awk-ward."

"You think?" Jackson grinned down at his nephew.

They got off on the tenth floor, the elevator doors opening to understated elegance. Old-fashioned wallpaper and dark wainscoting that alluded to men's clubs and secrets shared over a whiskey made Jackson think of trust funds and billionaires, way above his pay grade.

The door to the office opened, and a young man in navy blue slacks and a button-up Oxford shirt without a tie held out his hand in greeting.

"Welcome! Come on back." The man smiled at Matthew. "We've got a television in our waiting area with the Discovery channel. Juice and pretzels. I'll show you where it is, while your uncle is talking to Dr. Smith."

Matthew darted an anxious glance at Jackson, who felt the same nervousness but hid it behind a casual smile. "Sounds great, Matty. See you in a few."

The young man pointed to a partially open door to the left, as he and Matty went right. "Go on in, he's expecting you."

Jackson wished he could hang out and eat pretzels with Matty instead but knocked once on the polished dark wood door and pushed it all the way open.

A man about sixty with silver hair and silver-framed glasses looked up from a mug of tea. Orange spice wafted toward him.

"Welcome, Captain Hardy."

Dr. Leonard Smith got up from behind his desk with his hand outstretched. "Thank you very much for your service to our country."

Jackson froze. Not the response he was expecting. He shook the man's smooth hand. "Thanks. Not sure the VA expects to pay for this kind of service. Honestly, I thought I'd be in a shadier part of town. No offense."

"Call me Leonard." The shrink, no, doctor, gestured to a dark brown leather seat with brass studs creating a diamond pattern along the back cushion. "Talking with our soldiers means a lot to me. I served in the Air Force. During a peaceful time. Still stressful, though. Can't imagine…" He paused. "Well, I *can* imagine what you all are going through.

Which is why I do what I do."

"Which is?"

"Listen," the doctor said.

Jackson sat, and to his surprise, the psychiatrist grabbed his mug of tea and sat in the chair opposite him.

"Want a cup?"

"No, thanks."

"I love this. They sell it at Pike Street Market. I was glad when they made a decaf version." After a sip, he leaned back with a contented sigh. "Now, what can I do for you, Captain Hardy?"

"Jackson."

"Jackson."

He'd had a speech prepared about Livvie, about Matthew, about his commander. But under Leonard's compassionate gaze, Jackson said, "So, I guess I have these nightmares. My nephew told me about them, but I didn't remember them, really, so I figured he was exaggerating."

His heart raced, and he studied the brass stud on the armrest of the chair. The leather was more of a ripe Bing cherry color than wood, he decided.

"And?"

"Little turkey videotaped me having one. Couldn't deny it after that."

The sound of gunfire played in the back of his mind like mood music during a film. He put his hands over the armrests, centering himself by the feel of the leather beneath his fingers. Soft. The brass, cool.

He smelled blood instead of tea and turned his head.

"I guess not," Leonard agreed with a low chuckle. He cradled the mug between his hands and sat back, relaxed. "Did you bring the video?"

"Yeah."

"How did it make you feel?"

That was a shrink question, Jackson decided. "Shitty."

"Why? Because he took the video without your knowledge?"

"Partly." He pressed down on a brass stud as if it were a button and he could stop time. It didn't work. "And because then I couldn't deny it. Now, memories I thought I'd buried are right behind my eyes, taunting me." His voice cracked. "With sounds and smells and tastes." Remi's blood pooling over Jackson's boots. Iowa's bloody cot.

Leonard nodded and removed his glasses with one hand to set them on the desk. "Buried emotions rarely stay buried."

"I need to put them back," Jackson informed the doctor. Get to work. *Finish my time.*

"Why don't we examine them?"

"I can't afford to fall apart, Doctor, er, Leonard." He forced himself to meet the man's gaze. "My nephew is eleven. His mom is in a medically induced coma in Swedish Hospital with a brain injury after a car accident. His dad's out of the picture, and we have no other family. I am a career Marine. That's what I am."

The psychiatrist *hmmed*, the sound oddly comforting.

Jackson hadn't figured himself for the type to spill his guts, but his back was against the wall. All of the videos he'd watched last night on other Marines, other soldiers—some of those stories had ended up with vets being on the streets, homeless. Stuck in the vicious cycle of drugs and alcohol—to try to cope. Well, he might be stubborn, but Jackson knew he needed to ask for help to have a healthy life.

"How many years do you have in?"

"Ten."

"Halfway hump."

He missed his unit, his job. The guys were his brothers. "Retirement with full benefits is hard to pass up."

"Why do you say it like that?"

It terrified him, the idea of walking away from all he'd known. He was grasping at other options, desperate for an answer that fit. "Matty's worried about what will happen if Livvie"—he closed his eyes and breathed deep—"dies. We have no other family. I would have to take care of him, and that scares the crap out of me."

The doctor cradled his mug, eyes understanding.

"When I got the call that Livvie was in a bad accident, I was happy to take leave and care for Matty. We hadn't spent a ton of time together before now, but we are family." His throat clogged with emotion. "Now, I just love that kid—crazy, huh?"

Leonard smiled, the skin wrinkling at the corners of his mouth. "Parenthood. I've got three girls, so I do know."

"I'm not his dad, but even if things go back to normal, I can't imagine not being around."

"What does that mean to you?"

"I will be involved." As much as he could be. Maybe he'd buy a house nearby and stay for when he had time off. Two weeks, three weeks…would it be enough?

"You've mentioned your career in the military—why did you join?"

"Fourth generation."

"Besides that. Did your parents expect you to do so?"

"They died before I joined, but…" He thought of what Emma had said about his dad being proud of him, no matter what. He didn't believe that was true, but he would never know—how could he?

"I'm sorry to hear that. Did your sister feel obligated to join the military?"

"Livvie was in ROTC in high school, but she didn't continue in college—she's a dental hygienist. A great mom." He gritted his back teeth. "Was a great mom. Will be again. She has to get better."

"How do you feel right now?" Another shrink question. He'd have to warn Emma not to sound too much like a therapist when she talked to her patients.

He paused, digging deep. "Angry. Helpless. I'm used to acting."

He sighed. There was so much out of his control.

"You say you took leave?" Orange spice wafted upward in a ribbon of steam from the doctor's mug.

"Yeah." He sat back against the cushion of the chair and crossed his legs at the ankle. "Family leave—but my commander sent me an email that he'd like me back, sooner than later."

"Ah."

Ah? Jackson exhaled. "What?"

"Well, if I hear you correctly, you're getting bombarded with other people's wants. I'd love to hear what you want."

"Me? I'm the last guy on the totem pole."

Leonard chuckled and set his mug next to his glasses on the desk. "You hold everything else together, Jackson. The glue."

He slumped forward and tucked his feet beneath the chair. "It seems that way. Sometimes."

"So what are your options? If I were a wagering man, I'd bet you've thought of every possibility. Tell me."

Jackson lifted his gaze from the beige carpeted floor to the curtained window overlooking the city below. He lifted his hand and pressed one finger down. "First, and most important, is Livvie getting better."

"As you said, you have no control over that."

"Matthew's well-being." He put down a second finger. "My unit—you've served so you know what that's like—a different kind of family. I can't let them down." Jackson waited, but Leonard stayed quiet. "Third." Emma sprang to mind—tall, slender, strong. Freckles. He closed his eyes against the guilt that tore at his conscience. He'd pushed Emma away, knowing she was so much better a human being than he would ever be. He put his pinky flat to his palm. "I wonder if I could be a good civilian, after the things I've done."

Opening his eyes to the light in the room, he pressed his back into the brass studs in the cushion. "My nephew tried to steal a service dog to help me with my nightmares. Guess there's a way they can sense one's coming and wake you up?"

Leonard's expression held compassion, but he said nothing. Waiting. Listening. Making sure that Jackson was finished speaking. Jackson's throat was too clogged to do any more talking. Matty. Livvie. Even Emma. What wouldn't he do for his family?

"I knew you'd have some ideas," Leonard said, sitting up and resting his forearms on his thighs. "I can help you address all of these things, Jackson."

He sank into the leather seat.

The doctor *hmm*ed and sipped. "If you don't mind me saying, it sounds like your self-worth is wrapped up in your idea of serving our country."

Jackson eyed the man with caution. Was that true? What did that mean?

The doctor set the cup nonchalantly on the end table. "Who are you without the uniform?"

Jackson didn't know—it had been a given that he would do his twenty.

"You are strong enough to recall these memories, in time. And once you learn how to examine them without the emotion attached to the memory, you'll begin to heal. You don't need a dog to do that."

Jackson released a sigh of relief.

Chapter Thirteen

Emma drove home from the shelter, teary-eyed—and not because of Jackson's stubbornness, well, not *all* because of Jackson, or Lulu, but because the shelter was full to capacity and they'd had to turn a Maltese away.

People tried to drop the animal off at their no-kill shelter, but if they were full, they dropped off at the next available facility, which didn't always end well for the pup.

She popped a piece of dark chocolate into her mouth. Should she just ask Professor Collard about getting help for her grant? Was the money for the shelter worth getting booted from her doctorate program? The guilt for not saving the pup was awful, and the idea tempted her.

As she did every day before turning into her driveway, she focused her thoughts on the adjacent property's blue and gold FOR SALE sign. The dream of accomplishment it represented always cheered her.

The chocolate turned to ash in her mouth.

A bright orange SOLD sticker? She quickly pulled off the street and reversed down the dirt ditch to park in front of the

overgrown property. Blackberry brambles, pine scrub, ivy—
she had plans for the vacant land.

She got out of her SUV with disbelief. That property had
been for sale for years.

"Who bought my land?" Could this day get any worse?
She looked up at the sky. "Don't answer that."

Getting back into her vehicle, she drove home in dismay.
Pep was still gone, so she numbly did the chores with her dogs.
Checked the mail and wasn't at all surprised to see another
form letter telling her that her application had been denied.

It took all of her willpower to wash her face and get into
her office to gather what she had for her thesis. The goal was
an 80,000-word project showing how service animals eased
anxiety better than drugs. Despite all of the conferences
she'd gone to, and the articles published, she remained 20,000
words shy.

It seemed insurmountable, and for the first time, she
turned her back on her studies and shut the office door in
favor of a glass of wine on the back porch. Every door was
being closed. Jackson leaving Bandit, not trusting her to help,
Professor Collard giving her a deadline that loomed like the
Cascades, and another denial. The final straw was the sale of
her property.

Emma sat on the back porch with the glass of wine, a
plate of cheese, and crackers at her elbow on the picnic table.
The fountain gurgled peacefully in the background, the dogs
slept at her feet, and the cats dozed on top of the toolshed, in
the shade of an oak tree.

Tears fell in time with the splash of the fountain. How
much more could she take? Maybe she should have gone to
dinner with Sawyer after all. He'd offered after seeing how
sad she'd been to turn the Maltese away.

"You have a soft heart," he'd told her, his dark brown eyes
snapping with understanding. His dimples and thick dark

hair made Cindy blush every time he came into the shelter. "It hurts to see them go, but you are so good at finding just the right home." He'd offered to take her to dinner, which might have been construed as a date, and she didn't want to cross that line.

What made her pulse skip were brilliant green eyes and an eagle tattoo.

The dogs seemed sad, too, so she'd given everybody extra treats after their dinner. "We'll have a new recruit," she said to them. "Our job is to make people feel better."

Pedro and King exchanged licks; they'd been Lulu's boon companions.

She lifted the paperback and read the same page for the third time and finally set it down in exchange for a saltine cracker with thinly sliced sharp cheddar followed with a swallow of crisp white wine. Bandit lifted his head to check on her before laying his head back on the porch between his outstretched paws. Another hot tear trickled from her eye. She'd worked so hard. For what?

Was going to bed at 8:00 p.m. too early? She just wanted this awful day to end.

When her phone rang, she actually jumped. Princess's ears lifted, and she gave Emma a look. "Sorry, Princess." Emma checked the number. Jackson! She hadn't expected to hear from her soldier. "Hello," she answered. *Not yours.*

"Hey, it's Jackson."

"I know. Caller ID."

"There are no surprises anymore."

"Do you want to call again? I can pretend not to know who you are."

He chuckled. "Not necessary."

"How are *you*?" She put the book aside to give Jackson her full attention.

Bandit shifted his body, staring at the phone. Sweet.

Would Jackson want Bandit right away? She wasn't ready to lose another one so soon. But she would—Jackson needed Bandit.

"Fine. Well, all right. Matty and I stayed in the city for dinner. Clam chowder."

"Ivar's?"

"Yep. Did the Ferris wheel, too. First time either of us had been on it. What a view of the city, especially at night. Before that, we stopped by to see Livvie. Matty told me he's worried that she won't come home. I reminded him that he could talk to me, or you, about those feelings."

"Of course!"

She didn't prod him with the million questions running through her mind, and finally Jackson said, "The doc wasn't a bad guy."

"Who did you see?" she asked.

"Dr. Leonard Smith."

Shifting Princess on her lap, she said, "I know him." She brought to mind the older man with a stern demeanor and glasses. "He did a few lectures at the college." He was all about the science of mental health. Psychology, her field of study, was more about behavior patterns, why people acted the way they did. He was a *doctor*, thank you very much, and went strictly by the facts. The sort of person she was not...and didn't want to be.

Emma exhaled slowly to ease the tightness in her chest. Bandit lowered his ears.

"He offered some good suggestions. Dealing with the nightmares instead of burying them."

"That's important, I agree. What did he suggest?" She petted Princess.

"Revisiting the memories during the day so they won't bother me at night."

She nodded, then realized he couldn't see her. "Good."

Bandit inched closer to where she sat. She shook her head at him. She swore that the dog's brown eyes were sad.

"I brought up the therapy dog."

"Terrific," she said, hoping to sway him in a positive direction. "What did he say?"

"No harm can come from having Bandit at the house, but he didn't think it was *important*."

Her eyes watered, and she reached for her wine, taking a sip to clear the ache in her throat. She'd so hoped to help with Bandit. "Oh."

"Listen, I know you're disappointed. Matty is too, believe me. But I'd rather try it the doc's way, and maybe save us all some heartache in the long run when we'd have to give Bandit back."

She waited until she could talk without giving herself away. "I understand."

Bandit whined, and she reached down to scratch his ears. *It's okay, boy.*

"He suggested we see how things play out, so far as the bad dreams. I'll see him next week."

"I'm really glad you're talking to someone." She looked at the phone in her hand and rolled her eyes. "Professionally."

"Me, too. Thanks for being there for Matty, Emma. I really appreciate it. If he hadn't taken the video, I wouldn't have believed it. Doc said that the brain has a way of trying to protect us from the bad so, during the day, I had no recollection of what was happening at night. I know that now, and I can fix it."

What a typical male thing to say, she thought. "I wish you much success." Bandit laid his nose on her bare foot.

"Matty's in watching Spiderman cartoons. He's mad at me about the dog. Trying to understand, which is pretty grown up, considering." Jackson gave a light cough and said, "I told the doc about my commander needing me back soon."

She felt that news with a whoosh to her stomach. "How was that?"

"You know, you have all the right questions down, Em," Jackson chuckled.

"What?" Hearing him say her name like that, Em, would never get old.

"How do you feel, what do you think—those are shrink questions. I think when you get your own practice started you should ask different questions. Shake it up a little."

She laughed, drawing her knees up. "Those are the questions that work. Besides, I might not have a people practice." What she said surprised her, but she went with it, trying it out for size.

"Why the hell not?"

"Now *you* need to rephrase the question." Emma pressed her hand to Princess's fur, digging her fingers into the soft curls. "That's way too combative."

"That's what I do, combat. Fight. Win. I could never be a shrink. Takes too much inner peace. So, why not?"

Princess licked a crumb of cheese off Emma's finger. "I like what I do already."

"That's important." He waited a few seconds and then said, "But didn't you go to school for a long time? I can't believe how much education you need to mess with people's heads."

"Minds."

"Whatever." Jackson muffled the phone, possibly switching ears, and then asked, "How close are you again?"

"I'm on my final thesis. Then I have to intern for a year or two, and then have a mentor for another year or two." She curled her toes against the warm worn wood on the porch. "My professor gave me through the summer to finish but…I don't know. Today's been a rough day."

"Run out of ice cream?"

"Not funny, Jackson." She sniffed.

"I'm sorry. What happened?"

"It's nothing compared to what you're going through," she said, hesitant to complain when his sister was in a coma.

"It's okay, Em. I want to hear what's going on with you, I really do." His voice changed, and she felt as if he meant it.

"The property that I wanted to buy to build my shelter sold." The back of her nose filled with unshed tears. "And Lulu is gone, to a nice family, but still. And I got another denial for the grant. And we had to turn a dog away—"

"Geez, Em, that is a crappy day."

She wasn't even done with her list, which included him and Bandit. "I know." Princess gave the back of her hand a lick.

Then she sat up. "Hey, great job at changing the subject from you and your PTSD." She rubbed the silky tip of Princess's ear.

"It's not that simple," he said with a deep exhale. "I'm working on a decision that will be the best for everybody."

"Now, I know that is not what your Dr. Smith told you. Pretty sure he'd tell you to do what was best for you."

"Yeah." He chuckled. "You're pretty good, Em. I'm just thinking about what's best for Matty. I'd like to find a way to stay in the military, too. I'll figure it out. So much depends on my sister."

"True. I'm here, if you want to talk about it."

"I've done enough talking. Can't remember when I've *shared* so much."

She laughed at his heavy emphasis on the word. "That is how the healing begins."

"I'm sorry Bandit didn't work out. Do you still want Matty to come over on Thursday?"

"Yes. I love having him around. He owes me two more days." They'd agreed on four after the first day—Thursday would give Jackson two nights of writing out his dreams. "July fourth is the parade, and I have a booth downtown. I'd love his help with the dogs. It's a fun day, and he would have some free time, too. You're welcome as well."

"Sure," Jackson muffled the phone and then said, "Hey, Matty. Ready for some popcorn?"

She heard Matthew answer. "Yeah. Okay." Emma smiled, imagining a preview of the sullen teen years.

"I gotta go, Em. See you on Thursday."

"Bye, Jackson. Night to Matthew." Emma looked up at the dark blue starlit sky and said a prayer for the Hardy family, then picked up her book and stared at the page. Emerald green eyes and a sexy confident smile blurred the words.

• • •

Jackson shoved his phone into his pocket and got out the big popcorn bowl from the dishwasher. "Two bags?"

Matthew nodded. "I'm starving."

He'd grown in the last month, and Jackson anticipated another spurt. "You keep this up, and your mom will have to get a house with higher ceilings."

Matthew grinned self-consciously. "La-ame."

"I'm just saying. Maybe you should lay off the veggies."

"And be short like you?"

Jackson, at six feet, wasn't exactly pint-sized. "I may not be pro basketball player material," he said, "but I'm all right." He lobbed an empty juice box into the sink.

Matthew raced around him, pretending to dribble. "Block me if you can," he said, laughing with pure joy.

He blocked, and Matty whipped around him, then ducked under Jackson's outstretched arm for a perfect throw. "See that arc?" Matthew shouted. "Three for the win!"

"The win?" Jackson held his hands out to the side. "We are so buying a real basketball hoop tomorrow."

"Yeah?"

"I don't think your mom would mind, and if she does I can take it down before I leave. You look online for the best deal."

After the movie, Jackson insisted that Matthew take a bath. "You need to use soap, boy. Not the perfume stuff from your mom, but the bar of soap. Under your arms—everywhere, got it?"

Matthew stalked down the hall, mumbling about dirt and wasting his time in the tub. Jackson shook his head and powered up his laptop to check his emails. Maybe start on the list Dr. Smith had told him to write.

Another email from his commander—asking Jackson to hurry back. Hire someone to watch Matty. The unit needed their best sniper. He chose not to answer, confused by what was the right thing to do. There were many different "rights"—how to decide?

Dr. Smith had suggested writing a list of things he could control and things he couldn't. He opened a Word document.

First, Livvie. If she was out of the hospital, he would hire whatever she needed for physical therapy. In-home nursing, whatever it took for her to be well and able to care for Matty. Bonnie would be able to give him a list.

Then he could email his commander and let him know he'd join up with them overseas. With Dr. Smith's help, he should be able to return to his unit. Ten years would pass in the blink of an eye.

What do *I* want? He pushed the laptop aside and got up, walking into the kitchen for a bottle of water. Dr. Smith had also given him the same instructions that Emma had earlier: no booze, sleep in the bed, not the couch, no caffeine. Create a bedtime routine.

It's not about me.

He went back to the laptop and started writing out what he remembered about his dreams of being in battle.

If it meant preventing a nightmare, he'd do it.

But as he wrote, he stared at the accusing words. Remi. Dead. Blood. Iowa. Sniper. He couldn't breathe. *My fault?* Was there anything he could have done to prevent Remi's death?

The cursor blinked at him.

Blood.

Death.

My fault.

Jackson highlighted the paragraph and hit delete.

Chapter Fourteen

Thursday morning, Jackson was dragging ass. Exhausted did not even begin to describe the weight he felt, the cement in his boots as he took one sluggish step after another.

Perhaps Dr. Smith had underestimated the bite of his demons? It was a good thing he'd made sure to sleep in his room—or pretend to sleep, so Matty wouldn't know—because Jackson wrestled with ghosts all night long. After the second night of trying to conquer his dreams, the repetitive screams, the sounds of the dying, he caved and bought a case of Red Bull.

He downed pot after pot of coffee, shaking so bad that he dropped the keys to the truck. He didn't trust himself on the motorcycle with Matty.

"Ready?" he asked by their front door.

Matthew eyed him with concern. "Are you sick? I can stay home. Make you soup."

"I'm not sick." *Going out of my mind, but not sick.* "Let's go."

"I don't know." Matty hesitated, uncertain.

"*Move.*" His barked order came as a surprise, to both of them, and Matthew headed out the front door, letting the screen slam closed behind him.

He scrubbed the side of his face. The inch of beard on his jaw. His eyes felt gritty and his stomach soured from all the coffee. He'd agreed to help Mitch at the auto shop today, since Matty would be with Emma. Emma, who he couldn't stop wanting to kiss, even though it was wrong.

They passed the basketball hoop he'd bought and set up in the front driveway. Matty loved shooting hoops, and it was a good way to stay awake. Midnight, last night, before Jackson had declared bedtime.

"But it's summer," Matty had whined.

Jackson remembered saying the same thing to his dad. Lack of sleep was making him melancholy. His doctor's appointment was on Monday. Could he make it until then?

Maybe switch to Mountain Dew.

They drove to Emma's in silence, Jackson on autopilot and Matthew pouting. He parked by the gate and perked up at Emma's cheerful wave.

She wore khaki shorts and a light-blue polo with a Heart to Heart logo on the side. A mug in one hand and the whistle in the other. The dogs barked in welcome as he and Matthew got out.

His vision swam, but he covered by keeping his hand on the truck.

Or thought he'd covered until Emma's gaze narrowed in on him.

"How's it going?" she asked.

"Ask Uncle Jackson."

"That well?" Emma's auburn brows drew together.

Matthew opened the gate and closed it, shutting Jackson out. Matty burrowed his head in Romeo's fur, his back to Jackson.

Bandit barked at Jackson and wagged his tail.

Jackson squeezed the bridge of his nose and forced a smile.

"Morning, Emma. Matthew, don't be rude."

"Morning, Emma," Matthew said. He gave his uncle the stink-eye and continued petting Romeo.

Jackson gritted his teeth. "Kids."

She lifted her mug to her mouth, partially hiding a smile. "Hmm." Emma drank and lowered her cup, no doubt noticing his bloodshot eyes and the fact he hadn't shaved. "You look terrible, Jackson."

He held up his hand. "I know. You don't have to kick a guy when he's down."

"Sleeping?" She invoked concern with that one question.

"Yep."

"Liar." His nephew countered in a cool tone, "I know you aren't. I saw the Red Bull cans in the recycle bin."

Crap. "I see the doctor on Monday. Four days."

Emma nodded, looking from Matthew to Jackson. "Good." Bandit joined Emma, leaning against her long leg to stare at Jackson.

He was tired enough that he imagined resting his head under the shade of the cherry tree and Bandit chasing off the demons. It sounded awesome.

And delusional.

"I have to go."

Matthew didn't move from where he hugged Romeo.

Jackson looked at Emma, who gave a sympathetic shrug. "I'll be back at four."

"We're staying here today. We've got nails to trim and kennels to clean."

Jackson left, his heart heavy. His eyes heavier.

He stopped and picked up a liter of soda before going to the shop to work.

• • •

Matthew straightened as soon as the truck disappeared down the drive. "I am so mad, Emma. He's totally lying and hiding that he's not sleeping. I can't wait to tell that doctor that I think he's stupid. I'm going to, too."

Emma stepped back. "Whoa. Let's take this one piece at a time." This was the first she'd ever seen Matthew angry rather than sad or scared.

"Sorry." He crossed his arms and lifted his chin.

"Don't be sorry about how you feel." She motioned for him to join her in walking to the kennels. "We can clean and talk. It helps to direct the negative out of your body into something positive."

"I'm so mad I could clean the whole garage!" He shoved his hands into his pockets, and his sneakers scuffed the grass as they neared the building.

"I might take you up on that," she said. Anger was always better out than in. "Come on." Emma showed him how to take apart the kennels while she got the buckets of sudsy water prepared.

"Now, you don't agree with Jackson's doctor?" Because she didn't like Leonard Smith, either, she was determined to be fair. He practiced high-rise, old-school doctoring while she preferred a more open approach to a problem, and healing.

"No." Matthew, calmer now, said, "He told Uncle Jackson he didn't need a dog. It was like a teddy bear for grown-ups."

"A teddy bear?" She silently agreed with Matthew—having arrived at that opinion herself during Dr. Smith's lectures. He came off very arrogant as he relayed just the facts he wanted to, as if there was no room for emotion.

Matthew took a scrubber to the individual metal panels. "I mean, Uncle Jackson was so close to getting Bandit and bringing him home." He looked at Emma and scowled.

"That would've helped, I know it. Instead, I hear him in his bedroom, walking around in the dark and bumping into furniture." Taking a deep breath, Matthew added, "Dr. Smith told him to write about his nightmares." He sat back on the heels of his sneakers. "How can that help? It just makes him angry."

Emma lifted a panel. "There's a practice of looking at what is causing the bad dreams and facing it during the day. But maybe your uncle isn't ready for that yet. Dr. Smith isn't wrong, Matthew." It hurt to say that, but it was the truth. "There are many ways to solve a problem. Not all are going to fit everybody the same way."

"Uncle Jackson needs a dog, that's all. Bandit." He dismantled another kennel and started washing it down.

She rinsed off the suds with water from the hose and let the metal dry in the summer sun. Emma thought of all that Jackson was willing to put on the line to get healthy—his career in the military, his relationship with Matty. She knew from personal experience that facing your demons hurt, and a lot of people never took the risk. "I understand why you are angry. But I think your uncle is being very brave, too."

"Brave? He's not supposed to have coffee. Or Red Bull." Matthew dropped the scrubber and looked away. Romeo joined him, nudging Matthew's arm so it went around Romeo's neck.

Crying.

Ah, no. Tears filled her own eyes, and she joined them on the grass, sitting cross-legged. She touched his back, rubbing between his shoulder blades. "You must be really worried."

"I am." He petted Romeo's back, his face in the dog's thick neck. "And you know what double-sucks?" Sniffling, he lifted his chin.

"What?" She braced herself.

"I heard Uncle Jackson talking to Aunt Bonnie about

Mom. She's not getting better. Aunt Bonnie was crying."

Emma closed her eyes as she accepted his anguish, calming him through her touch on his back.

"What if she *dies*?" His lower lip quivered, and Romeo gave his cheek a lick with a long pink tongue. "I need my mom. She has to come home."

How to help without joining him in tears? Acknowledge the facts, and deal with them.

"Right now, the doctors are making sure that your mom has a chance to heal. I understand that it is very scary. It isn't that the doctors are hiding things from you, Matthew. I don't think they have answers. It is better to wait and give your mom time."

His chin quavered. "They won't let me bring her flowers, and I know she likes them. Or hold her hand. I promised to be so careful…"

"Your mom loves you, don't forget that." Emma got to her feet, before she completely lost her composure. "Come on. We've got a few more crates to do. Then I say we go inside and have some ice cream. I think we have chocolate."

Matthew looked around, his expression confused as his tears dried. "Where's Lulu? And Princess?"

"They've been placed in homes." She brushed the grass off the bottom of her shorts.

"They're *gone?*"

She nodded, tugging him up to stand next to her, sneaking in a side hug. "Yes. That's our job, to get the animals ready for good homes where they can offer a special brand of comfort. A little more complicated than a teddy bear."

Emotions rippled across his young face. Sadness, grief, understanding. "I didn't get to say goodbye."

Loss. "They knew you cared."

"Really?"

"Really." She put her hand over his heart. "Do you know

that Romeo cares about you?"

He nodded.

"The other dogs feel that, too. Maybe not as much as Romeo—you're his favorite, I think, but it's like that."

He stared at the ground.

How to cheer him up? The world was sometimes very heavy, but she was showing him how to cope. The dogs, keeping busy, and looking at a problem head on helped. Being useful.

"Matthew, would you like to help me run the Heart to Heart Dog Kennel booth during the July fourth festival downtown? During the day, you'll be free to wander around and be with your uncle for the fireworks at night."

"Yes!" He swiped the shaggy brown bangs off his forehead. "I'll ask. What do I need to do?"

She'd discovered that helping others brought light to the shadows inside. Maybe it would for Matty, too.

"Sit with me. Walk the dogs, show them off. Try to match them with people who are looking for an Emotional Support Therapy Dog. They trust you and will listen to you, so I feel very comfortable having you there. You've been a huge help to me."

"Thanks, Emma. I'll do a good job."

"I know that." She snuck in another quick side hug and finished rinsing the crates.

After double scoops of chocolate chip ice cream, Emma made grilled cheese sandwiches for lunch, with diced apples and cabbage in a slightly sweet coleslaw.

"When is Aunt Pepita coming home?"

Emma hid a smile, amazed at how well Matthew fit in her day-to-day. Had Pepita felt the same, when she'd had Emma dumped on her doorstep? "She's on a two-day trip. Last I heard, she's up a hundred bucks."

"I bet I could play." Matthew rested his elbows on the

kitchen table, the dogs arrayed around his feet just in case something dropped.

"Ask her to teach you blackjack when she comes back; it's fun. We played with jellybeans instead of money. Helped me with math."

It got hot later in the afternoon, so she set up the sprinklers and they all ran through them on the grass. Bandit liked to gulp the water as it spurted close from the base, while Sweetie stayed back and barked at the rainbow colors in the mist.

Emma discreetly checked her watch and realized that it was almost five. No word from Jackson about being late.

She sent him a text.

No answer.

Worry nagged at her like a sore tooth, and she told Matthew to keep playing as she ran inside and called Mitch at the auto shop.

Nothing.

Concern over his obvious exhaustion overcame her sense of professional boundaries. She *liked* him, dang it. Now she tossed a sundress on, slipped her feet into flip-flops, and grabbed her purse and the keys to her SUV. "Hey, Matthew? Let's go to your house and see if your uncle wants Fabio's pizza."

Matthew gave a fist pump in the air, his anger forgotten. "Pizza!"

Bandit waited by the fence, as if determined to go with them. She turned off the sprinklers and got the dogs in the kennel. She fed them half a cup of dry kibble for a quick dinner, promising extra treats later.

She didn't question bringing Bandit with her—he stayed on her heels.

Matthew, his hair damp, a towel around his wet shorts, climbed into the SUV. "I'm starving. Uncle Jackson says

Mom might need to get a bigger house—you know, 'cause I'm growing so fast."

Emma smiled, but her heart wasn't in it. She drove the five minutes to their house. The blue truck was there, next to the motorcycle and a shiny, new basketball hoop.

"We've been shootin' hoops," Matty informed her, then noticed the time on the clock of the SUV. "Five thirty. Why didn't he come and get me?" He frowned.

She parked, and before she could come up with a reason for him to wait for her and to let her go in first, Matthew was out of the passenger side door, with Bandit at his side.

Oh, no.

She got out, slammed her door, and ran in after them.

"Uncle Jackson!" Matthew shouted.

Emma ran up the steps of the porch and into the house. Jackson was sprawled on a large blue sectional couch, his feet out and his hand over his head. He'd somehow knocked the black and white lamp over, breaking the glass that crunched beneath Emma's thin flip-flops. Bandit had no protection, but he made his way to Jackson and licked his face.

Matthew was barefoot, and she quickly set him away from the glass. "Careful. The lamp is broken."

Jackson, eyes squeezed shut, pushed at Bandit. "Get back, Remi! Get down!"

Who was Remi?

She slipped the training clicker out of her front pocket and clicked it as Bandit licked Jackson's cheek, then nudged his shoulder to wake him up.

"Good dog," she said. *Wake him up.*

Jackson kicked his foot to the side, barely missing Matthew.

Matthew got out of the way, his stance angry, scared, and determined, and Emma glimpsed how he'd look when grown. "Wake up!"

Muttering unintelligible words in a harsh tone, Jackson turned to his side, and then onto his back again, his arm flung wide.

Bandit barked loudly next to Jackson's ear. Once. Twice. *Woof.* Jackson sat up, eyes open but unfocused. "What? What's going on?"

His breaths came fast. She sat on the edge of the couch, holding his wrist, letting him know that he was not alone. Matty darted out of sight.

"You're okay," she said in calm tones. "In your house. On your couch."

"What are *you* doing here?" Jackson's bristled jaw grew tight as he eyed her, then looked around for Matthew. His hand rested on Bandit.

"We came to check on you." It was good that they'd come, though she knew Jackson didn't agree. Her heart raced in fear, in empathy.

"You didn't pick me up." Matthew's eyes were round and scared as he held a glass of water he'd gotten from the kitchen out to his uncle.

"What time is it?" Jackson scuffed the side of his head with the palm of his hand before accepting the glass.

"Five thirty," she answered in a steady voice.

"I didn't mean to sleep." Jackson stared into the clear liquid, a slight tremor in his hand making the water shake. "I had to rest for a bit." His voice deepened with layers of guilt. "Set the alarm for an hour. Overslept. Sorry."

"You can't deprive your body." Emma leaned closer to him, keeping her tone gentle, though she wanted to yell and shake him to get his attention. He didn't have to suffer like this.

Bandit waited, sitting on his haunches by Jackson's feet, watching each move Jackson made as he tilted his head back and drank until the glass was empty.

Jackson started to get up, but Emma held out her hand. "Careful, broken ceramic. You must have kicked over the lamp," she said. "When you were dreaming."

Jackson looked at the black side table where the lamp had once resided.

"Busted," she said in a soft voice, touching his leg. "Here, I'll take the glass. Want more?"

Jackson shook his head. "No thanks."

Emma set the glass down by her feet, focusing on the situation, on Jackson.

Bandit whined and set his head on Jackson's knee. Jackson absently put his hand in the dog's ruff.

Good boy, Bandit, she thought. *Good boy.*

After a few minutes, the color returned to Jackson's tanned face, and his breaths evened. Matthew perched on the opposite side of the L-shaped couch and watched his uncle as intently as Bandit.

"I think we should implement Plan B."

"What's that?" Jackson's scowl didn't scare her any as she sensed his underlying tumult.

"Plan Bandit." She jerked her chin at the dog and Jackson's hold on Bandit's neck. "He'll work better than any *teddy bear*, I guarantee it. What do you have to lose?"

"I don't know." He planted his feet on the floor, looking around the living room as if for hidden answers.

"Uncle Jackson, you have to," Matthew shouted.

Jackson raised his palm against the words. "I go to the doc on Monday."

"So, try this until then," Emma said. "It doesn't negate the work you are doing with Dr. Smith. Just gives you a buffer. Your body fights sleep because your mind is bringing up awful memories when you have no control. Therefore, it seems like you should fight sleeping and stay in control. But you can't." She gestured to the white shards littering the living room. "As you can see."

She clasped his wrist, the muscle jumping beneath her fingers. *Please, Jackson, accept the help.*

Jackson looked down at where she held him, and then at her, confusion radiating from every pore.

"Bandit can wake you up before the dreams get to this point," Emma said. "You are so exhausted you can't rouse yourself from them."

Jackson exhaled and closed his eyes, his hand still in Bandit's ruff. "We can't keep a dog."

Matthew started to cry, burying his face in his knees. "If Mom were here she would understand about Bandit."

"We can try," Jackson said gruffly. "I know this is a scary time for you. I don't want you to be afraid."

Matty lifted his face and wiped his eyes. "Promise?"

Jackson looked at Emma. "I'll try the dog." He scrubbed at his cheek. "But can he do something different than lick my face, Em?"

Her heart surged with hope and affection. She loved it when he called her Em, as if they were on the same team rather than on opposite sides.

"Sure. We can teach him to nudge you with his nose. Or bark in your ear. Jackson, we can take this as slow as you need to go. For right now, why don't you guys just get used to having a dog in the house?"

Matty stared at Jackson, as if afraid to believe he'd actually do it.

"Okay." He nodded again.

Matthew leaped across the couch, throwing his arms around Jackson's neck. "Thanks, Uncle Jackson. I will take good care of Bandit, and you."

"You already do." He pulled back and said, "I need to take care of you."

Emma blinked away tears of gratitude. "Jackson, you

won't have to do it alone."

He reached for her hand, interlacing their fingers to send a thrill through her, a longing for something that she knew she couldn't have. A partner. A family. Not with this man, anyway. Too bad nobody else had ever come close.

Chapter Fifteen

Jackson got Matty set up with *Scooby-Doo* on television, one arm looped around Bandit's neck, the other hand free to dig into the popcorn bowl. One piece for Matthew, one for Bandit.

"I have to make a few phone calls," he said. "You okay?"

Matthew nodded. Bandit gave a *woof* before turning his attention back to the popcorn. "Are you going to call Emma? Tell her that I didn't tell the doctor that he was stupid, okay?"

"What?" Jackson asked with surprise.

"She'll know." His nephew went back to watching the cartoon that never seemed to go out of style.

Jackson took the phone into his bedroom but then decided to see if there was a breeze on the small wooden deck at the back of the house. He opened the slider and figured it was cool enough—his bedroom was not a place where he liked to hang out these days. He sat at the round bistro table with three matching chairs and dialed Emma's number.

She answered on the first ring. "Jackson? How did it go today?"

"Hello to you too," he said with a chuckle. It warmed him to know she cared. "I'm supposed to tell you that Matty didn't call Dr. Smith stupid?"

Emma burst out laughing, the sound bringing a smile to his face after what had been a rough few days. "Good."

He'd have to press for that story later. Jackson sat back, kicking his boots off and arching his toes. It was that eerie time of dusk, right before dark after the sun had gone down, when it was easy to believe in ghosts and things that go bump in the night. As a soldier, his job was to protect against the boogeyman.

The small backyard was fenced with six-foot wooden planks that wrapped around the back and sides, with the garage at the rear of the property. Plenty of room for Matty to run around. Some of the boards were loose; two were missing. It had been on the list of things for him to eventually get to, but now that they had Bandit, it had jumped to the top.

"Hey, can dogs have popcorn?" he asked.

Emma was quick to answer. "A few pieces won't hurt."

"With extra butter, you know, movie style? At the rate Matty and Bandit are sharing the bowl, it's about a half bag each."

"I'm glad I don't have pooper-scooper duty."

"You're my witness. Matty said he'd do it." He stretched his legs out and lifted his face to the soft wind through the trees. Night jasmine and pine, with a hint of skunk.

"True." She laughed softly, encouraging confidences. "How's Bandit doing?"

"He's a good dog. As you know." Look at him, telling her that her own dog was good. *Nice, Jackson. Smooth.* "Thanks for dropping off the crate and dog food. Matty's got two of those clicker things. Says he's going to 'work' with me and Bandit tomorrow." Matty had told him this with no small amount of pride.

"He's got the instructions on how to practice with Bandit. It shouldn't take more than a week or two of training before the dog understands what you need. But after seeing him the other night? I'd say Bandit's already got a good idea of what to do. I'm glad that I was there and able to click when he licked your face to wake you up. It's a start, and Bandit is very smart."

"It's got to be something besides a lick." He scrubbed his cheek with his palm.

The tone of her voice dropped to husky as she said, "Since when do you not like kisses, Jackson?"

Was she being flirty? He eyed the phone—maybe he'd caught her after a glass of wine. "I prefer any tongue exchanges to be with a female human—as you know."

She laughed so hard that the dogs started barking on her end of the phone.

"So what are you doing home? You're single, pretty, intelligent. Shouldn't you be out on the town on a Friday night?"

"Ha! I am in the living room with my research books, a mug of herbal tea, and five dogs all around me, waiting for me to accidentally drop a piece of cracker."

"Way to live it up, Em."

"Professor Collard's deadline has made me realize how much I've put into this. I'd forgotten that I have *ten* articles published on various dog-person relationships, and how dogs are a viable alternative to medicine. Not that the pharmaceutical companies want to hear that, and don't get me started on insurance. Grr."

"I can relate. Nothing can happen with Livvie without it being cleared through the insurance company, which seems backward. Shouldn't the doc get the last word? I've already got major bills coming in. The accident happened a month ago, and Livvie's got great health insurance."

"That's one good thing, then, huh?" She shifted the phone, and static crackled. He pictured her on the couch surrounded by hopeful pups.

"When do you need your thesis done?" He saw the stress she was under, and it amazed him how well she handled it all—he'd be a mess. He only had to juggle Matty and was still behind on laundry.

"I've got all of July, all of August, then he wants the rough draft. Can you believe I turned in an assignment with a paw print on the back?"

Jackson started to laugh. "Was that the catalyst?"

"Yeah. I can't blame him."

He hated to ask, but he hoped for something positive. "What's new on the grant front?"

"I'm up to nine rejections. But what's the point? My property sold. Dream gone, just like that." She snapped her fingers.

"You can get other land, can't you?" He saw parcels for sale all over Kingston.

"This was perfect, though. No buildings on it, and right next door to Aunt Pep's place so we could combine them. I'm sounding like a whiner, Jackson. This could be the real reason why I don't have a date." She laughed.

He loved how she never took herself too seriously. "Where's your aunt?"

She sighed. "Out with Harold at a dance at the senior center, while my last date was…" She stopped, and he imagined her brow furrowed as she thought back. "Right before last Christmas."

"Six months is too long, Em."

"I keep telling myself that I will make time after I get my doctorate."

He could see her in the middle of a laughing household, then imagined himself as the man next to her. He bit his tongue before he offered to take her out to dinner.

She cleared her throat as if embarrassed. "I've shared my lame story. What was your last date like?"

Jackson reached back into the memory banks but nothing story-worthy jumped out—most free time was spent cleaning gear or playing video games in the tent. "Dating isn't my thing."

"I thought you'd be a Romeo," she said in low drawl. "A handsome soldier like you."

She thought he was handsome? He puffed his chest a little. "I've always put my career first. Don't get me wrong, I've dated, but I've kept things casual." Nobody compared to Emma Mercer.

"Don't you ever get lonely?" Her gentle voice was as soft as the feel of her hair between his fingers.

"No time. It's all about the job."

"You can't work twenty-four hours a day, Jackson. Even I take beach breaks with Aunt Pep. What else did you do?"

"Overseas is where I learned to love motorcycles. Some of the other guys and I take 'em apart and put them back together again. For speed."

She groaned. "And here I was worried about you getting shot. Now I can add reckless driving over sand dunes to my imagination."

"We're careful." Sort of. "You say the word and I'll come take you for a ride." He imagined the feel of her arms around him and almost stood to grab his keys.

"I don't know…" she said.

"I've been all over the world, seeing the sights. It's an amazing place."

His sessions with Dr. Smith had made him examine his reasons for joining the military, and for staying—he was, subconsciously, nothing without the military. His dad's death had cemented that path for him in his mind, and the love he'd had for Emma, who loved with her whole heart, had scared him. She had made him want something different, which would have disappointed three generations of Hardy men.

At the time, he'd convince his teenaged self that he'd broken up with her so she would fly. "I really thought you'd leave Kingston."

"You've said that before. Why would I leave Aunt Pep?" She scoffed into the phone. "I didn't have a happy home until she took me in at fourteen. No mom, no dad. You know this."

He did. Their grief over having no parents had been a tragedy in common. Which made him think of his strong, loving sister, who would not abandon her son, not even in death. Not if she could help it.

"I talked to Livvie's neurosurgeon. He wants to meet face-to-face on Wednesday." How long could they keep her going with no change, or hope?

"Will you take Matty with you?" She paused, and he heard her take a sip of tea.

"I'll ask him, but I see his frustration—the doctor doesn't think he should be there at all, and he's gruff with Matty, when Matty just wants his mom, you know?"

"I do understand."

He'd been tempted to text or call Emma on many different pretenses over the weekend but had stayed strong. Therapy had shown him why he'd broken up with her so abruptly in high school—he had known, on a heart level, that Emma could be The One. And that didn't fit his life plan back then. Knowing the woman she was now brought fantasies of what they might be like if he hadn't left. Would it be a life of lasagna, chicken salad, and romantic comedies? Stargazing at the beach? Saving dogs? He straightened in the stiff-backed metal chair. Kids?

She was his Achilles heel. He could be a super soldier, proving his mettle against the enemy, but one welcoming smile from Emma and he was tempted to toss it all.

He could recall each time she'd put a hand on his knee or a comforting touch on his wrist. Her pink mouth releasing warm breath against his cheek, the light floral scent of her perfume.

Emma was a hundred times smarter than him, genuinely cared about other people, and smelled like flowers. He was all boots, jeans, God, and country. He did not do feelings especially well—hence, the nightmares, according to Dr. Smith.

"So," she said, as if on cue. "What did the good doctor say?"

"He wants me to continue writing down what I remember from my dreams. Even if it doesn't make any sense, eventually, ideally, it should all come out." The doctor had asked him to be patient and not give up the work.

"Will you see him again next week?"

"Yeah." His goal was to get better. Emma's remark that his dad would be proud of him, no matter what he did for a career, made him question his actions. Was he proud of himself? There were things he'd done in the name of war that happened in the line of duty. There was guilt because he hadn't saved Remi, or McMahn, but in that situation, nobody could have. It was time to let go.

He was very aware of wanting to be his best self in caring for Livvie and Matty and not just to make his parents proud, but because he loved them.

"And you told him about Bandit?"

Jackson squirmed guiltily on the bistro chair. "No."

"Why?" Her tone rose with surprise.

"I didn't want to start a discussion on 'reasonable expectations,' like last time. I get it already." Having a service dog would not provide a miracle.

He heard her suck in her breath. "Reasonable

expectations. In regards to what you get from a service animal?" Her exhale rattled the earpiece. "I will have you know that studies prove—"

Jackson's laugh rumbled from his belly as he pictured her sitting on the floor surrounded by books and dogs and fuming because of Dr. Smith's referral to her working animals as teddy bears.

"You are so easy, Em. I'm giving Bandit a try. I'm also going back on the 'no caffeine after noon' regime. And yeah, listing out what I remember from the dreams." It wasn't easy, but he was determined.

Her breathing returned to normal. "You have it together."

"No, but I'm trying." It was so comfortable talking with Emma. He wished they were sitting next to each other—here, or at her place, so he could see her nose crinkle or her smile widen before she tilted her head back to laugh.

"Oh, I put Sawyer's phone number on the paper I left with the training instructions, in case you had a question and wanted to talk to a guy about it."

"Uh, no." He crossed his stretched-out legs at the ankle. "The reason I was uncomfortable," he gritted his teeth but admitted, "was because I didn't want to seem weak to you."

"That could never happen, Jackson. Your emotions do not make you a weak person. Every time you share it's a sign of strength." Her voice thickened. "Thank you."

A crash sounded, and Jackson jumped up, peering through the sliding glass door. "Dang it. Looks like I'll be buying *two* new lamps tomorrow."

"Oh no! Is everybody okay?"

"Boys will be boys," he said, not too upset as he watched Matty with the broom and Bandit following with the dustpan. "I'll see you Wednesday."

"All right. Call me if you need anything before then."

• • •

Emma hung up the phone, regretting her words. Call me if you *need* anything? How about just call? To talk, to share stories, and get to know each other again?

King plopped his nose into her lap and stared at her with compassionate canine eyes. "I know," she said. "Unrequited affection sucks."

She and Jackson had chemistry—the sizzle of heat from just a slight touch was enough to make her hot all over. But there were a hundred reasons why she couldn't act on that attraction; she had to protect her heart.

Looking back over the years, she'd sometimes wondered if their relationship had been built on mutual tragedy, and here they were again, with his PTSD and Livvie in the hospital, she stressed to her maximum capacity. The difference being that now she understood Jackson's bravery, and seeing how he put his family first? She sighed.

Cramped after sitting so long, Emma brought her empty mug to the kitchen to concoct a half-herbal, half-black tea to keep her focused instead of sleepy.

It didn't help that her research subject was on sleep apnea—she was fascinated that the dogs could be trained to wake the sleeper, and she'd emailed the author of the paper to ask a few questions for her training program at Heart to Heart Dog Kennel. It tied in to her thesis subject on dog-human interactions, which was another step closer to getting her project finished.

If she didn't fall asleep first. Was Jackson watching a movie with Matty? Kicked back on the blue couch...

Blue, like Professor Collard's eyes. His disappointment prodded her to keep going. She couldn't let him down.

Grabbing a bag of unsalted almonds, she took her tea back to the couch and curled up with Sweetie at the crook of her knees, Pedro and Cinnamon on the opposite end of the couch, Romeo by the door, and King on the floor at her end of the couch. She was proud of Jackson for not sounding angry about Matty breaking that lamp...

Focus on something other than Jackson.

At eleven o'clock, Aunt Pepita waltzed, literally, through the front door. In an aqua velvet gown, floor-length and off the shoulders, her aunt was a reminder of 1950. Lawrence Welk. Big band era.

Emma set the pamphlet she was reading down on the coffee table. "Have fun?"

"As always." Her aunt swirled across the floor, somehow missing Romeo's wagging tail. "You should come next week."

"I'm not even thirty."

"I'll loan you a dress."

Emma wouldn't be caught dead in aqua velvet. "Thanks. I'll pass."

Emma heard Aunt Pepita open the refrigerator and entered the kitchen to see her aunt bent over, poking around the bottom shelf.

"Harold asked me to marry him."

Emma froze and stared at Aunt Pepita, who'd discovered a bottle of sweet Moscato behind the cranberry juice and lifted it up.

Appropriate responses flitted around her mind but soon disappeared. "What?"

Aunt Pep grinned and nudged the fridge closed with her hip. "Join me in a toast?"

"Uh, congratulations!" Emma got down two glasses and set them on the kitchen table, took the wine before her aunt dropped it, and gave her a huge, heartfelt hug. Married? Free-spirit, love 'em and leave 'em Aunt Pepita, married?

Pep pushed free with a coy smack to Emma's arm. "And what makes you think I said yes?"

Speechless, Emma decided she'd better just pour the wine.

"He claims to love me, but I think he's jealous."

Emma thought back to the men at the senior center. Women outnumbered them four to one, so available guys were nabbed immediately. "Of who?"

"Ernie."

"The bus driver?" Ernie was in his late sixties, to her aunt's eighty-something.

"He can dance. I had no idea." Her aunt sipped her wine, her eyes half closed with some memory that made her glow.

"Ernie," Emma clarified. Fat and bald with a mustache?

"There was music and the lights were low…" Pep's voice trailed off. "Ernie and I were dancing, and then Harold cut in."

Emma could imagine Harold's surprise at having to fight for Pepita's affections.

"When I admonished him, he clutched his chest. I thought he was having a heart attack, but as it turned out"—she displayed her left hand, which remained devoid of jewelry— "he was reaching into his jacket for a ring."

"Where is it?" Emma grabbed her aunt's fingers.

"Aren't you listening? I didn't say yes."

Emma downed her wine and poured a second glass. Heck, she might need another bottle.

"Ernie drove me home."

"In the senior center bus? Like always?"

"Pfft. He saved my stop for last." Pepita closed her eyes and twirled, bumping into the kitchen table and making the dogs *woof* in warning. "He kissed me."

Emma's eyes welled, and she blinked back tears. Her aunt looked so happy that it made Emma wish for a love of her own. A man without green eyes or broad shoulders. No eagle tattoo. A man who wouldn't choose his career over her.

"Poor Harold," she said. "You really do care for Ernie."

"I do." Pep opened her eyes and held her wineglass close to her chest. "I really, really do."

"I'm happy for you, Aunt Pepita."

Her aunt offered a dreamy smile, held out her glass for a refill, and then danced her way down the hall. "Sweet dreams, Emma."

She lifted her glass toward her aunt's back, crushed velvet hips swaying from one side to the next. "Sweet dreams."

Emma finished her wine on the back porch, looking up at the moon and stars. Stars always made her think of Jackson, their very hot kiss in the kitchen, the way they'd fit as if no time had passed at all. Her hand on his muscular arms, her hip to his, his fingers caressing her lower back. The musky scent of his cologne.

Just like that, desire for him had rekindled—but not a thing had changed between them. If anything, the chips were stacked even higher. Now, she had a business that needed to expand in order to save dogs, a doctorate her own professor wasn't sure she wanted—and the stirring of her heartstrings when she thought of Jackson and the man he'd become.

She might not survive a second broken heart, and he would break it—just by doing what he needed to do, who he'd been raised to be, which was finish his career in the military. He would not choose her—again.

A shooting star whisked across the night sky, and she closed her eyes to make a wish.

I want true love with a man I can trust to pick me first. Which crosses Jackson Hardy off the list.

Chapter Sixteen

July third, Emma logged on to her computer before Jackson and Matty were due to arrive. She almost spit out her coffee when she saw an email from her professor. The subject read: CALL ME. Capital letters equaled shouting in the cyber world.

Would he kick her out of the doctorate program? He'd given her until September first. She *did* want to finish, and after gathering all of her studies and published works, she knew, if she stayed at it, that she could just make that rough draft. Minus the paw prints. But she did have concerns and had to be realistic about them.

She had some hard thinking to do but not now. It was the last Wednesday with Matthew and Jackson, and she dreaded the void their absence would leave. Forget the psych talk—she was going to miss them terribly.

She closed down the computer, refilled her coffee, and went outside to wait for Jackson and Matthew by the gate. Jackson had texted her yesterday that he'd convinced Matty to stay with the pups while Jackson talked to Livvie's doctors;

it was sure to be a tough meeting.

She'd thought they might go to Kingston Animal Shelter, but she would play the activities by ear to see what Matty needed most.

They arrived in the truck with Bandit, who immediately joined the other dogs and raced around the cherry trees.

"Morning, guys." Emma forced cheer into her voice. Sometimes getting answers, even unwelcome ones, allowed you to move forward, and she prayed that things went well at the hospital today.

Jackson shuffled up to the chain link fence. "Morning. Did you know that the SOLD sticker is off that property sign?"

"It is?" She clamped down the hope that rose like a phoenix. "Probably just fell. I'll have a look later."

Matty had followed Bandit into the yard, leaving his uncle on the opposite side of the fence. He was careful to close the gate and latch it.

Emma noticed that Jackson looked less haggard today. His jaw was cleanly shaved, his green eyes clear. Bright. He wore blue denims and a gray T-shirt instead of the previous black on black. He was letting the sides of his hair grow past the usual one-inch bristles, and the light brown looked soft to the touch.

She moved her gaze to Matty, who stood next to her, his ears more prominent. "Did you get a haircut?"

"Yes," he grumbled, running a palm over the back of his neck where the skin wasn't tanned. "Looks dumb."

"It's very nice. I like it."

"You do?"

"I swear." She held up her hand.

He looked away with a slight smile. "I got new shoes, too."

Emma glanced down at the gray and red sneakers. "Nice. I hope you don't mind getting them dirty."

"He outgrew the other ones and refused to wear them with the toes cut out." Jackson shrugged to show he was teasing.

"I'd like you both to stay for dinner tonight," she said, wondering if she could come up with other ways for them to stick around. "Grilled chicken on the barbecue." Emma studied Jackson's face, imagining the scruff of his jaw beneath her lips. "Aunt Pepita is back, and I know she'll want to see you, too, if you want." Could Emma offer Matty a job for the rest of the summer? Or would Jackson see right through her ploy? He had to know she cared. Very much. Too much.

She'd have to be a fool not to realize how careful he'd been not to touch her, or be alone with her, since she'd come over with Bandit. His admission of seeming weak had come as a surprise when he was so strong. She swallowed her longing and chased it with a swallow of coffee.

He patted the four-foot-tall fence between them. "Sounds great."

Matthew flung a red Frisbee and then took off after it, Romeo on his heels.

"How did your weekend go?" she asked, searching for signs of distress, but his posture was easy confidence. "Are you sleeping?"

"It's all right. I have Bandit in my room, with the crate door open. He sleeps in there." Jackson rubbed his cheek and scowled. "We're still working on the not licking, though."

"Keep practicing. It takes more than a week, you know." She touched his arm, drawn to him like a flower to the sun. His skin at the wrist was warm, the hair soft beneath her fingertips. Before she realized what she was doing, she caressed her thumb down the back of his hand.

He sucked in a breath and looked down. She pulled back as if she'd done something wrong. Hadn't she?

Jackson's green eyes stared into hers. The air between

them charged with sensual awareness, and it was hard for her to think.

"I'm going to miss seeing you." His deep voice caused her to shiver.

Emma's mouth dried as she stared at his lower lip, knowing the firmness of his skin, the teasing warmth of his tongue. She swallowed over the lump in her throat. "Me too."

She didn't recognize her own voice, and her heart sped up.

He gestured with his finger for her to come closer, and she did, so that they were nose to nose with the fence between them. Her body yearned for his touch; her skin prickled as she looked into his eyes.

With the lightest pressure, he gently, sweetly, put his mouth to hers. His breath mingled with hers, coffee, and toothpaste, Emma and Jackson. Her eyes fluttered, and she was tempted to hop the fence. But she'd jumped into the man's arms once already, and that was probably enough.

He eased back, maintaining his gaze. She brought her hand to her throat to calm the speeding pulse. Jackson broke the spell between them by shouting a goodbye to Matthew, who waved and went around the tree again.

"Good luck today, with Livvie."

He swaggered to his truck with a wave.

Her adrenaline pumped so hard she could've chased after his royal blue Dodge Ram and caught up before he reached the end of her driveway.

It took at least ten minutes before she could focus. Matthew ran around chasing squirrels with Romeo while she tried to understand what had just happened. She warned herself to get her emotions together—didn't she know the statistics on desire? The perils of following the libido? Oh, yes she did.

• • •

Jackson walked into the sterile-smelling Swedish Hospital and headed to the ICU, reliving the sweet heat of Emma's kiss. He drew on that for warmth, as the chill of the hospital doused his hopeful spirits.

He washed with antibacterial soap harsh enough to remove a layer of skin and entered his sister's room, her face somehow paler than ever. He covered her hand with his, willing his warmth and life force into her. Bowing his head, he prayed for her recovery and that she would remember her son, her reason to live.

The doctor came in with Bonnie at his heels. He'd met her a few times over the years, a sturdy blonde, today dressed in red, white, and blue scrubs.

"Good morning. This is a difficult situation," the doctor said. Tall, mid-sixties, with a slim build, the man had a white jacket with lots of pockets. "And the reason that we wait, sometimes, as long as we do with a coma patient."

Bonnie's mouth twitched.

Confused, he looked from his sister, supine and still, to the doc, to Bonnie. "What are you saying? The simpler the better, please?"

"The recent MRI shows the wound is closing. If your sister continues to improve, we can start preparing her to breathe without the machines."

Jackson stood and stumbled, his eyes welling as he dashed hot tears free. "She's improving? Will she be okay? Can she come home? When can we—?"

Bonnie started laughing and grabbed him in a teary hug. "Take a breath, Jackson."

The doctor shrugged but gave a cautious smile. "There is still a long road ahead. These things don't happen overnight."

Bonnie pointed to the beeping machines with numbers

that Jackson didn't understand and then touched Livvie's forearm, in a tiny spot that wasn't covered in tubes or tape. "I know our Livvie, and she's a fighter."

Jackson stepped to the side of his sister's bed and kissed her forehead. Her pale skin was cold beneath his lips, and it scared him that he couldn't see any difference. What was he missing? "Keep fighting, Livvie. Matty and I love you."

He sat at her side for hours, willing her his strength. *Soon, Liv, you'll be home.*

That evening, Jackson drove his truck to Emma's house, his mood lifting as soon as he turned down the tree-lined drive. The paperwork required for the insurance company was daunting, but as soon as the day after tomorrow, his sister could be awake.

The yellow rancher welcomed him as he parked next to Emma's silver SUV.

He'd purchased a dark purple orchid that seemed like it might fit on the back porch, a box of designer dog treats, and had a deep hunger to see Emma that wouldn't go away. He'd held on to their kiss that morning through the rough patches.

Around the back, the six dogs, counting Bandit, barked in greeting in the yard with the fountain. Aunt Pepita, in a red and white checked apron, tended the smoking cedar chips at the grill. The savory smell of grilled sausage wafted toward him.

Emma, still in her shorts and shirt from earlier, wore a harried expression as she talked on the phone.

Matty tossed a ball to Romeo and King, his back to Jackson. He and Bonnie had discussed whether or not to tell Matty about his mother's improvement. By tomorrow, the doctors might know if her healing continued, and then they'd lower the dosages of the medicines keeping Livvie unconscious. He didn't understand all they'd told him, but fortunately Bonnie relayed the medical lingo in everyday language afterward.

Emma waved and returned to her phone conversation, her shoulders rigid and mouth turned down.

"Hello, Aunt Pepita. I brought something for the porch." He leaned in to kiss her weathered cheek. Bright rainbow earrings dangled from stretched lobes.

"Welcome, Jackson." She smiled through the smoke. "We've got chicken breast, or Italian sausage, or both."

"Sounds terrific. Why choose, when you can have it all?"

"Exactly!" She pointed at the porch with her tongs. "Go ahead and get yourself something to drink. Tea, lemonade, wine, or beer."

He walked up the steps and centered the purple orchid on the picnic table. Emma slammed out of the kitchen to the porch and stopped short when she saw him. Her cheeks were pretty pink, her hazel eyes snapping with temper.

"You will never believe what the VA is trying to do now." She went back inside and gestured for him to follow.

He did, and she faced him in the kitchen. Instead of jumping into his arms for a kiss, she raised her chin—upset and not wanting to share it with everybody else.

"This concerns you," she said with a fervent nod. "Well, it could, if you had to go through the regular channels for a dog to help you with your nightmares. They're refusing to grant funding for EST dogs for vets. They seem to agree with your Dr. Smith that dogs are just pets. Teddy bears! Regular old dogs you can find off the street." She slowed down, her hands on his forearms. "Well, let me tell you, if the dog has the right temperament, it can be trained. But it does need to be trained! You can't just willy-nilly decide. Our dogs help people, Jackson."

Her foot stomp at the end of her tirade made him chuckle, which was the wrong response. He realized his mistake right away—when tears welled in her hazel eyes.

"You're laughing at me?"

Jackson gently pulled her into a comforting hug, running his hands up and down her stiff spine. "Never, Em. I know how important your work is to you and to anybody lucky enough to get one of your dogs."

It took a minute, but she finally relaxed into his embrace, her cheek naturally settling against his chest. They fit together like two parts of a whole.

"I'm sorry," he said, his fingers stroking her hair. She smelled like roses and fresh air. He should not be holding her, knowing now that he *would* be leaving, probably within the month.

He couldn't move away. This time he understood fully what he was leaving behind, picnics for rations, and that made the sacrifice even harder.

Emma sniffed, her voice muffled against his T-shirt. "I guess you think I'm being silly."

"No, you surprised me, that's all. You were just so *passionate.*"

Passionate was perhaps the wrong word, he thought, with her already in his arms—it wasn't enough. She wasn't close enough. He pressed a kiss to the top of her hair. Soft, silky.

Still not enough.

He leaned back and tipped her chin up. Her expression changed from confused to wanting, and he didn't think about anything else but kissing her. She parted her lips, maybe to protest, but he didn't give her time. Instead, he took advantage and pressed his mouth to hers. Gently, but insistently.

Emma tasted like watermelon, like white wine, like grapes. Her tender skin gave way beneath his, and she sighed with pleasure against his mouth. His hand cupped the back of her head, and he walked her backward until she reached the sink. He leaned both hands on either side of her, anchoring them to the counter. His knees braced on either side of her legs, and he deepened the kiss, sharing with each press his unspoken feelings.

She pulled her mouth free, her head resting above his wildly beating heart. "Jackson," she whispered.

"This morning's kiss was just a tease. I've wanted to do this all day." He smoothed his rough palm down her arm, watching her shiver, needing her close. Would she tell him to take a hike?

Emma stood on tiptoe, her mouth a hair's breadth away from his. "I've wanted it, too, even though it can't go anywhere."

She reached for him, her fingers tickling the hair at the back of his neck as she wrapped her body around his. She was right, yet he was trapped by their feelings, too. He held her so that she wouldn't let him go. There was no way they weren't going to be hurt at the end of this affair.

Jackson deepened their kiss.

Emma returned his ardor, tightening her arms around his shoulders before she slowly eased away, her cheeks pink and rosy. "I love your kisses."

"I practiced with a master at the beach," he said teasingly. They'd spent hours just kissing.

"We should get back to the party. I smell barbecue." She exhaled and gave a slight shake of her head. "How did the visit go?"

He got the message—time to join the others. "Come on, it's good news, actually." They went out to the picnic table and the waiting feast.

"I could use some good news," she said, her pinky skimming the outside of his hand.

"Uncle Jackson!" Matty sank down on the bench. "I didn't see you get here."

"I just did." He stood behind Matty and ruffled his hair.

"How's Mom?" Matty glanced up as he reached for a roll.

"There's been some improvement, Matty."

His nephew froze in place. Jackson sat next to him and looked him in the eye, knowing the shock he must be feeling. After weeks of no change, it was an emotional wallop.

"The doctor said that if she continues to heal, then we can see about getting her breathing on her own."

Aunt Pepita whooped, and Emma clapped. The dogs barked excitedly.

Matty slammed his arms around Jackson, and Jackson rocked backward, happy to accept the weight of his hug. Glad to be here for Matty. He didn't share with them the doc's warning that her recovery could be difficult. He would take care of it, no matter what.

Right now, they needed the joy of Livvie's coming back to life.

Chapter Seventeen

Emma woke before dawn on July fourth and stretched her arms above her head, not the least bit tired though her sleep had been filled with cautionary dreams. Jackson made her want to push aside her studies for a family *right now*. To build a home, in addition to the dog shelter, as if time had no constraints. To open her heart to love, when she knew for a fact that the man who brought her joy was not the kind to stick around.

Emma showered and dressed, knowing that makeup would be a waste of time. Braiding her hair with red and blue ribbons was the fanciest she could muster in the July heat. Blue shorts, light blue polo, and red, white, and blue sneakers for a festive touch. The booths would be set up along Main Street, one block up from the bay, but if last year was anything to go by, the breeze wouldn't be enough to squelch the summer's heat.

As early as she'd woken, the smell of frying bacon let her know Pep was up earlier. Emma poked her head into the kitchen. Sure enough, her aunt, dressed in denim short coveralls over a scarlet tank top, a stars and stripes bandana on her head, stood at the oven.

"Morning," Emma said. "I'll let the dogs out into the yard, let them run around a little before we need to pen them up."

"I froze watermelon cubes for treats," her aunt said.

"Great idea. I was going to do that yesterday and totally ran out of time."

Her aunt turned on her with a knowing smile. "Because you were too busy whispering with Jackson?"

"What?" she asked, unable to hide a smile.

Pep lifted a few strips of bacon from the pan to a waiting paper towel. "I think it's wonderful. And about time, too."

"He's been around only a few weeks. Jackson and I are friends, that's it, Aunt Pepita."

"Friends that make out in the kitchen, by the window, where everybody can see?"

She'd seen that? Emma's cheeks flamed with embarrassment. "You might have mentioned that before now."

"Why?" Pep popped a crumble of bacon into her mouth. "I think it's great."

"Don't get the wrong idea. Jackson's going back to the service, and now that Livvie is improving, who knows when that will be?" She'd forced her heart back under lock and key to focus on finishing her thesis. Everything else was out of her control.

After taking care of the dogs, Emma filled the coolers with ice. She filched a piece of bacon when Pep's back was turned and couldn't hide her laughter at doing something so silly. "What did you do?" Aunt Pepita asked.

"Nothing." Emma covered her mouth.

"You have never been able to resist bacon." Her aunt waved the spatula at her as if she were in trouble.

"Who can?" Emma shrugged.

"Good point. I've had two pieces already. Maybe I should fry up another package, so there will be enough for sandwiches?"

Emma held up her hands. "I promise, no more." A knock sounded at the front door, and Emma opened it wide, welcoming Jackson and a very sleepy Matthew. "Just in time."

Matthew sniffed the air and perked up. "Bacon?"

She exchanged a glance with Pep. "Universal. If we ever get attacked by aliens, we need to offer them bacon in exchange for peace."

"I think I missed something," Jackson said, stepping into the house and closing the door behind him.

He took Emma's hand, and she resisted the urge to pull it free.

Her brain reminded her that he'd be gone in three weeks; her heart whispered to take a chance. Her mind remembered the bliss on Aunt Pepita's face as she'd twirled around the kitchen in her velvet gown. Her words of wisdom that love makes you do stupid things. In Emma's line of work, that was not *real* love. Real love needed to be able to stand the test of time. She squeezed Jackson's fingers and then freed her hand as they reached the kitchen table.

Biscuits, English muffins, fried eggs, cheese, and bacon were arrayed in the center so they could build their own sandwiches.

"Coffee, Jackson?" Pepita asked.

"Please." He sat next to Matthew, who was stacking together a sizable sandwich with both a biscuit and a muffin. "What is that, a quad-decker?"

Matthew shrugged and squished it down with the palm of his hand. "Delicious." He bit into the creation, cheese dripping down the side.

She made a more traditional sandwich with egg and

bacon on a biscuit, then went into her office to check her email one last time, searching for something from her professor in response to her last email.

Not ready to call Professor Collard back, she'd taken her possible career choices—including dog trainer, to be fair—and laid it all out for him to see. The years of study, her grades, her love for dogs, her desire to create a training shelter. Her drive to help people with anxiety, like her mom. She'd even complained about her grant requests not getting approved, which might be the boot he was looking for to kick her out of the program. Where did she fit, as a psychologist, with what she wanted to do?

Maybe he'd have an answer that she was too close to the problem to see.

Slinging the bag of dog adoption records, personality tests, and the matching questionnaires over her shoulder, Emma left her office and joined the rest of the group outside. Jackson and Matthew had corralled the dogs, getting all of them into her SUV. "Matthew, want to ride with me?"

"Yeah!"

She handed him a stack of rubber-banded brochures. "Go ahead and get in. I'll be right there."

Jackson had loaded the individual crates in the back of his truck, along with the coolers, the shade for the gazebo, and the folding table and chairs. He was in the truck and rolled the window down as she neared. "Thanks, Jackson. Looks good."

"I wanted to help you for all you've done for me and Matty," he said, his sunglasses in hand. She hated for him to cover the gorgeous green of his eyes.

"I was just thinking that I owe you big for your help today."

He winked before sliding the glasses on. "I have a way you could pay."

She blushed and hurried back to her SUV. Now she'd be thinking of his kisses when she should be focused on her dogs and finding them homes.

Starting the engine, she turned to Matthew. "Ready?" she asked.

"Yep." Matthew grinned, early morning sunshine sprinkling rose and gold through the dark pine trees, coloring his face. "We're going to find these pups a job."

Downtown had a wide main street with shops on one side, and then a sidewalk and the parking lot for the beach and park, next to the pier. The bay was at their backs and their tent faced the street, which would be perfect for the Fourth of July parade later.

Between the three of them, they were ready for business by eight.

"This looks great." Emma eyed the six large crates along the back wall of the tent for the dogs, complete with individual fans to keep them cool. They were content enough for the moment with their chewy rawhides. She had a long folding table with four chairs set up. Brochures, Heart to Heart Dog Kennel T-shirts and baseball caps were at one end, with the cash box on the other. She handed Jackson and Matthew a hat. "Here. Walking advertising, and it will keep you from getting sunburned."

"Cool!" Matthew said.

Jackson shoved the hat in his back pocket. He wore a beige collarless tee, plaid board shorts, and leather flip-flops. Handsome.

But not hers. He belonged to the military, first and foremost.

As she looked at him now, his soldier's body at ease, she wanted him with a pang of longing that went beyond desire.

"What are you thinking?" Jackson asked, his mouth close to her ear.

She shivered at his breath tickling her skin. "Nothing."

"Liar." He smiled with a touch of male arrogance. "Your eyes have a glint in them when you kiss me. Is that what you're thinking about? Kissing? Or what happens after that..." He ran a finger down her lower back, and she considered tossing him to the dog beds and showing him that glint again.

Thankfully, the next few hours were busy with folks stopping by, and she didn't obsess—too much—over the feel of Jackson's mouth against hers.

Matthew talked eloquently to potential customers about the dogs. "I want to hire him," Emma said from her seat beneath the shaded canopy.

"I'd like for him to finish high school," Jackson countered, his hand on her chair.

"Very funny." Emma peeked at him from behind her bangs. "I was thinking two mornings a week."

He ran a hand over his short hair and rubbed the back of his head. "We can see how it goes, but Livvie will have to decide."

She grabbed her water bottle and took a quick drink to erase the taste of rejection. "I'm sorry," Jackson said. "I don't mean to be abrupt. You are the bright spot in my days, Emma, and I am very reluctant to let you go."

She smiled, but when he didn't smile back, her stomach tightened with apprehension.

"I *will* have to let you go." Jackson's tone left no room for discussion.

Emma was the first to look away.

Honest to a fault, that man.

Chapter Eighteen

Around noon, she and Matthew had the dogs run through some of their tricks. Playing dead was popular with the folks walking by, as was waving a paw. She made sure the pups had plenty of water and weren't overheated. She secured Romeo in the kennel after giving him a frozen watermelon cube.

"Why is this a support dog?" Emma turned to look at a young man, mid-twenties, with fine brown hair in a bowl cut. He pointed at Sweetie.

The golden Chihuahua sat up at the attention, his tail wagging against the floor of his crate.

"He's very lovable. And extremely well-trained. Naturally compassionate. He'd be a terrific companion for someone with anxiety."

The young man seethed, seeming to want an argument. "I mean, it looks like a regular dog." He pulled one of her brochures from his pocket with a list of prices. "And it would be a lot cheaper, too."

Jackson, all six feet of Marine muscle, straightened up in his seat across the open tent, but Emma shook her head and kept her attention on the young man. His inability to meet her eyes let her know that he was agitated on a deeper level.

"You sound like you're familiar with service animals." She put her hands behind her back and waited. If there was a chance to educate, she would.

He nodded, looking at the ground or over her shoulder, his gaze darting around the booth before he gestured to Sweetie. "Everybody knows what a Seeing Eye dog is—that ain't it."

Emma bristled but held on to her temper. "As it says in the brochure, a service dog provides a specific task for a person that they can't manage for themselves. You're right, a guide dog is a familiar service animal." She turned to disengage and end the conversation, realizing that the man just wanted to argue. Since she wouldn't approve an application from him, it was pointless to draw the confrontation out.

"I don't think this little rat dog is going to help anybody cross the street." He chuckled at his own joke. Sweetie plopped down with a whine.

"An emotional support dog is another option for treating anxiety. Sweetie here senses when a person is emotionally vulnerable, like having a panic attack, and will nudge the person back to the present moment and away from what was causing the anxiousness." Right now, this guy was making the dog tremble. Emma gave Sweetie a bacon-flavored piece of kibble.

"That sounds dumb."

Emma breathed in, out. Smiled. "Well, it's not to the person needing the assistance."

He dropped her twisted brochure on the table and walked out into the street with a smug expression—as if he'd won something.

"You all right?" Jackson asked. He came up behind her to put his hand on her shoulder. "That guy was a jerk."

Emma was upset with herself for letting the man get to her. "I know better. Anxiety isn't something that's going to cause alarms or get government assistance. But mental health disorders are rampant, and a trained animal can be much more helpful than drugs." She hugged her waist as she watched the young man disappear into the crowd.

Jackson planted a kiss to the top of her head, offering his own brand of comfort.

Emma looked up at him. "People have so many prejudices against mental health. One in every fifty-nine kids is diagnosed with autism. Dogs offer unconditional love and can be trained to soothe an outburst before it happens. PTSD isn't just for war veterans. Rape victims, brain injuries"—she thought of Livvie—"car accidents." *Agoraphobia.*

Jackson rubbed her back and whispered against her temple, "You talked to him. Not everybody is going to get it. You care, Em."

She held her palm to her heart. "Being able to train a dog to help a person matters. If only my grant would get approved, then I could do more, reach more people." Save more dogs.

Jackson smoothed circles with his palm. "I'll be home on leave. I have serious skills with a hammer and nails. You wouldn't believe what we have to cobble together out in the desert sometimes."

He was leaving. But he might be back? To check on his sister and nephew? Her?

"You're shaking, Emma. What's wrong?"

"I'm fine." *I'm not fine.*

He lifted her chin to look into her eyes. "Now why don't I believe you?"

She had no defense against his caring looks. She melted when she should be strong.

He took her hands and squeezed them, then pulled her close. "I owe you three kisses as soon as we're alone."

Emma smiled against his chest. "You're keeping track?"

"Each time I've wanted to kiss you but had to hold back. It's all I'm thinking about." He brushed his knuckles along her cheek. Not that he'd asked her, but she'd thought about ways being with Jackson might happen. She could join him on base, wherever he was—but what would she do? Her business she'd built was here. Could she give up all she'd poured her heart into? A dog facility and a people practice required being in one place.

Jackson moved all the time.

Would he be willing to visit her in Kingston when he had leave or vacation? What about Livvie and Matty? Or the fact that he'd broken her heart before?

Emma moved back from his embrace with regret.

Jackson didn't pressure her but dropped his hand to his front pocket, hooking his thumb inside. "I've been thinking, Em, since you want to build so badly, why not do it on Pepita's property?"

Emma held out her arms to the sides. "It's not big enough for what I want to do, which is a training shelter, not just a kennel."

"And no other land will work?"

"You have no idea how much debt becoming a doctor accumulates," she said with a light tone she didn't feel, her muscles tensing up. "So I need the grant, even to make the garage bigger."

He winced. "Got it."

Cindy showed up with another vet tech from the shelter, stopping their conversation.

"Jackson, Matty, this is Cindy. She's my right hand at the shelter."

The bubbly brunette waved to each of them. "You guys must be dying—the food smells are all blowing this way." Her hair was down to her shoulders today, her scrubs red.

Grateful for the reprieve, Emma patted her stomach, turning her back to Jackson. "I could eat." She gestured to the cash box. "Price sheet is taped to the top, although so far we've mostly handed out dog treats and brochures."

Cindy sat down. "We've got this."

"Matthew, Jackson?" Emma asked. "Ready for a break?"

Matthew popped out his earbuds with a grin. "Yeah." They left, and it seemed completely natural for Jackson to slip his hand over hers. She leaned her shoulder in to him, and they walked between the booths.

They ordered three specials from a guy with a red, white, and blue chef's hat cooking meat over a black barrel grill— ribs, cornbread, slaw, and roasted corn, taking their plastic plates to the seawall and finding a place to sit on the cement. The seagulls squawked, in scavenger heaven.

One dove toward Jackson's plate, and he jumped backward, the barbecue spilling on his shirt. "Oh man," he said, wiping at the red smear.

"That bird wanted some lunch." Matty giggled nervously and covered his own plate with his forearm.

Emma pointed to the wooden bathroom facilities. Crowds of people wandered around, everybody enjoying downtown and the pre-parade activities. "You can rinse the sauce off before it stains."

"Good idea," Jackson said, stripping off the beige T-shirt. Her mouth dropped at the expanse of tanned abs before her. He caught her looking and grinned before hurrying off toward the restroom.

She watched until his broad shoulders disappeared, then she and Matty gathered their trash and tossed it on the way to the bathrooms.

Emma washed the barbecue from her hands and got a look at the train wreck that was her hair. She smoothed it back in the braid as best she could and noticed the sparkle in her eyes. Did they really shine when Jackson kissed her? Get a grip, Emma Mercer. *He is leaving. Jackson Hardy is not the man for you.* Being around him, she couldn't stop herself from touching him or wanting him.

There was something about knowing their time together was short, that it couldn't be more, that made her want to store up each kiss. Dancing with fire? She knew she'd be burned, but she couldn't stay away.

Chapter Nineteen

After lunch, and food overload, Matty napped in the corner on a stack of dog blankets, curled up with Romeo, fast asleep. He looked six instead of eleven, Jackson thought as he ended the call with Bonnie and slipped his phone into his back pocket.

Her news, though hoped for, still shook him—Livvie was off the machines tomorrow. So much could go wrong. What if it was too soon? There was no guarantee, but Bonnie seemed certain that this doc knew his stuff.

Emma met Jackson's eyes and smiled. She reached out and squeezed his hand, offering solace and strength. "Are you okay?"

He brought her fingers to his lips and kissed them. "Yeah. That was Bonnie. Livvie's procedure is scheduled for tomorrow afternoon." His stomach knotted, but he breathed out through the tension.

"Do you want to go? Matty can hang out with me."

She was kind, always. "I think I'll take Matty down the market in Seattle. We'll be five minutes away from the hospital, close enough without being in the way." In case things went crazy, as life tended to do. You planned, but plans went haywire. Hopefully Livvie would wake up without complications. If she crashed...well, he couldn't let that happen.

"That's smart."

"We'll see." He shifted restlessly. "I'll let you know what's going on."

Cindy, seated on a dog crate, turned to Emma. "Hey, that cute little pug was adopted yesterday."

"I have dibs on the spaniel mix," Emma said. "Don't forget. She's going to be really special."

"I don't know how you know," Cindy said. "But you're right on the money." She got up to pet King, who dozed in the largest crate they had. "He's socialized and follows the commands, and I thought he'd be too shy."

"Gentle soul, that's all." Emma relaxed in the plastic chair, the breeze from the fan lifting her braid and ruffling Bandit's fur at his spot by her feet. "Sawyer will test both King and Romeo next week for their AKC Good Citizen certificates."

Jackson admired her patience and dedication. That, combined with her innate compassion, surely translated into an excellent psychologist. People and dogs. And why couldn't Emma, with her empathy and grace, help animals and people? Why was she so hung up on one or the other?

Cindy said, "If you guys are staying for the fireworks, you should keep your parking spot here. It'll be a madhouse later on tonight."

"Good point. When do we need to have the tent down?" Jackson asked.

Emma smoothed the tip of her auburn braid—Jackson liked it when she wore her hair loose, though she didn't do it often. "We can tear down the booth after the parade at four.

Then maybe take the dogs back? Pepita is going to sit with them at home during the fireworks tonight. You can leave Bandit with her, too, if you want, but he was fine with the loud noises last year. He, of course, aced his AKC tests." She reached down, gently tugging on Bandit's ears.

Bandit was fun for Matty to have around. Oh hell, he admitted. The dog was a good companion. "We'll see." The truth was that Bandit, even by just sleeping in the same room, offered another heartbeat, another live being, to combat the war that waged in his mind. With each passing night, he got more actual rest.

Over the past week, he'd increased his sleep to four solid hours before Bandit jumped on the bed and pawed his shoulder. Might not seem like much, but a week's worth of four hours a night of nightmare-free z's made him feel like a new man.

He understood how it worked—the body resisted sleep because it knew what the mind was getting up to—memories that were to be avoided at all costs. So, instead of getting relaxed and sleepy, his body tensed and subconsciously prepared for the worst.

The more he trusted that Bandit would wake him before things got too bad, the more he'd trust himself to sleep. The dog intuitively knew.

He wasn't sure how to explain it to Dr. Smith to make it sound like science, so he didn't bother. Jackson checked his watch. Two in the afternoon. "It's good that Matty's catching some shuteye. He'll enjoy the fireworks. Can't believe he can be comfortable all twisted up like a pretzel."

Emma reached her hand out to him from her plastic chair. "Sit, Jackson, it's okay."

But he couldn't be still. He was used to acting without spending so much time in his own head. "I'm gonna take a walk. I'll be back in a few minutes."

However, no matter how many times he paced the park, Jackson couldn't outwalk his stupid words to Emma—telling her that he had to let her go. He felt no better equipped now than he'd been ten years ago to be the man she deserved. She deserved kids and a family. She deserved a husband who was her equal.

She deserved marriage, but by offering that, he would take her away from the life she'd built here. Not in any position to make promises, Jackson didn't want to let her down, yet he couldn't stay away. How was that for a cluster?

• • •

Jackson strode into the crowd, probably to walk off some of the apprehension he had to be feeling about Livvie. There would be a risk involved in taking her out of the coma, and that had to be worrisome.

He cared about his family. Emma knew he cared for her, in his own way. He was a good man—a *worthy* man who had told her that he would let her go; he'd done it once before so she knew it to be true.

Matty, awake, brought Romeo to the front of the booth and encouraged people to interact with the dog; they both loved the attention.

Emma got up from the plastic chair and stepped over Bandit to refill the stack of brochures. Was there any way to make Jackson see that she was worth fighting for?

As if thinking of Jackson had conjured him, he was suddenly right behind her, and he slid his hand down her lower back. "You all right?"

"Yes, Jackson." She laughed softly. "You don't have to take care of me."

"Sorry."

She tilted her head with a teasing smile. "I don't think

you can help it."

"Do you mind, so much?" His fingers caressed her wrist.

"No." She glided her hand along his and then stepped away before she foolishly kissed him in front of everybody. "But I should."

She covered her heart with a glossy brochure as if the paper were armor.

Jackson looked at the front toward Matty, who chatted easily with an older man about Romeo and golden retrievers, and back to her. The intensity in his gaze made her think of hot nights under a starry sky, the two of them entwined.

Emma steered the subject to safer waters. "So, it seems that our Cinnamon has found a family."

"You've helped three dogs find homes in the last two weeks." Jackson brought his arms to his sides. "Is that a normal turnaround?"

She noted that he didn't include Bandit in his count. "It ebbs and flows. You can't predict how many dogs will come into the shelter that will be a good fit for Heart to Heart. Training varies—King took a while longer, while Romeo zoomed through. I was hoping Sawyer would stop by today, so you two could meet."

"Why?" Jackson asked warily.

"He's the one who helped me with Bandit," Emma said. "If I had some open spaces, I'm sure he could find me qualified dogs from shelters all over. Right now, though, I've been forced to keep under ten dogs at my kennel."

"Emma, I've watched you," Jackson said. "You say you prefer pets to people and I admit that folks can be"—he glanced at Matthew, now talking to a bald guy eating a hotdog—and said, "difficult."

She bit her lower lip to keep from laughing.

"But you are good with everybody. You were even nice to that jerk earlier. You have a talent with matchmaking. There's no reason you can't incorporate both into your practice. Maybe you see people a couple days a week. Maybe you only see kids with autism, or folks with anxiety. You can choose."

Emma ran her finger along the crisp folded edge of the glossy brochure. Heart to Heart Kennel. It's where her heart was… Could she create a practice where she worked only a few days a week with people?

The idea was foreign to her. "That's not how it's done, Jackson. I mean, tell me about your Dr. Smith's office. Pretty fancy, right? I don't work like that."

The doctorate program was solid lines and boundaries. People telling her what was and wasn't acceptable.

The rules stifled her, and it came as a surprise to realize that those boundaries were an issue—maybe the number one issue.

Emma dropped the brochure to the table, looking out at the people walking by. Many were dressed in something red, white, and blue. Patriotic. She reached for Jackson's hand, running her thumb along the hard ridge of his knuckle.

"I went into psychology because I thought I could help people like my mom, who refused to step outside the house… she was so afraid of what might happen that she taught me to be afraid of the mailman, the grocery delivery guy, the park across the street." Emma braced against the avalanche of negative memories. "You know all that already."

Jackson brought her fingers to his lips and kissed the back of her hand. "You are the bravest woman I know. You could have let your childhood cripple you, but instead you took all that pain and figured out a way to help others."

Her brow lifted. "Brave?" She shook her head. "Determined, maybe."

Jackson propped his hip against the table and crossed his arms. "I believe that you will find your own path. If anybody can do it, it's you. I've always believed that."

Was there another way? A third option that suited her temperament and ideals?

"Thanks, Jackson." His unwavering support gave her a boost of added confidence she needed after being called on Professor Collard's carpet. "I'll figure it out."

He held up his palms. "Sorry if I pushed. You seem like you've got it all together." He winked. "You're pretty, too."

Her cheeks heated in a rush as she recalled his hand on her hip, the way he savored her kiss and made her feel beautiful.

"Uncle Jackson," Matthew groused, walking to the table with Bandit for a few brochures to hand to the people passing by. "Lame."

"What?" Jackson's brows lifted in question as he looked from his nephew to her and back.

"Emma doesn't want a boyfriend." Matty smacked the brochures against his open palm. "No time."

Emma laughed with surprise.

"And you know this, how?" Jackson teased.

"We talked about it," Matthew said. "I told her that I'd take her to the movies if she wanted to see one, but she has to buy the popcorn."

"Oh." Jackson's laughing green eyes speared her. "So my nephew already staked his claim."

Emma giggled, the sound unexpected and freeing.

"Emma?"

She turned to Aunt Pepita, who barreled through the crowd, her striped kerchief over her orange hair a beacon.

"I'm here," her aunt quipped, her lips slashed with cherry red lipstick. "Sorry to be late."

"No worries. Where's Ernie?"

Her aunt's chin trembled. "We broke up."

"Oh." Emma pulled her into a hug. "I'm so sorry."

Pep stepped free and blinked the dampness from her

eyes. "I'll miss the way he dances, but any man who has a wandering eye is not the man for me. Margaret can have him, the old biddy."

All Emma could think about was the bliss on her aunt's face the other night, the look that made Emma wish for something more. And now it was just gone? What chance did that give her feelings for Jackson?

"Are you sure you're okay?" Emma watched her aunt's face closely.

"Better to have danced and lost, my dear," Pep said.

"There's always Harold." She patted her aunt's plump shoulder.

Pepita shook her head. "We're just friends, and that is fine with me."

"How'd you get here?"

"I called a cab." Pep fixed a button on her coveralls, the white stripe in her American flag earrings flashing in the sun.

Pepita's independence was something Emma had always admired. No hiding from the world for her. "Thank you for coming anyway."

"Wouldn't miss it." Pep gave the rest of the dogs a pat and received hugs from Jackson and Matthew. "So, which dogs are celebrating the fireworks with me at home tonight?"

"Watch the fireworks with us downtown, Aunt Pepita."

"No, Emma. I plan on having champagne and curling up on the couch with the fur babies and a new novel. No better medicine for a broken heart." She huffed. "Not that mine was broken. I was swept away by romance. Ernie sure could dance."

Once the parade was over, Emma and Jackson, with Matthew and Pepita's help, started to dismantle the booth—taking it down always took longer than setting things up.

Pepita drove the SUV and dogs to the rancher after a promise from Emma not to come back early, because she didn't need a babysitter. They slid the dismantled canopy into the rear bed of Jackson's truck. What a day of highs and lows. If only Jackson wasn't leaving, then she wouldn't hold back on her feelings for him. *I wouldn't trade today for the world.*

"You guys want fish and chips?" Emma asked, digging hand sanitizer from her purse and offering it around. "My treat."

"I'm hungry," Matthew said.

"Now why am I not surprised?" Jackson reached for Matthew's hair, and Matthew ducked out of the way with a laugh.

Bandit stayed with the three of them as they ate their dinner on the pier. Emma bit into the crispy white halibut, watching the reflection of early fireworks over the bay—folks who couldn't wait for the big show at nine.

Deep pinks and vibrant oranges splayed across the darkening sky as the sun set behind the mountains, casting a rosy net over the blue water. Emma took it all in before zeroing her focus on Jackson, the shadow along his jawline, the fullness of his mouth, and shifted on her bench.

"Thank you for today. I couldn't have done it without you." She thought of the pups she'd trained and cared for and the jobs they'd perform for their new owners with a pang of happy sorrow. She broke off another piece of fish and swiped it through the malt vinegar. "King and Cinnamon both found new homes!"

Matthew dipped his fries into some tartar sauce and popped them in his mouth. "We need to get more dogs, Emma."

"We do." She nudged Jackson's arm—he sat so close on the bench that their thighs touched, that she could smell his aftershave.

Matthew's sneaker kicked at the metal table leg. "Emma, did Uncle Jackson tell you about Mom getting better?"

"He did! You must be so excited." She was so happy for them.

"I wish it was tomorrow already. I mean, the fireworks are going to be cool, but this is worse than Christmas Eve, waiting for presents in the morning."

"I know what you mean," she said, impressed with his analogy.

"Uncle Jackson said if Mom wakes up, we're going to sneak her in a flower. She likes them."

Emma glanced at Jackson, who explained, "ICU rules. No flowers."

"Got it." She rested her forearm on the table. "I say it's worth the risk." Emma smiled, just imagining how wonderful their reunion might be.

Matthew grinned and "accidentally" dropped a fry toward Bandit. The dog wasn't picky and snapped it up.

After their dinner, they spread a blanket on the beach and listened to the band play top forty covers. Jackson bought them all huckleberry iced tea and sugared almonds. She and Jackson hummed along to the songs. "Want to dance?" Jackson asked, his tone low, his gaze on her legs stretched out in front of her.

"No, thanks," Emma said quickly. "I'm not much of a dancer."

"Two left feet, don't you remember?" Matthew jumped up and shook his backside before taking off to run toward the seawall and startling the gulls.

"The kid pays attention," Jackson said with approval. He scooted over to sit behind her and lightly massage her neck. "I remember our first dance and how you felt in my arms. You smelled like strawberry lip gloss, and I was so nervous that I kept wiping my palms on my jeans because I didn't want you to know my hands were sweaty."

She chuckled, remembering how nervous she'd also been.

His touch traveled down her body like a rush of wildfire, hopping from one sensitive nerve to the next, and she leaned in to him. Jackson pressed a light kiss to her neck, and she shivered.

Bandit and Matthew raced back and plopped on the blanket, interrupting the tender moment. With reluctance, Emma straightened and took a sip of tea to quench her thirst—it didn't work. She had a feeling the only thing to satisfy her would be more of Jackson. "What do you have there?"

"Bandit found a Frisbee," Matthew said, tugging on one end while Bandit had the other.

And then the dog and boy were off again, leaving Emma and Jackson alone on the blanket. They each sat cross-legged, facing one another.

"Why did you warn me that you have to let me go?" She stared into his eyes, not letting him off the hook.

"I don't want to hurt you, Em." He leaned across the few inches between them to lift her braid and nuzzle her collarbone. His mouth created goosebumps on her skin. "I can't stay away." He nipped, creating a wave of sensation. "I can't be in Kingston and not see you. Fair warning."

Her body thrilled at his words and his actions. She was glad that she wasn't the only one to feel so out of control. "Well, I can't stay away from you, either." She turned to rest against his chest, and he stretched his legs alongside of hers.

Jackson smoothed her braid down her back, sighing with pleasure. "Mom used to say that home was where the heart is—I think to find a way to make moving all the time okay. But I understand why you've built your own community here."

Emma curved her palm on Jackson's knee, needing to be connected by touch. And since kissing on the blanket in front of everyone wasn't a good idea, she'd sit close and whisper sweet talk. Would they spend the next few weeks together, and damn the consequences? "Jackson, I've missed you." There'd never been anyone else she'd connected with like him.

"I'll tell you a secret," he said in her ear. "You are the woman I dream about, when things are quiet and I'm looking up at the stars. It's you, on our place at the beach, snuggled together under a blanket."

Her heart cracked at his admission. "Why?" Why hadn't he told her that before now?

He wouldn't let her turn around to look at him as he finished his confession. "I knew that I'd hurt you that day, and I never forgave myself for it. I promised that I would be the best soldier I could be, to make the sacrifice worthwhile."

It was a good thing that she was sitting down already, because his words took all strength from her body and left her speechless. Vulnerable.

Tears spilled over and splashed on his hand. "Em?"

His eagle tattoo flexed as he shifted and tightened his arm around her, but she hid her face. "Why didn't you talk to me about this?"

He scooted backward and came around to face her, on his knees, sitting back on his heels. "It wouldn't have changed anything, don't you understand? But I never stopped loving you."

He tilted his head so that their mouths were inches apart, his eyes staring deep into hers as if demanding that she see his feelings for her—and she did. It made her head swim, and she clasped his shoulder to steady herself. The shield around her heart buffeted in the storm of her emotions.

"I've never met anyone like you." He feathered his lips across hers, and Emma sighed at the longed-for contact of his mouth. They kissed, and she didn't care who watched in the crowd. She reveled in the rightness of it, ignoring the wrong.

"Just being here with you eases something in me." He

tucked her close.

As if by silent agreement, they watched the world from their blanket, content to be together for this moment with no expectations.

As the sunset faded to dusk and then into night, the white caps of the Cascades glowed in the moonlight. By nine, the music stopped, and the fireworks were set to begin. Jackson made sure they sat hip to hip. Her body hummed at the heat of his thigh next to hers, the touch of his pinky finger skimming her hand.

Casual. Electric. God, how she craved more.

Fireworks sparked before them, and she jumped back, her hand to her throat as she laughed nervously. Bandit and Matthew raced over to the blanket, Bandit dropping the slobbery Frisbee in her lap.

Jackson met her gaze, a smile dancing along that sexy mouth, his eyes promising a million pleasures—later.

Later. Emma grinned and hugged Bandit close. She didn't know what the future might bring, and even if it wasn't a happy outlook, she couldn't turn her back on what she felt right now. *One day at a time.*

Matthew scooted next to Jackson, searching the sky for a brilliant flash, but there was nothing. Then suddenly a sparkling array of color crossed the night sky, followed by booms as more rockets were launched, one after the other.

"Beautiful," she said, staring upward into the night.

Bandit left her to join Jackson and Matthew. She noticed Bandit put his head in Jackson's lap with a whine. Jackson gave an imperceptible wince at the explosions of light, noise, and color.

Emma hadn't considered what the fireworks might bring on for a man used to war. She watched with concern, but Jackson dug his hand into Bandit's ruff and petted the pup, his shoulders tight, as he handled the display. Her heart flipped with emotion as she saw him study Matty's excited face as each new brilliant shower of sparkling light decorated the sky—as if that made the explosions bearable.

When the last firework faded, Emma got to her feet, her eyes bright with tears. "Spectacular." She held out her hand to Jackson to pull him up, maintaining eye contact. "Every year it gets better." *Not just the fireworks, but the anxiety. I'm so proud of you.*

Jackson's tense shoulders eased the slightest bit. "Ready to go?"

Emma folded the blanket and they walked back to the truck.

Bandit and Matthew climbed into the rear seat while she sat in the front next to Jackson. Jackson reached across the console for her hand, giving her a single squeeze before starting the truck.

Was he sorry that he'd shared his feelings? She was sorry only that he hadn't shared them before now.

"Is Aunt Pepita going to be sad?" Matthew asked, his head over the seat between them. "Because of dumb Ernie?"

Maybe. "I bet she's read an entire love story and eaten at least two bowls of ice cream. She'll feel better tonight but have a tummy ache in the morning."

Matthew frowned. "When I had a stomachache, Mom made me chicken soup."

"That's a good idea." Emma smiled at Matthew and then Jackson. "I'll keep that in mind. But you two are going to have a busy afternoon."

Matty sat back, arms crossed as his expression turned pensive. "I know."

Jackson drove out of downtown; the normally quiet area was congested, but he was patient. Controlled.

"I'll be around if you want to talk about things, okay?" She made sure to look at Matty until he nodded. "Whatever you're feeling is all right. Scared, or excited, maybe a mix of everything."

Matty gave a quick nod and looked out the window, his chin quivering.

Jackson drove up the winding mountain road. "It's too late to unpack tonight, so let's do it in the morning."

"Okay." Turning down her long driveway made her wish the night didn't have to be over. But it did. She eyed Jackson's profile, his strong jaw, his slim nose. Being together had reawakened her passion for him, only him.

But at what cost? It was going to hurt, she knew that, either way. Was she brave enough to open her heart? What a joke, she realized with a pang. She'd been acting like she had a choice in the matter, but her heart had already accepted that her soul mate was home again.

The epiphany didn't make her feel very intelligent.

Jackson pulled to a stop next to her SUV.

"Night, Bandit. Don't get out, guys. Tonight was really fun. Thanks for everything."

Jackson leaned over to kiss her, and she turned so that his mouth grazed her cheek. She was in trouble, emotional trouble. Emma stuck her purse strap over her shoulder, getting out of the truck alone.

The porch light beckoned, but she didn't want to leave.

She blew them a kiss, her eyes locking with Jackson's. Love blazed, and she stepped backward at the impact. He loved her, yes. She loved him too.

But he was still going to leave her.

"How much of a fool are you, Emma?" She watched their taillights disappear down the drive. *Love made you stupid.*

Chapter Twenty

Emma woke cranky the next morning after an angst-filled night. She kicked the covers back and crawled out of bed, going to the bookshelf and her high school yearbook—the one she shared with Jackson.

She took it to her comfy chair that overlooked the fountain in the yard—the sun's morning rays caught the drops and created rainbows on the grass. She loved this spot, loved this house that had welcomed her as a frightened girl and guided her to the woman she was right now.

Flipping the pages, she found the picture he'd set aside of them, kissing at the Harvest Dance. Was he her fate? Did she believe in that? *Love always.* Another page showed a candid shot of Jackson laughing after a football game, head back, carefree. As a man, he had burdens now that he hadn't then, but the integrity he carried them with made him stronger and more desirable in her eyes.

Her phone *ding*ed. Her heart skipped. It was Jackson.
Can you talk?
She picked up the phone and typed. *Yes.*

He called, and Emma answered on the first ring. "Morning. How are you?"

"Fine," he answered in a subdued tone. "I was wondering if I could come over about ten?"

"Sure." She hesitated at the undercurrent of emotion in his tone. "Are you all right?"

"Yeah. I just wanted to see you before heading to Seattle today with Matty, for Livvie."

He wanted to talk in person? Wary, she said, "I'll help you unpack the truck."

"I've been up for hours and already did that. Matty's headed over to a soccer game with a friend. I thought I'd stop by."

"I'll be ready."

She hurried into the shower, dressing in shorts and a lightweight T-shirt. By nine she'd made coffee and there was no word from Aunt Pep, who must still be sleeping in her room.

Emma let the dogs out and thumbed through her mail, opening and reading one letter in particular. And yet, even that good news couldn't dent the apprehension of what Jackson might want to discuss.

What would she say if he wanted to continue a relationship? How could she honestly say no? It wasn't smart, but this was *Jackson*.

At ten, she was waiting outside when he pulled up on his motorcycle—he offered a spare helmet. Her stomach clenched. "Hi!"

"Hi," he rumbled, looking sexy as he stayed on the bike. "Thought I'd take you for a ride down to the beach. Should we see if our old place is there?"

She looked back to the house, but Pepita was not in sight. Her aunt had told her to give the hottie on the bike a chance. Getting on the back of Jackson's motorcycle took a big dose of positive self-talk and yes, trust.

"Sure."

"It will be fun, Em. I promise not to take any sharp curves at less than a hundred miles an hour."

"Funny."

"You think I'm joking?"

She accepted the helmet he handed her and lifted her chin so that he could adjust the strap—all from his seated position on the leather seat. His green eyes challenged her, and she couldn't back down.

Didn't want to. The pad of his thumb lingered at her lower lip.

She climbed on behind him and wrapped her arms around his waist as the engine rumbled to life. The power of the motorcycle beneath her was a thrill, but not as thrilling as the feel of Jackson's torso between her thighs.

She closed her eyes as the bike jetted down the road, and after a few minutes she dared to look around her at the passing landscape. Pine trees, ivy, blackberry bushes, the feel of the wind against her face, the scent from the bay.

"Their" spot was an older park with an overgrown emerald-green path that led down to a rocky beach. Driftwood collected in grayish heaps, and white shells dotted the thick gray sand. Jackson helped her off the bike and onto her wobbly legs.

He caught her to him, and she looked up. Just the two of them, walking hand in hand to the shore. He dusted off a log and they sat, hip to hip, facing the cresting dark water. Pine trees shaded them from the heat of the summer sun.

"I can't believe this is still here." She looked around in surprise.

"Waiting for us," Jackson said.

As if time had stood still, but that wasn't possible. Ten years had passed since they'd been here last. "You broke up with me here."

He sucked in a breath and turned to look at her. "I *am* sorry."

"I know." She shifted and leaned down to pick up a white shell, smoothing the edges with her thumb, fighting back tears.

"I thought you would be long gone right afterward." He scanned the water. "You were smarter than me. Driven to get an education. I know that you loved me enough to stay in Kingston and get married. If I hadn't left for the military, you wouldn't have accomplished everything that you have."

She bristled. "You don't know that, Jackson." He was right that she would have married him. Would she have given up her education? That didn't seem possible. "You should have asked me. You chose for us."

"For you."

"It wasn't just for me," she countered. "You had an agenda. To make your dad proud."

He scraped a hand over his hair in frustration. "I wanted to be worthy of you, to make you proud, too."

"I am. I was then." She rubbed the shell, loosening flecks of dried sand. "Why are we here, Jackson? Do you regret telling me that you loved me?" And here she'd been thinking he might want to move forward. *Fool.*

He picked up a round dark gray rock and tossed it into the water where it landed with a splash. "I wish I would have waited."

"For what?" Tears burned her eyes, but she held herself stiff with pride. "You want to break up with me again?" Her laugh was hollow. "We never agreed to date. You are safe." She threw the shell into the bay. "What are you so afraid of?"

"Nothing." His jaw clenched tight.

"I'm calling you out on that, Jackson." Her body numbed against the pain of his pushing her away. Because he thought she deserved better? Ha. "I am not some love-struck teenager who is going to let you call the shots. I have a say."

He leaned forward, his forearms on his knees, and stared out at the water. "What are you talking about?"

"You. You think you aren't good enough, and I happen to disagree. The military is a career, a job, but it does not define you."

Jackson scoffed.

"Have you thought about who you could be outside your unit? Without constantly putting your life in danger? Your life matters to me, to Matty, to Livvie."

He folded his hands together, not looking at her. "Men like me are needed on the front line."

She briefly closed her eyes. "I'm not taking that away from you, Jackson. You are so brave. I don't have your courage to stand up for what is right in the middle of a war. I try to do my part right here."

He chose another rock and tossed it up and down in his palm. "Just how do you think a sniper would find a job in Kingston, Washington?"

"You told me you were good with your hands. Help me build Heart to Heart."

Before she could tell him her good news, Jackson stood and chucked the rock into the surf. "That's not who I am."

"It could be." She also got to her feet, taking his hands, the sun bright at the back of his head as it dappled through the trees.

"Em. I'm a soldier. It's who I've always been meant to be. Don't you see that who I am would only hold back who you are?"

"I don't believe that, and I wish you wouldn't." She grasped his upper arms, demanding that he listen to her.

"My commander expects me back with my unit by August first."

He'd told her that he trusted her, but it wasn't true—he guarded his heart. Just as she had guarded hers. Not fated lovers, but ill-fated.

In a daze, Emma kissed him for all she was worth, holding him and memorizing him. Knowing that this was goodbye.

• • •

Emma spent the rest of the afternoon cleaning the house and mowing the lawn. She had a ride-on mower, and it soothed her mind to make the neat rows in the grass.

Pep mopped the floors and didn't question Emma's mood, which was just as well, since Emma couldn't pick one emotion to feel. She ran the gamut between sadness and anger and a smidge of self-pity.

She washed the dogs and brushed them out, crying between the strokes through their fur. At dusk, she went inside to find that Pepita had created a lavish spread of flatbread pizzas with various toppings. Sliced tomatoes, black olives, onions, and sweet peppers from their garden.

"I saw you run over the begonias twice," Pep said, handing her a tall glass of iced tea. "You're a master on the John Deere. Time to tell me what's wrong."

Emma accepted the tea and cringed. Twice? "Sorry about that."

"Those are just flowers. It's you I'm worried about." Her aunt motioned for her to sit down at the long kitchen table. "Comfort food. Melted cheese. I figure this has to do with Jackson."

She started to protest, but her aunt raised a hand.

"Don't waste your breath. I have eyes, and I saw you together yesterday. You are meant for each other, Emma."

Hot tears poured down her cheeks. "Nothing has changed," Emma choked out. "He's going back to

Afghanistan as soon as Livvie is situated."

"Any word from the hospital?" Aunt Pep cut a piece of the flatbread and added sliced black olives, putting it on a small plate.

"No. If Jackson hasn't texted me before bed, I'll call. Just because Jackson and I can't make it work doesn't mean that I won't be there for Matty, or Livvie, if she wants."

Emma took another drink of the tea, hoping to cool the rush of emotion flushing her system.

"He thinks he isn't good enough for me. I tried to reassure him, but he won't let his guard down enough to believe it."

Pep stared at her over the rims of her orange glasses. "Jackson Hardy loves you."

"I know," she said, her words catching on an awful sob.

Aunt Pep crumbled her napkin. "It's obvious that you love him." She took a bite of flatbread.

"I do."

Her throat closed with hurt, and she picked an olive into tiny pieces. "To be fair, I am not willing to let my guard down, not after he broke my heart before." She dropped the olives. "And he would do it again, for my own good." Anger dried her tears. "How am I supposed to fight that?"

Pep frowned. "I really hope you aren't hiding behind the kennel, because you know we could find a way to run it without you being here."

Her mouth dropped and she quickly snapped it closed. "I was thinking about that, actually." She got up and retrieved the letter she'd opened earlier, bringing it back to the table. "My grant was approved."

Pepita lifted her fist and whooped with victory. Sweetie barked from under Pep's feet. "Wait, does Jackson know?"

"He didn't give me the chance to tell him. Well, that's not true. I asked him to stay with me and build Heart to Heart." She scanned the approval letter again with disbelief. She'd never seen so many zeroes. "He said no. But this gives us funds to hire Cindy, and Sawyer, to get started, if I was to travel with Jackson. I mean, I've never left the United States."

She looked at her aunt and blinked back tears. "I thought it was a good plan." Home was where the heart was…and she wanted to give Jackson hers. Stubborn man didn't realize it was right there.

"It is—it still is," Pep insisted. "Only this time when you talk to Jackson, be clear, Emma."

She shook her head. "I don't think so. We just aren't meant to be."

Her cell phone *ding*ed, and all emotions turned to joy within her. She leaped up from the table. "Aunt Pep! Livvie is breathing on her own."

Chapter Twenty-One

Jackson zeroed in on the guy in the mirror and faced his biggest enemy—himself. Writing down his dreams had helped, just as Bandit had helped, and now he was able to accept that he was not guilty of killing Remi. He was not responsible for Iowa's death. He'd been lucky as a soldier, but he'd also taken precautions.

Emma's hazel eyes came to mind. He didn't want regrets in his life, and losing her would be the ultimate in bad decisions. She loved him and yet he'd walked away from that love once before. How stupid could a man be to do it twice?

He shaved the scruff from his neck, angling to make sure he hadn't missed any rough patches. In the past week, Livvie had come around quickly—the doc said it was miraculous, but Jackson knew it was because of her love for her son. She was in a private room at the hospital, and Matty read out loud to her for hours.

She would need physical therapy to help relearn some motor functions, but she would be home next week. He'd hired a team of people to be with her at the house whenever she was ready to transfer.

They'd talked about being in the service. Well, he had talked while she had listened. Speech was something that was slow to return, but the doc was certain it would. If her eyebrows were anything to go by, then she was supportive of his decision to find a home here in Kingston and transfer to a desk job in Seattle. Dr. Leonard was helping facilitate that.

He'd told Livvie about Emma, and she'd squeezed his hand, a lopsided smile forming as he shared his plan to woo her.

Bandit scratched outside the bathroom door, and Jackson leaned down to splash water over his skin, then patted it dry with a towel. He opened the door, and Bandit eyed him with canine approval. He'd ask Matty, but he was at his friend's house for the day.

Jackson dreamed of a future with Emma Mercer—not that she knew it. He prayed that she wouldn't slam the door in his freshly shaved face.

He called, and Aunt Pep answered the house phone. "Is Emma there?"

"Jackson?"

"Yes, ma'am."

The older woman huffed and said, "She isn't here right now."

He could face an enemy army, but Emma Mercer had the ability to slay him with one tear. He'd felt the goodbye in her kiss last week but refused to accept it. "Do you know where she is? The shelter?"

"She took Romeo to the dog beach."

"Thank you," he said.

"Good luck. You're going to need it." She hung up with a knowing chuckle.

Jackson wouldn't surrender until Emma was his.

...

Emma sensed someone staring from the pier and shaded her eyes. She should have known from the tingling in her spine that it was Jackson. She was tempted to grab Romeo, jump into her SUV, and drive away, but that would reek of cowardice, and this time she would not back down.

She'd been here practicing her speech to get him back anyway. It wasn't quite ready, but it seemed the time was now.

She quickly stuffed the notes in the pocket of her shorts and uncapped her water bottle, taking a fortifying drink.

Jackson entered the dog park, handsome in a navy-blue T-shirt and cargo shorts. His hair had been trimmed and he smelled like home from twenty paces.

"Hey, Em." He strode toward her, eyes focused and intent.

"How'd you find me?"

"I called your house. Aunt Pepita told me you were here."

Her sweet aunt needed to stop meddling. "Oh."

Jackson sat opposite her at the table, giving Romeo a nice scratch behind the ear. The dog went back to dozing, since she'd worn him out already playing fetch.

"I wanted to catch up with you," he said, reaching for her hand.

She couldn't be swayed from what she needed to say and wished she could peek at her notes. His gentle clasp of her fingers, twined with his, made her belly heat and her mind race.

"I'm actually glad you're here," she said. "How is your sister? Matty? I've missed him this last week."

"Really great. He's been spending hours a day reading out loud to Livvie. All of those reading assignments were practice, I guess." Jackson swept his thumb across her knuckles.

"That is good. And how is she?"

"Coming home next week." His tone held a note of impatience that he tried to hide with a chuckle.

"What?" she asked, searching his face.

"I want to know how you are. I regret how we ended things last week and I..." Jackson trailed off.

"Yes?" Emma sat forward on the bench seat.

"This is the hardest thing I've ever done, and I've traveled miles across the desert, set up camp in the dark, survived being shot at, but telling you that I love you, and that I want to spend my life with you, is..." His green eyes were stormy with emotion.

"You do?" Elated, Emma jumped up from her side of the table and ran around so they were next to each other. "Jackson, I want to be with you. I will travel the world and see it with you." She curved her hands over his shoulders, hanging on tight. "I just want to be at your side. I thought I was being so safe and smart, keeping my heart under lock and key, but you've had it all this time."

Jackson swept his arms around her and brought her to sit on his lap on the bench. Looking into her eyes, he searched, until he found the truth of her love blazing within—it couldn't be contained. He cupped her head and kissed her so thoroughly she saw stars.

"Are you sure?"

She slowly nodded to clear her dazzled mind. "Oh, yes." Pulling a sheet of paper from her pocket, she said, "I have notes. A plan."

He smoothed one on the table, his left arm tight around her hips as he kept her close. He read, "Love me."

Jackson lifted her chin and held her gaze. "I do love you, and I was a fool for ever leaving."

"I should have told you that you were what mattered most. I didn't know." Her brow scrunched. "I think we were too young then, but now?" She pressed her hand against his thumping heart. "Now is the best time for us."

"You're not the only one with a plan," he said, reaching into his back pocket. Emma made no move to leave the comfort of his lap.

"What do you have?" She rested her open palm above his heart.

"This is for you." He handed her an envelope, and she carefully pulled out the deed to the piece of land next door to her aunt's property. The one she'd wanted for her shelter.

"Jackson!" Her body trembled with a torrent of emotion. "How?"

He smoothed a hair back from her cheek. "I heard how upset you were by the sale, the loss of your dream, and I called and offered a higher bid on the property. I want to make sure that you know how important you are to me."

She'd never been more certain of anything in her life. "I'm willing to move with you, though. If you want... Wherever you want to go. *You* are what I need."

"What about your doctorate?" His arm tightened around her waist.

"I went to see Professor Collard yesterday, and he gave me the names of three different psychologists willing to work with me, without a nine-to-five schedule. He confessed that he'd given me that deadline to make me realize what I wanted, which is to be a doctor."

He eased back a fraction to really look at her with pride. "You did it all—the studying, the work. I'm glad you figured out *your* perfect solution."

"With your nudge." Emma put her hand on his thigh, and the muscle jumped the slightest bit at her touch. She rubbed her thumb softly over the fabric. His eyes dilated as her thumb circled his sizable quad. Jackson stood from the bench and pulled her up, into his arms, holding her so close her breath hitched.

He looked down into her eyes, his expression serious—his embrace making her feel infinitely precious.

"What would you think if I transferred to Seattle?"

"Are you joking?" She was afraid to look away. "Can you?"

"Yes, Dr. Leonard is helping me with a letter about my PTSD. I will stay in the Marines, but I won't be going on deployment. That is, if you're okay with that? I want us to make these decisions together. You were right that I never gave us a chance to talk ten years ago."

His words were a balm to her heart.

"I love you," she said. He covered her mouth with his, capturing her words and taking them with the firm press of his lower lip. He tilted her back, firing kisses down her throat, up to her waiting mouth again. His whole being exuded love. She felt it in his caress, in the protection of his arms as he cradled her close to his wildly beating heart.

"I love you, Emma." His hand dropped to her hip, and she snuggled cheek to cheek.

Tears filled her eyes and she blinked them back.

He gently sucked her lower lip, and her knees buckled.

The rush of feelings made her thankful for the table at her back. How was she supposed to stand up straight? He trailed warm kisses across her collarbone. She sighed and tilted her head back.

"I can take care of you," he said. "And when I'm not working, I will help you build your training shelter."

"I can take care of you," she countered, balancing on one elbow. "I'm a doctor, you know." Close enough, she thought, to take it seriously.

Joy erupted, and she couldn't stop grinning. A lifetime of Jackson Hardy?

Oorah.

Acknowledgments

Thank you to Alethea and Entangled for this wonderful opportunity! My thanks to Evan Marshall, who is the best agent ever, and my thanks to our military and all who serve or who have served our country.

About the Author

With an impressive bibliography in an array of genres, *USA Today* bestselling author Traci Hall has garnered a notable fan base. She pens stories guaranteed to touch the heart while transporting the reader to another time and place. Her belief in happily ever after shines through, whether it's a romantic glimpse into history or a love affair for today.

Find your Bliss with these great releases...

ROMANCING HIS RIVAL
an *Accidentally Yours* novel by Jennifer Shirk

Elena Mason doesn't often hate people, but she *hates* her ex-fiancé's insufferable best man, Lucas Albright III. She just knows Lucas is the one who talked her ex out of getting married—so Lucas is clearly the cause of all her problems. And now she's expected to *work* with him? Oh, heck no. But it turns out he had a great reason to end her engagement... So what happens when fighting starts feeling a whole lot like falling in love?

HOW TO SEDUCE A BAD BOY
a *Point Beacon* novel by Traci Douglass

Melody Bryant has heard it all before. Sure, she's the epitome of the librarian stereotype. Loves rules and deadlines. Loves books. But what she doesn't love is still being a virgin at twenty-four. Now her birthday is fast approaching and she can't take it any longer. She needs to ruin her reputation. And she knows the perfect guy to help her: the baddest bad boy in town. This Army vet won't know what hit him...

COWBOYS NEED NOT APPLY
a novel by Robert Tate Miller

Prima donna ballerina Jessica Carmichael is *not* interested in the cowboy she met in physical therapy. In fact, she'd love to strangle him...if she wasn't so busy thinking about kissing him. Matt needs to get back on the rodeo circuit, even if he has to get there in tights. To do so, he'll need to convince Jessica to train him—and to finally let loose and live a little.

DATING FOR KEEPS
a *Pine Falls* novel by Coleen Kwan

Lily Baker is trying to get back in the dating game. But then her first night out ends in disaster. Typical. And worse, Caleb Willmett witnessed the whole thing. All Caleb wants is a business partnership with Lily's father, but the man is impossible to reach. So if Lily can arrange a meeting for him, Caleb will help her find a guy worth dating. But when Lily unexpectedly captures his heart, playing matchmaker gets complicated.

CPSIA information can be obtained
at www.ICGtesting.com
Printed in the USA
BVHW030216160719
553568BV00001B/25/P